Editor: Julie Schnittka
Art Director: Ellen Lloyd
Food Editor: Mary Beth Jung
Assistant Food Editor: Coleen Martin
Test Kitchen Assistants: Judith Scholovich, Sherry Smalley
Assistant Editors: Julie Buchsbaum, Robert Fojut
Photography: Scott Anderson
Food Photography Artist: Stephanie Marchese
Photo Studio Coordinator: Anne Schimmel
Illustrations: Jim Sibilski

5400 S. 60th Street, Greendale, WI 53129
International Standard Book Number: 0-89821-158-1
Library of Congress Number: 95-73093

Printed in U.S.A.

Pictured above. Strawberry Cream Pie (p. 75).

Pictured on front cover. Clockwise from bottom: Lemon Barbecued Chicken (p. 8), Cinnamon Apple Cake (p. 67) and Roasted Red Potato Salad (p. 46).

Pictured on back cover. Clockwise from top: Spaghetti 'n' Meatballs (p. 7), Crispy Beef Tostadas (p. 7), Pasta Meatball Stew (p. 20) and Meatball Pie (p. 7).

THE VERY BEST COOKING IN THE COUNTRY? YOU'VE GOT IT!

HOW do you make the best even better? By listening to the experts—experts like *you*.

For almost an entire decade, the cookbooks in our annual *A Taste of the Country* series have been among the most popular across North America. That's never been truer than in the past couple years, since—based on numerous suggestions from readers—we began organizing recipes by handy category.

Now, we've listened again. And you're holding the results in your hand—the biggest and very best *A Taste of the Country* edition ever!

Readers told us they wanted even *more* recipes. So this ninth edition includes *over 350* family-approved and kitchen-tested recipes from country cooks coast to coast.

Readers told us they wanted even *more* completed dishes shown in full color. So the mouth-watering photography in this ninth edition includes over 180 of them!

What's more, to ensure this enlarged edition—bigger than any previous edition—remains an attractive addition to your kitchen even after years of regular use, we've put the pages between a heavy hard cover that resists everyday kitchen spills...and bound them in to stay using an extra-durable process that's the most advanced yet developed.

With all that, though, we haven't changed the "user-friendly" features that make *A Taste of the Country* so convenient for cooks. As always, you'll *never* have to turn a page to finish a recipe in this book. And you'll find you can devote *both* hands to cooking—once you open this book to the recipe you want, it stays open lying on the counter.

But, most importantly of all, we haven't changed the "heart" of *A Taste of the Country*... the most delicious down-home food you can find anywhere!

Turn to Meaty Main Meals for a stick-to-your-ribs roundup of oven dishes, skillet suppers and more, including Hoosier Pork Chop Supper (the most "finger-lickin'-good" entree in Frances Cory's Rockville, Indiana kitchen).

When cool weather comes calling, the Stews & Soups chapter will help you warm your family with hearty one-dish dinners like Southwestern Meat and Potato Stew from Linda Schwarz of Bertrand, Nebraska.

Fudge Pudding Cake—in Cakes, Cookies & Bars—is a richly old-fashioned dessert that wins raves for Roxanne Bender in Waymart, Pennsylvania. And Raspberry Ribbon Pie from Victoria Newman, Antelope, California, is a fruity finale to any meal.

Those are only a tiny fraction of the tried-and-true recipes in this taste treasury. You'll also find an appealing assortment of breakfast foods guaranteed to get the day off to a great start...a *mmm-mmm-good* medley of oven-fresh muffins and breads...country-style condiments to top off favorite foods...and a satisfying selection of side dishes and salads.

Want more? There's *plenty*:

- Six complete meals that go from start to finish in *less than 30 minutes*!
- Recipes with the flavor of the past from eight cooks who share their most memorable menu items.
- A special section featuring delectable dishes perfectly portioned for just the two of you.
- Dozens of recipes labeled "Quick and Easy" that you can make *anytime* your clan is hungry.
- "Restricted diet" recipes marked with this check ✓ that use less salt, sugar and fat—and include *Diabetic Exchanges*.
- Proven "helpful hints" from great cooks to save you time, money and work in the kitchen.

So turn the page—the *best* taste tour of country kitchens is about to begin!

AS THIS ASSORTMENT of recipes tastefully proves, "ground beef" does not by any means mean "boring". Give your spaghetti 'n' meatballs a face-lift...present a new Mexican meal at your table...bring a new twist to stew...or make a hearty meat-filled pie. Best of all, each of these delicious recipes is easy to prepare. So start stirring up some new excitement with an old mealtime standby.

GROUND BEEF BESTS. Clockwise from the top left: **Spaghetti 'n' Meatballs** (p. 7), **Crispy Beef Tostadas** (p. 7), **Pasta Meatball Stew** (p. 20) and **Meatball Pie** (p. 7).

Meaty Main Meals

Win rave reviews for mmm-many years to come with this hearty roundup of oven entrees...skillet specialties...grilled foods...and more!

Spaghetti 'n' Meatballs

Mary Lou Koskella, Prescott, Arizona

(PICTURED AT LEFT AND ON BACK COVER)

1-1/2 cups chopped onion
3 garlic cloves, minced
2 tablespoons olive *or* vegetable oil
3 cups water
1 can (29 ounces) tomato sauce
2 cans (12 ounces *each*) tomato paste
1/3 cup minced fresh parsley
1 tablespoon dried basil
1 tablespoon salt
1/2 teaspoon pepper
MEATBALLS:
3 pounds ground beef
4 eggs, lightly beaten
2 cups soft bread cubes (1/4-inch pieces)
1-1/2 cups milk
1 cup grated Parmesan cheese
3 garlic cloves, minced
1 tablespoon salt
1/2 teaspoon pepper
2 tablespoons cooking oil
Hot cooked spaghetti

In a Dutch oven over medium heat, saute onion and garlic in oil. Add water, tomato sauce and paste, parsley, basil, salt and pepper; bring to a boil. Reduce heat; cover and simmer for 50 minutes. Combine the first eight meatball ingredients; mix well. Shape into 1-1/2-in. balls. In a skillet over medium heat, brown meatballs in oil; drain. Add to sauce; bring to a boil. Reduce heat; cover and simmer for 1 hour, stirring occasionally. Serve over spaghetti. **Yield:** 12-16 servings.

Crispy Beef Tostadas

Joy Rackham, Chimacum, Washington

(PICTURED AT LEFT AND ON BACK COVER)

3 cups all-purpose flour
5 teaspoons baking powder
1-1/4 cups milk
1 pound ground beef
2 garlic cloves, minced
1 can (4 ounces) chopped green chilies
1 envelope taco seasoning mix
3/4 cup water
1 can (16 ounces) refried beans
Cooking oil for deep-fat frying
Picante sauce *or* salsa
Shredded lettuce
Finely chopped green onions
Diced tomatoes
Shredded cheddar cheese

In a large bowl, combine flour and baking powder; add the milk to form a soft dough. Cover and let rest for 1 hour. About 30 minutes before serving, brown beef and garlic in a skillet; drain. Stir in chilies, taco seasoning and water; simmer for 10 minutes. Stir in beans; heat through and keep warm. Divide dough into sixths. On a lightly floured surface, roll each portion into a 7-in. circle. In a deep-fat fryer, preheat oil to 375°. Fry tostadas in hot oil until golden, turning once; drain on paper towels. Top each with meat mixture, picante sauce or salsa, lettuce, onions, tomatoes and cheese; serve immediately. **Yield:** 6 servings.

Meatball Pie

Susan Keith, Fort Plain, New York

(PICTURED AT LEFT AND ON BACK COVER)

1 pound ground beef
3/4 cup soft bread crumbs
1/4 cup chopped onion
2 tablespoons minced fresh parsley
1 teaspoon salt
1/2 teaspoon dried marjoram
1/8 teaspoon pepper
1/4 cup milk
1 egg, lightly beaten
1 can (14-1/2 ounces) stewed tomatoes
1 tablespoon cornstarch
2 teaspoons instant beef bouillon granules
1 cup frozen peas
1 cup sliced carrots, cooked
CRUST:
2-2/3 cups all-purpose flour
1/2 teaspoon salt
1 cup shortening
7 to 8 tablespoons ice water
Half-and-half cream

In a bowl, combine first nine ingredients; mix well (mixture will be soft). Divide into fourths; shape each portion into 12 small meatballs. Brown meatballs, a few at a time, in a large skillet; drain and set aside. Drain tomatoes, reserving liquid. Combine the liquid with cornstarch; pour into skillet. Add tomatoes and bouillon; bring to a boil over medium heat, stirring constantly. Stir in peas and carrots. Remove from heat and set aside. For crust, combine flour and salt in a bowl. Cut in shortening until the mixture resembles coarse crumbs. Add water, 1 tablespoon at a time, tossing lightly with a fork until dough forms a ball. On a lightly floured surface, roll half of dough to fit a 10-in. pie plate. Place in ungreased plate; add meatballs. Spoon tomato mixture over top. Roll remaining pastry to fit top of pie. Place over filling; seal and flute edges. Cut vents in top crust. Brush with cream. Bake at 400° for 45-50 minutes or until golden brown. If needed, cover edges with foil for the last 10 minutes to prevent overbrowning. Let stand 10 minutes before cutting. **Yield:** 6 servings.

Pork Chops with Stuffing

Margaret Pache, Mesa, Arizona

6 pork chops (1/2 inch thick)
1 tablespoon cooking oil
3 cups cubed day-old bread
1 can (10-3/4 ounces) condensed cream of mushroom soup, undiluted
1 cup chopped celery
1 cup chopped onion
2 garlic cloves, minced
1 egg, beaten
1/4 teaspoon poultry seasoning
1/4 teaspoon pepper
1/2 cup shredded cheddar cheese, optional

In a large skillet, brown pork chops in oil. Place in an ungreased 13-in. x 9-in. x 2-in. baking pan. Combine bread cubes, soup, celery, onion, garlic, egg, poultry seasoning and pepper; spread over pork chops. Bake, uncovered, at 350° for 45-55 minutes. If desired, sprinkle with cheese and return to the oven for 5 minutes or until melted. **Yield:** 6 servings.

Lemon Barbecued Chicken

Rodella Brown, Hanover, Pennsylvania
(PICTURED ON FRONT COVER)

2/3 cup lemon juice
1/3 cup vegetable oil
1/3 cup vinegar
1 tablespoon soy sauce
2 teaspoons sugar
1 teaspoon salt
1 teaspoon paprika
1 teaspoon chili powder
1/2 teaspoon pepper
1/2 teaspoon garlic salt
1 medium onion, chopped
1 broiler/fryer chicken (3-1/2 to 4 pounds), cut up

Whisk together the first 11 ingredients; set aside 1/4 cup. Pour remaining marinade into a large resealable plastic bag. Add chicken; seal bag. Refrigerate at least 8 hours or overnight, turning occasionally. Drain, discarding marinade. Grill the chicken, covered, over medium coals for 45 minutes or until juices run clear, turning and basting with reserved marinade every 8-10 minutes. **To bake chicken:** After marinating, place chicken in a greased 15-in. x 10-in. x 1-in. baking pan. Pour all of the marinade over it. Bake, uncovered, at 350° for 1-1/4 hours or until juices run clear, basting occasionally. **Yield:** 6 servings.

Italian Shepherd's Pie

Rosanne Reynolds, Kissimmee, Florida

✓ This tasty dish uses less sugar, salt and fat. Recipe includes *Diabetic Exchanges*.

1 cup Italian bread crumbs
1 cup cold water
4 medium potatoes, peeled
1-1/4 pounds uncooked ground round
1/2 cup finely chopped onion
1/2 cup finely chopped celery
1 can (8 ounces) tomato sauce
1 can (4 ounces) mushrooms, drained and finely chopped
1 garlic clove, minced
1/4 teaspoon pepper
1-1/2 cups frozen peas and carrots
1/2 cup shredded low-fat mozzarella cheese

Combine crumbs and water; let stand for 5 minutes. Cook potatoes in boiling water until tender. Combine meat, onion, celery, tomato sauce, mushrooms, garlic and pepper. Stir in crumb mixture. Spread into an ungreased 11-in. x 7-in. x 2-in. baking dish. Top with peas and carrots. Drain the potatoes; mash with cheese. Spread over vegetables, sealing to pan. Bake at 375° for 45-60 minutes. **Yield:** 6 servings. **Diabetic Exchanges:** One serving equals 3-1/2 lean meat, 2-1/2 starch, 1 vegetable; also, 398 calories, 976 mg sodium, 80 mg cholesterol, 43 gm carbohydrate, 34 gm protein, 11 gm fat.

Barbecued Beef Pizza

Lisa Buglass, Bancroft, Wisconsin

1 package (6-1/2 ounces) pizza crust mix
1 pound ground beef
1/4 cup chopped onion
1 can (15-1/2 ounces) sloppy joe sauce
1/2 cup shredded cheddar cheese
1/2 cup shredded mozzarella cheese

Prepare crust according to package directions. In a saucepan over medium heat, brown beef and onion; drain. Add sloppy joe sauce; bring to a boil. Reduce heat; simmer, uncovered, for 5 minutes. On a floured surface, knead dough several times; pat into a greased 12- to 14-in. pizza pan. Bake at 425° for 10 minutes. Spread with meat mixture; sprinkle with cheeses. Return to the oven for 8 minutes or until the crust is brown and cheese is melted. **Yield:** 6-8 servings.

Beef Noodle Casserole

Grace Lema, Winton, California

2 pounds ground beef
1 large onion, chopped
1 medium green pepper, chopped
1 can (14-3/4 ounces) cream-style corn
1 can (10-3/4 ounces) condensed tomato soup, undiluted
1 can (8 ounces) tomato sauce
1 jar (2 ounces) sliced pimientos, drained
2 tablespoons chopped jalapeno pepper
1-1/2 teaspoons salt
1/2 teaspoon chili powder
1/4 teaspoon dry mustard
1/4 teaspoon pepper
1 package (8 ounces) medium egg noodles, cooked and drained
1 jar (4-1/2 ounces) sliced mushrooms, drained
1-1/2 cups (6 ounces) shredded cheddar cheese

In a large skillet, cook beef, onion and green pepper until the meat is browned and vegetables are tender; drain. Add the next nine ingredients and mix well. Stir in noodles and mushrooms. Transfer to a greased 13-in. x 9-in. x 2-in. baking dish. Sprinkle with cheese. Bake, uncovered, at 350° for 45 minutes or until heated through. **Yield:** 8-10 servings.

Deviled Corned Beef Buns

Helen Kennedy, Hudson, New York
(PICTURED ON PAGE 40)

1 cup crumbled canned corned beef
1/2 cup shredded process American cheese
1/3 cup chopped stuffed olives
1/3 cup ketchup
2 tablespoons finely chopped green onions
1 tablespoon finely chopped green pepper
1 tablespoon Worcestershire sauce
1/4 teaspoon pepper
4 submarine *or* hoagie rolls, split

In a medium bowl, combine the first eight ingredients. Divide and spoon onto bottom of rolls. Replace tops; wrap each tightly in foil. Bake at 325° for 20 minutes or until heated through. **Yield:** 4 servings.

Mexican Spaghetti

Vicki Jernas, Knox, Indiana

1 pound ground beef
1 small onion, chopped
3 cups water
1 can (8 ounces) tomato sauce
1 envelope taco seasoning mix
1 package (7 ounces) spaghetti
1 cup (4 ounces) shredded cheddar cheese

In a skillet over medium heat, brown beef and onion; drain. Stir in the water, tomato sauce and taco seasoning; bring to a boil. Break spaghetti into thirds; stir into sauce. Reduce heat; cover and simmer for 20-25 minutes or until spaghetti is tender and sauce is desired consistency. Sprinkle with cheese. **Yield:** 4-6 servings.

VITAMIN PACKED. Lasagna takes on a whole different twist if you spread a 15-1/2 ounce can of well-drained spinach on the middle layer. It's a deliciously new way to sneak vegetables into your family's diet.

Swiss Steak

Linda Stiles, Baltimore, Ohio

- 2 pounds beef round steak (1 inch thick)
- 3 tablespoons all-purpose flour
- 1/2 teaspoon salt
- 1/4 teaspoon pepper
- 2 tablespoons cooking oil
- 2 medium onions, sliced
- 2 celery ribs, chopped
- 1 can (16 ounces) tomatoes with liquid, cut up
- 2 tablespoons Worcestershire sauce
- 1/4 teaspoon dried oregano
- Hot cooked noodles, optional

Cut meat into serving-size pieces and dredge in flour. Sprinkle with salt and pepper. In a skillet or Dutch oven, brown meat on both sides in oil. Top with the onions and celery. Combine tomatoes, Worcestershire sauce and oregano; spoon over vegetables. Cover and simmer for 1-1/2 to 2 hours or until meat is tender. Serve over noodles if desired. **Yield:** 6 servings.

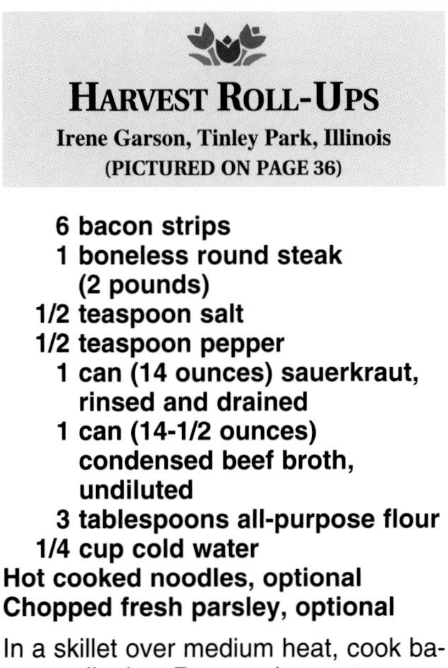

Harvest Roll-Ups

Irene Garson, Tinley Park, Illinois

(PICTURED ON PAGE 36)

- 6 bacon strips
- 1 boneless round steak (2 pounds)
- 1/2 teaspoon salt
- 1/2 teaspoon pepper
- 1 can (14 ounces) sauerkraut, rinsed and drained
- 1 can (14-1/2 ounces) condensed beef broth, undiluted
- 3 tablespoons all-purpose flour
- 1/4 cup cold water
- Hot cooked noodles, optional
- Chopped fresh parsley, optional

In a skillet over medium heat, cook bacon until crisp. Remove bacon to paper towel to drain; discard all but 2 tablespoons drippings. Cut the steak into six pieces and pound to 1/4-in. thickness; sprinkle with salt and pepper. Place 1/3 to 1/2 cup sauerkraut and a bacon slice on each piece of meat. Roll up; secure with a short skewer or toothpicks. Brown roll-ups in drippings. Add broth; bring to a boil. Reduce heat; cover and simmer for 50-60 minutes or until meat is tender. Remove roll-ups; keep warm. Combine flour and water to form a smooth paste. Bring cooking liquid to a boil; add flour mixture, stirring constantly. Cook and stir for 2 minutes or until thickened and bubbly. Remove skewers or toothpicks from roll-ups; serve with gravy over noodles if desired. Sprinkle with parsley if desired. **Yield:** 6 servings.

Herbed Pork Roast

Jean Harris, Central Point, Oregon

(PICTURED ON PAGE 72)

- 1/4 cup packed brown sugar
- 1 tablespoon dried thyme
- 1 teaspoon *each* garlic salt, pepper, dried rosemary and crushed sage
- 1 boneless pork loin roast (3 to 4 pounds)
- 1/4 cup all-purpose flour

Combine brown sugar, herbs and seasonings; rub over entire roast. Place roast, fat side up, on a rack in a roasting pan. Place in a 500° oven; immediately reduce heat to 325°. Bake, uncovered, for 2 hours or until a meat thermometer reads 160°. Remove roast from pan. Pour pan drippings into a large measuring cup; add water to equal 2 cups. Pour into a small saucepan; add flour. Cook and stir over medium heat until gravy comes to a boil; cook and stir 2 minutes more. Slice roast and serve with gravy. **Yield:** 6-8 servings.

Rosemary Chicken

Carol Fischer, Pewaukee, Wisconsin

✓ This tasty dish uses less sugar, salt and fat. Recipe includes *Diabetic Exchanges.*

- 1 can (14-1/2 ounces) chicken broth, *divided*
- 3 garlic cloves, minced
- 1 tablespoon finely chopped fresh rosemary *or* 1 teaspoon crushed dried rosemary
- 1 tablespoon vegetable oil
- 1 tablespoon soy sauce
- 1 teaspoon sugar
- 1/2 teaspoon pepper
- 6 boneless skinless chicken breast halves
- 1 cup uncooked long grain rice
- 1/2 cup water
- 10 asparagus spears, blanched and cut into pieces
- 1 teaspoon grated lemon peel
- 1 teaspoon lemon pepper
- 1/2 teaspoon salt, optional

In a shallow glass baking dish, combine 1/4 cup broth, garlic, rosemary, oil, soy sauce, sugar and pepper. Add chicken; turn to coat. Cover and refrigerate at least 1 hour. In a saucepan, cook rice in water and remaining broth until soft and fluffy, about 20 minutes. Meanwhile, in a skillet, cook chicken in marinade over medium-high heat for about 7 minutes per side or until chicken is brown and juices run clear. Remove rice from the heat; add asparagus, lemon peel, lemon pepper and salt if desired. Spoon onto individual plates. Cut chicken into strips; arrange in a fan shape over rice. **Yield:** 6 servings. **Diabetic Exchanges:** One serving (prepared with low-sodium broth and soy sauce and without added salt) equals 3 lean meat, 3 starch; also, 297 calories, 165 mg sodium, 73 mg cholesterol, 29 gm carbohydrate, 31 gm protein, 8 gm fat.

Cheeseburger Casserole

Sherilyn Charlton, Rockford, Illinois

- 1 pound ground beef
- 1/2 cup chopped onion
- 2 cups water
- 2/3 cup ketchup
- 2 tablespoons prepared mustard
- 1 teaspoon salt
- 1/4 teaspoon pepper
- 2 cups uncooked instant rice
- 2 slices cheddar cheese, cut into 1-inch strips

In a skillet over medium heat, brown the beef and onion; drain. Add water, ketchup, mustard, salt and pepper; mix well. Bring to a boil. Stir in rice. Cover and remove from the heat; let stand for 5 minutes. Top with cheese; cover and let stand for 3-5 minutes or until cheese is melted. **Yield:** 4 servings.

Beef and Pepper Kabobs

Janet Wood, Windham, New Hampshire

- 3 tablespoons lemon juice
- 2 tablespoons vegetable oil
- 1 large onion, finely chopped
- 1-1/2 teaspoons dried thyme
- 1/2 teaspoon salt
- 1/4 teaspoon pepper
- 2 pounds sirloin, cut into 1-inch cubes
- 1 *each* green, yellow, orange and red peppers

In a glass bowl or heavy-duty plastic bag, combine lemon juice, oil, onion, thyme, salt and pepper. Add meat; stir or shake to coat. Cover or seal and refrigerate 6 hours or overnight. Cut peppers into 1-in. squares and thread onto skewers alternately with meat. Grill over hot coals, turning often, for 12-15 minutes or until the meat reaches desired doneness. **Yield:** 6-8 servings. **Editor's Note:** Boneless lamb can be substituted for the beef.

WHAT A WONDERFUL surprise your family's taste buds are in for! Could sloppy joe use added spark at your place? Try it as a pie instead of sandwich filling. Is your standard taco dip starting to seem a little tired? Whip up a meaty one instead. And, to give chili a charge, fix one with an unexpected ingredient—potato dumplings! All this and more is in store for you with these mouth-watering recipes.

GOOD TASTE, BASICALLY. Clockwise from lower left: **Beef and Sauerkraut Dinner**, **Cajun Burgers**, **Ground Beef Turnovers**, **Sloppy Joe Pie**, **Inside-Out Brussels Sprouts**, **Beefy Taco Dip**, **All-Purpose Meat Sauce** (all recipes on p. 12 and 13) and **Chili with Potato Dumplings** (p. 20).

Beef and Sauerkraut Dinner

Marilyn Dietz, White, South Dakota

(PICTURED ON PAGE 10)

1-1/2 pounds ground beef
1 egg, lightly beaten
1-1/2 cups soft rye bread crumbs
1/3 cup milk
1/4 cup chopped onion
1 tablespoon cider vinegar
1-1/2 teaspoons caraway seed
1 teaspoon salt
1 tablespoon cooking oil
2 cans (15 ounces *each*) sliced potatoes, drained
2 cans (14 ounces *each*) sauerkraut, undrained
2 tablespoons minced fresh parsley
1/4 cup *each* mayonnaise and horseradish, optional

In a bowl, combine beef, egg, crumbs, milk, onion, vinegar, caraway and salt; mix well. Shape into 1-1/2-in. balls. In a Dutch oven over medium heat, brown meatballs in oil; drain. Add the potatoes and sauerkraut and mix well. Bring to a boil. Reduce heat; cover and simmer for 15-20 minutes or until heated through. Sprinkle with parsley. If sauce is desired, combine mayonnaise and horseradish; serve on the side. **Yield:** 6-8 servings.

Quick & Easy

Cajun Burgers

Julie Culbertson, Bensalem, Pennsylvania

(PICTURED ON PAGE 10)

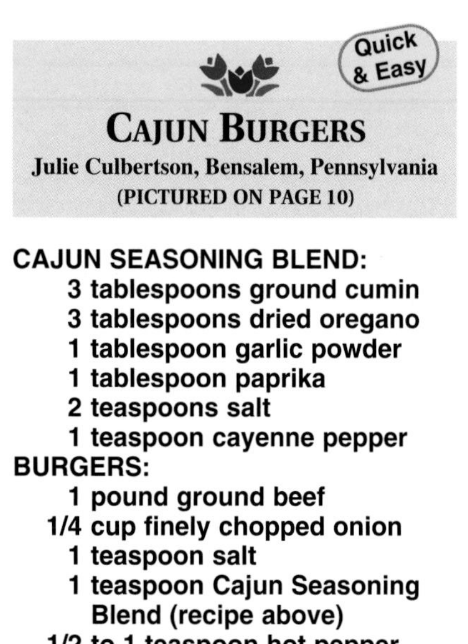

CAJUN SEASONING BLEND:
3 tablespoons ground cumin
3 tablespoons dried oregano
1 tablespoon garlic powder
1 tablespoon paprika
2 teaspoons salt
1 teaspoon cayenne pepper
BURGERS:
1 pound ground beef
1/4 cup finely chopped onion
1 teaspoon salt
1 teaspoon Cajun Seasoning Blend (recipe above)
1/2 to 1 teaspoon hot pepper sauce
1/2 teaspoon dried thyme
1/4 teaspoon dried basil
1 garlic clove, minced
4 hamburger buns
Sauteed onions, optional

Combine all seasoning blend ingredients in a small bowl or resealable plastic bag; mix well. In a bowl, combine the first eight burger ingredients; shape into four patties. Cook in a skillet or grill over medium-hot coals for 4-5 minutes per side or until burgers reach desired doneness. Serve on buns; top with sauteed onions if desired. Store remaining seasoning blend in an airtight container. **Yield:** 4 servings.

Ground Beef Turnovers

Wendy Tomlinson, Echo Bay, Ontario

(PICTURED ON PAGE 10)

4 cups all-purpose flour
1 tablespoon sugar
2 teaspoons salt
1-3/4 cups shortening
1/2 cup ice water
1 egg, lightly beaten
1 tablespoon vinegar
FILLING:
2 pounds uncooked lean ground beef
1 cup diced carrots
2 medium potatoes, peeled and cut into 1/4-inch cubes
1 medium onion, chopped
1 to 2 teaspoons salt
1/4 teaspoon pepper
Half-and-half cream

In a bowl, combine flour, sugar and salt; cut in shortening until mixture resembles coarse crumbs. Combine the water, egg and vinegar; mix well. Add to shortening mixture, 1 tablespoon at a time, tossing lightly with a fork until mixture forms a ball. Cover and chill for 30 minutes. Meanwhile, combine the first six filling ingredients. Divide pastry into 15 equal portions. On a lightly floured surface, roll out one portion into a 6-1/2-in. circle. Mound a heaping 1/3 cup filling on half of circle. Moisten edges with water; fold dough over filling and press edges with a fork to seal. Transfer to a greased baking sheet. Repeat with remaining pastry and filling. Cut three slits in the top of each turnover; brush with cream. Bake at 375° for 35-40 minutes or until vegetables are tender and crust is golden brown. **Yield:** 15 turnovers.

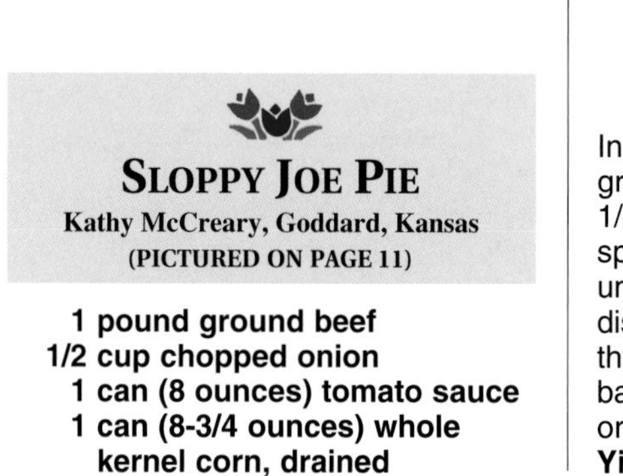

Sloppy Joe Pie

Kathy McCreary, Goddard, Kansas

(PICTURED ON PAGE 11)

1 pound ground beef
1/2 cup chopped onion
1 can (8 ounces) tomato sauce
1 can (8-3/4 ounces) whole kernel corn, drained
1/4 cup water
1 envelope sloppy joe seasoning mix
1 can (10 ounces) refrigerated biscuits
2 tablespoons milk
1/3 cup cornmeal
1 cup (8 ounces) shredded cheddar cheese, *divided*

In a skillet, brown beef with onion; drain. Stir in the tomato sauce, corn, water and sloppy joe seasoning; cook over medium heat until bubbly. Reduce heat and simmer for 5 minutes; remove from the heat and set aside. Separate biscuits and roll or flatten each to a 3-1/2-in. circle; dip both sides into milk and then into the cornmeal. Place seven biscuits around the sides and three on the bottom of an ungreased 9-in. pie plate. Press biscuits together to form a crust, leaving a scalloped edge around rim. Sprinkle with 1/2 cup cheese. Spoon meat mixture over cheese. Bake at 375° for 20-25 minutes or until crust is deep golden brown. Sprinkle with remaining cheese. Let stand for 5 minutes before serving. **Yield:** 7 servings.

Inside-Out Brussels Sprouts

Shirley Max, Cape Girardeau, Missouri

(PICTURED ON PAGE 11)

2 pounds ground beef
1-1/2 cups uncooked instant rice
1 medium onion, chopped
2 eggs, lightly beaten
1-1/2 teaspoons garlic salt
1/2 teaspoon pepper
1 package (10 ounces) frozen brussels sprouts
2 cans (15 ounces *each*) tomato sauce
1 cup water
1 teaspoon dried thyme

In a large bowl, combine the first six ingredients and mix well. Shape a scant 1/4 cupful around each frozen brussels sprout to form a meatball. Place in an ungreased 15-in. x 10-in. x 1-in. baking dish. Combine tomato sauce, water and thyme; pour over meatballs. Cover and bake at 350° for 1 hour and 15 minutes or until meatballs are cooked through. **Yield:** 8-10 servings.

Beefy Taco Dip

Faye Parker, Bedford, Nova Scotia

(PICTURED ON PAGE 11)

1 package (8 ounces) cream cheese, softened
1 cup (8 ounces) sour cream
3/4 cup mayonnaise
1 pound ground beef
1 envelope taco seasoning mix
1 can (8 ounces) tomato sauce
2 cups (8 ounces) shredded cheddar *or* taco cheese
4 cups shredded lettuce
2 medium tomatoes, diced
1 small onion, diced
1 medium green pepper, diced
Tortilla chips

In a small mixing bowl, beat the cream cheese, sour cream and mayonnaise until smooth. Spread on a 12- to 14-in. pizza pan or serving dish. Refrigerate for 1 hour. In a saucepan over medium heat, brown beef; drain. Add taco seasoning and tomato sauce; cook and stir for 5 minutes. Cool completely. Spread over cream cheese layer. Refrigerate. Just before serving, sprinkle with cheese, lettuce, tomatoes, onion and green pepper. Serve with chips. **Yield:** 16-20 servings.

All-Purpose Meat Sauce

Sonja Fontaine, Winnipeg, Manitoba

(PICTURED ON PAGE 11)

1 pound ground beef
1 to 2 garlic cloves, minced
1 can (15 ounces) tomato sauce
1 can (10-3/4 ounces) tomato soup, undiluted
1/4 cup grated Parmesan cheese
1 tablespoon Worcestershire sauce
1-1/2 teaspoons dried oregano
1 teaspoon dried basil
1/2 teaspoon sugar
1/2 teaspoon salt
1/2 teaspoon dried parsley flakes
1/4 teaspoon crushed red pepper flakes
Pinch *each* dried thyme, tarragon and ground cinnamon
Hot pepper sauce and cayenne pepper to taste

In a large skillet or Dutch oven, cook beef and garlic until beef is browned; drain. Stir in remaining ingredients. Simmer, uncovered, for 30 minutes or until sauce is as thick as desired, stirring occasionally. Serve over pasta or rice, or use for making lasagna, pizza, chili dogs, tacos or sloppy joes. **Yield:** 4 cups.

Hearty Bean Casserole

Mrs. Kenneth Kneut, Port St. Lucie, Florida

1-1/4 pounds ground beef
1 large onion, chopped
1 large green pepper, diced
1 garlic clove, minced
1 can (16 ounces) pork and beans, undrained
1 can (16 ounces) kidney beans, rinsed and drained
1 can (15 ounces) garbanzo beans, rinsed and drained
1 cup ketchup
3 tablespoons brown sugar
3 tablespoons vinegar
2 tablespoons prepared mustard
1 teaspoon salt
1/2 teaspoon pepper
3 bacon strips, cooked and crumbled

In a Dutch oven, brown ground beef; drain. Add onion, green pepper and garlic; cook until tender. Stir in all of the beans. Combine ketchup, brown sugar, vinegar, mustard, salt and pepper; add to bean mixture and mix well. Pour into a greased 2-1/2-qt. casserole. Top with bacon. Bake, uncovered, at 350° for 45 minutes or until heated through. **Yield:** 6-8 servings.

Golden Fish Cakes

Madeline Waldron, Walhalla, South Carolina

1 pound flaked cooked whitefish, cod *or* haddock
1-1/2 cups soft bread crumbs
3 eggs, beaten
2 to 4 tablespoons water
1 medium onion, chopped
2 tablespoons mayonnaise
1-1/2 teaspoons dry mustard
1 teaspoon dried parsley flakes
3/4 teaspoon salt
1-1/2 cups Italian-seasoned bread crumbs
2 tablespoons cooking oil
Tartar sauce and lemon wedges, optional

In a bowl, combine the first nine ingredients; mix well. Shape into 12 patties, adding additional water if needed; coat with the Italian bread crumbs. In a large skillet, cook the patties in oil for 4-5 minutes on each side or until lightly browned. Serve immediately with tartar sauce and lemon if desired. **Yield:** 4-6 servings.

Hoosier Pork Chop Supper

Frances Cory, Rockville, Indiana

(PICTURED ON PAGE 22)

1 medium onion, sliced
3 tablespoons cooking oil
3 tablespoons all-purpose flour
1 teaspoon salt
1/2 teaspoon pepper
4 pork chops (1-1/2 inches thick)
2 large potatoes, peeled and sliced
1 large carrot, sliced
1 can (16 ounces) tomatoes with liquid, cut up
1 cup frozen peas

In a large skillet, saute onion in oil until tender. Remove with a slotted spoon and set aside; reserve drippings in pan. Combine flour, salt and pepper; coat the pork chops. Brown on both sides in the drippings. Add potatoes, carrot, tomatoes and onion; bring to a boil. Reduce heat; cover and simmer for 1-1/2 hours, adding the peas during the last 10 minutes. **Yield:** 4 servings.

Hawaiian Ham Sandwiches

Alice Lewis, Red Oak, Iowa

(PICTURED ON PAGE 58)

8 submarine rolls *or* hoagie buns (8 inches)
8 slices Swiss cheese, halved
1/2 medium sweet red pepper, julienned
1/2 medium green pepper, julienned
6 to 8 green onions, sliced
2 teaspoons cooking oil
1 pound sliced fully cooked ham, julienned
1 can (20 ounces) pineapple tidbits, drained
1 cup (4 ounces) shredded mozzarella cheese

Cut thin slices off tops of rolls. Hollow out bread in the center, leaving 1/4-in. shells; set aside tops and discard hollowed-out bread (or save for another use). Place rolls on a baking sheet; line the inside of each with Swiss cheese. In a skillet, saute peppers and onions in oil for 3 minutes. Add ham; cook for 3 minutes. Add pineapple. Remove from the heat; drain. Spoon into rolls. Bake at 450° for 5 minutes. Sprinkle with mozzarella cheese; return to the oven until cheese melts, about 1 minute. Replace tops of rolls. Serve immediately. **Yield:** 8 servings.

WHEN THE WEATHER starts turning cooler, celebrate the tastes of the season. Plan a "do-ahead" meal featuring a tender pork roast with barbecue flavor or quick-cooking chicken topped with tangy salsa. For a flavorful side dish, stuff some of those extra garden tomatoes. And for dessert, this apple pie recipe needs the oven for only a few minutes—just to bake the crust.

TIME FOR THE HARVEST. Clockwise from the bottom: **Lime Ginger Chicken**, **Pork Roast Barbecue** (both recipes on p. 15), **Icebox Apple Pie** (p. 70) and **Broccoli Tomato Cups** (p. 38).

Lime Ginger Chicken

Patti Billet, Missoula, Montana
(PICTURED AT LEFT)

✓ This tasty dish uses less sugar, salt and fat. Recipe includes *Diabetic Exchanges*.

1/3 cup fresh lime juice
3 garlic cloves, minced
1/2 teaspoon ground ginger
1/2 teaspoon dried red pepper flakes
1/4 teaspoon salt, optional
4 boneless skinless chicken breast halves, cut into 1-inch strips

SALSA:

2 cups diced fresh plum tomatoes
1 cup diced green pepper
1/2 cup diced red onion
1 tablespoon chopped fresh cilantro *or* parsley
1 tablespoon olive *or* vegetable oil
1 tablespoon fresh lime juice
2 garlic cloves, minced
1/4 teaspoon salt, optional

In a glass bowl, combine lime juice, garlic, ginger, red pepper and salt if desired. Add the chicken and toss lightly. Cover and refrigerate for 2-4 hours. Meanwhile, combine all salsa ingredients; cover and refrigerate until ready to serve. Drain chicken; discard marinade. Brown in a large nonstick skillet until no longer pink, about 10 minutes. Serve with salsa. **Yield:** 4 servings. **Diabetic Exchanges:** One serving (prepared without salt) equals 3 lean meat, 3 vegetable; also, 250 calories, 80 mg sodium, 73 mg cholesterol, 20 gm carbohydrate, 31 gm protein, 7 gm fat.

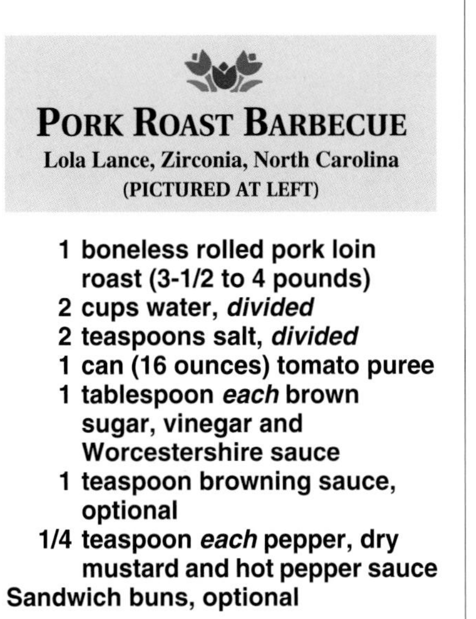

Pork Roast Barbecue

Lola Lance, Zirconia, North Carolina
(PICTURED AT LEFT)

1 boneless rolled pork loin roast (3-1/2 to 4 pounds)
2 cups water, *divided*
2 teaspoons salt, *divided*
1 can (16 ounces) tomato puree
1 tablespoon *each* brown sugar, vinegar and Worcestershire sauce
1 teaspoon browning sauce, optional
1/4 teaspoon *each* pepper, dry mustard and hot pepper sauce
Sandwich buns, optional

Place roast in a heavy 5-qt. roaster or Dutch oven. Combine 1 cup water and 1 teaspoon salt; pour over meat. Cover and simmer for 2 hours. Drain, reserving 1 cup broth. Cool roast for 15 minutes. Cut into thin slices; place in an 11-in. x 7-in. x 2-in. baking dish. In a 2-qt. saucepan, combine tomato puree, sugar, vinegar, Worcestershire, browning sauce if desired, pepper, mustard, hot pepper sauce, remaining water and salt and reserved broth. Bring to a boil; cook and stir for 3 minutes. Pour over meat. Cover and refrigerate overnight, turning the meat once. Remove from the refrigerator 30 minutes before reheating. Bake, covered, at 350° for 1 hour. Serve on buns if desired. **Yield:** 10-12 servings.

Quick & Easy

Catfish Parmesan

Mrs. W.D. Baker, Starkville, Mississippi

3/4 cup dry bread crumbs
3 tablespoons grated Parmesan cheese
2 tablespoons chopped fresh parsley
1/2 teaspoon salt
1/4 teaspoon paprika
1/8 teaspoon *each* pepper, dried oregano and basil
6 fresh *or* frozen catfish fillets (3 to 5 ounces *each*)
1/2 cup butter *or* margarine, melted

In a shallow bowl, combine the bread crumbs, Parmesan cheese, parsley and seasonings. Dip catfish in butter, then in crumb mixture. Arrange in a greased 13-in. x 9-in. x 2-in. baking dish. Bake, uncovered, at 375° for 20-25 minutes or until fish flakes easily with a fork. **Yield:** 6 servings.

Quick & Easy

Pizza by the Yard

Jean Johnson, La Veta, Colorado
(PICTURED ON PAGE 47)

1 pound lean ground beef
1/2 cup sliced ripe olives
1/2 cup chopped onion
1/2 cup grated Parmesan cheese
1 can (6 ounces) tomato paste
1 teaspoon dried oregano
1 teaspoon salt
1/8 teaspoon pepper
1 loaf French bread (20 inches), halved lengthwise
3 medium tomatoes, sliced
2 cups (8 ounces) shredded mozzarella cheese

In a bowl, combine the uncooked beef, olives, onion, Parmesan cheese, tomato paste, oregano, salt and pepper. Spread to the edges of the cut surface of the bread. Broil 6 in. from the heat for 8-10 minutes or until the meat is fully cooked. Top with tomatoes and cheese. Broil 2-3 minutes more or until cheese is melted. Serve immediately. **Yield:** 6-8 servings.

Sweet 'n' Sour Chops

Shirley Ramsey, Wymore, Nebraska

2 tablespoons butter *or* margarine
1/2 cup packed brown sugar
2 tablespoons cornstarch
1/8 teaspoon salt
1-1/2 cups pineapple juice
1/2 cup cider vinegar
1 tablespoon soy sauce
2 teaspoons Worcestershire sauce
1/2 teaspoon liquid smoke
1 cup lemon-lime soda
6 pork loin chops (1 inch thick)

In a saucepan over medium heat, combine butter, sugar, cornstarch and salt. Add pineapple juice, vinegar, soy sauce, Worcestershire and liquid smoke; mix well. Bring to a boil, stirring constantly. Cook for 2 minutes or until thickened. Pour the soda into a 13-in. x 9-in. x 2-in. glass baking dish. Add 1/2 cup of the sauce; mix well. Add chops and turn to coat; cover and refrigerate overnight. Cover and refrigerate remaining sauce. Remove chops, discarding marinade. Grill chops, covered, over hot coals for 10-15 minutes per side or until juices run clear or the internal temperature reaches 160°. Heat reserved sauce and serve over chops. **Yield:** 6 servings.

Crispy Picnic Chicken

Joanie Elbourn, Gardner, Massachusetts

20 butter-flavored crackers, crushed
2/3 cup grated Parmesan cheese
2 teaspoons dried parsley flakes
3/4 teaspoon garlic powder
1/2 teaspoon paprika
1/8 teaspoon pepper
1 broiler-fryer chicken (3-1/2 to 4 pounds), cut up
1/3 cup butter *or* margarine, melted

In a small bowl, combine the first six ingredients. Dip chicken in butter and then roll in crumb mixture, coating both sides. Place in a greased 13-in. x 9-in. x 2-in. baking pan. Bake, uncovered, at 350° for 50 minutes or until chicken is tender and juices run clear. Serve hot or chilled. **Yield:** 4-6 servings.

THERE'S NO NEED to heat up the kitchen in summer when you have recipes at hand for grilling. A marinated beef tenderloin will satisfy even the most hungry family. By grilling your vegetables, they remain tender and flavorful. The cool, creamy ice cream is so simple that you don't even need to hassle with an ice cream maker.

OUTDOOR BARBECUE. Pictured are: **Herbed Beef Tenderloin** (p. 17), **Marinated Grilled Vegetables** (p. 39) and **Special Chocolate Ice Cream** (p. 71).

Herbed Beef Tenderloin

Paul Verner, Wooster, Ohio
(PICTURED AT LEFT)

1 beef tenderloin (4 to 5 pounds)
2 garlic cloves, minced
2 green onions, finely chopped
1 tablespoon Dijon mustard
1 tablespoon red wine vinegar *or* balsamic vinegar
1/2 cup olive *or* vegetable oil
1 tablespoon *each* dried basil, thyme and rosemary
1 teaspoon salt
1 teaspoon pepper

Place tenderloin in a large resealable plastic storage bag. Combine remaining ingredients; pour over meat. Seal bag and gently squeeze marinade over the meat. Refrigerate overnight, turning bag occasionally. Remove meat and discard marinade. Sear (brown) the meat over medium-hot coals, turning frequently, for 20 minutes. Cover and continue to grill for 10-20 minutes or until meat reaches desired doneness (for rare, internal temperature should be 140°; medium, 160°; well-done, 170°). Let stand 10 minutes before slicing. **Yield:** 8-10 servings.

Creamy Ham Rolls

Becky Carcich, Littleton, Colorado

1 medium onion, chopped
1/2 cup butter *or* margarine
1/2 cup all-purpose flour
1 teaspoon dill weed
1/2 teaspoon garlic salt
1/2 teaspoon pepper
1 can (14-1/2 ounces) chicken broth
1-1/2 cups light cream
1 tablespoon Dijon mustard
3 cups cooked wild rice
1 can (8 ounces) mushroom stems and pieces, drained
12 thin slices fully cooked ham (about 3/4 pound)
1/2 cup shredded cheddar cheese
Minced fresh parsley

In a large saucepan, saute onion in butter until tender. Stir in flour, dill, garlic salt and pepper until smooth and bubbly. Gradually add broth, cream and mustard; cook until thickened. Pour 1 cup into an ungreased 13-in. x 9-in. x 2-in. baking pan; reserve another cup for topping. To the remaining sauce, add rice and mushrooms; spoon 1/3 cup onto each ham slice. Roll up and place with seam side down over sauce in pan. Top with reserved sauce. Bake, uncovered, at 350° for 25-30 minutes or until heated through. Sprinkle with cheese and parsley; serve immediately. **Yield:** 12 servings.

Southwestern Beef Burritos

Jacqueline Hergert, Payson, Arizona

2 to 2-1/2 pounds round steak, cut into 1-inch cubes
2 tablespoons cooking oil
2 large onions, chopped
2 garlic cloves, minced
1 can (15 ounces) enchilada sauce
1 can (14-1/2 ounces) diced tomatoes, undrained
1 to 2 cans (4 ounces *each*) chopped green chilies
1 teaspoon salt
1/4 teaspoon pepper
2 tablespoons all-purpose flour
1/4 cup cold water
8 flour tortillas (10 inches)
Diced tomatoes, sliced ripe olives, shredded cheddar cheese, sour cream, chopped green onions, shredded lettuce and/or guacamole, optional

In a large skillet over medium heat, brown meat in oil; drain. Add onions and garlic; cook and stir for 2 minutes. Add the enchilada sauce, tomatoes, chilies, salt and pepper; bring to a boil. Reduce heat; cover and simmer for 2 hours or until meat is tender. Combine flour and water; add to beef mixture, stirring constantly. Bring to a boil; cook and stir for 1 minute or until thickened. Warm tortillas; spoon 1/2 cup filling, off center, on each one. Fold sides and bottom of tortilla over filling, then roll up. Spoon a little more filling over top of burritos. Serve immediately. Garnish with tomatoes, olives, cheese, sour cream, onions, lettuce and/or guacamole if desired. **Yield:** 8 servings.

Tarragon Skillet Chicken

Sarah Patterson, Little Rock, Arkansas

1-1/2 pounds boneless skinless chicken breast halves
Salt and pepper to taste
1 teaspoon lemon-pepper seasoning
1/4 cup butter *or* margarine
2 tablespoons minced green onions
1 cup heavy cream
2 tablespoons lemon juice
1 teaspoon dried tarragon
Hot cooked rice

Pound chicken to 1/4-in. thickness; cut each half into three pieces. Season with salt, pepper and lemon pepper. In a large skillet, saute a third of the chicken at a time in butter until browned and no longer pink. Remove and keep warm. In the same skillet, saute onions until tender. Add cream, lemon juice and tarragon; bring to a boil. Cook and stir until thickened, about 5-6 minutes. Serve over chicken with rice. **Yield:** 4 servings.

Honey-Garlic Pork Chops

Helen Carpenter, Marble Falls, Texas

4 boneless center pork loin chops (1-1/2 to 1-1/4 inches thick)
1/4 cup lemon juice
1/4 cup honey
2 tablespoons soy sauce
2 garlic cloves, minced

Place pork chops in a shallow dish. Combine lemon juice, honey, soy sauce and garlic; pour over chops. Cover and refrigerate for 4-8 hours. Remove chops; discard marinade. Grill, covered, over medium coals for 15-20 minutes or until juices run clear. **Yield:** 4 servings.

Festive Ham 'n' Cheese Bread

Dona Bass, Aberdeen, Maryland

1 loaf (1 pound) French bread
2 cups cubed Monterey Jack cheese (1/4-inch pieces)
2 cups cubed fully cooked ham (1/4-inch pieces)
1/2 cup finely chopped red onion
1/2 cup butter *or* margarine, melted
2 tablespoons lemon juice
2 tablespoons poppy seeds
2 teaspoons prepared mustard

Slice bread diagonally about every 1/2 in., not cutting all the way through bottom crust. Place loaf on a piece of foil large enough to wrap it completely. Insert cheese, ham and onion evenly between every other slice. Combine remaining ingredients; drizzle between slices and over top. Wrap foil tightly. Bake at 350° for 35 minutes. Cut bread between unstuffed slices; serve warm. **Yield:** 6-8 servings. **Editor's Note:** This recipe may easily be doubled.

KEEP IT TOGETHER. To prevent leftover meat loaf from crumbling when you slice it for sandwiches, knead the uncooked mixture before shaping and baking.

WELCOME friends and family into your home with a simple-to-prepare stew simmering on the stove. It's the perfect way to satisfy hearty appetites. Whether it spotlights beef, chicken, pork or sausage, a steaming-hot stew is sure to delight everyone at your table.

ONE-DISH DINNERS. Clockwise from bottom: **Herbed Beef Stew and Dumplings**, **Creamy Sausage Stew**, **Skillet Chicken Stew** and **Pork and Winter Squash Stew** (all recipes are on p. 19).

STEWS & SOUPS

Country-style cooking couldn't be easier—or more delectable—with this super selection of savory stews and soups.

CREAMY SAUSAGE STEW

Rosemary Jesse, Cabool, Missouri
(PICTURED AT LEFT)

8 to 10 medium red potatoes, cut into 1-1/2-inch pieces
2 large white onions, quartered
1 large green pepper, cut into 1-inch pieces
1 large sweet red pepper, cut into 1-inch pieces
2 pounds smoked Polish sausage, cut into 1-inch slices
1/3 cup cooking oil
1 tablespoon dried basil
2 teaspoons salt
1 teaspoon pepper
1 pint heavy cream
3 tablespoons cornstarch
3 tablespoons water

Place potatoes in a 5-qt. roasting pan. Add onions, peppers and sausage; toss gently. Combine oil, basil, salt and pepper. Pour over the meat and vegetables; toss well. Cover and bake at 350° for 45 minutes; stir. Add the cream; cover and bake 30-40 minutes longer or until potatoes are tender. Combine cornstarch and water; stir into stew. Place on stovetop and bring to a boil, stirring constantly until thickened. **Yield:** 10-12 servings.

HERBED BEEF STEW AND DUMPLINGS

Madeleine DeGruchy, Antigonish, Nova Scotia
(PICTURED AT LEFT)

1 pound lean beef stew meat, cut into 1/2-inch cubes
2 tablespoons cooking oil
2 medium onions, chopped
2 garlic cloves, minced
3-1/4 cups water, *divided*
1 teaspoon dried basil
3/4 teaspoon dried thyme
1/2 teaspoon rubbed sage
1/2 teaspoon ground cinnamon
1 to 2 teaspoons salt
1/4 teaspoon pepper
1 pound baby carrots
3 medium parsnips, cut into 1-inch pieces
1/2 teaspoon browning sauce, optional
2 tablespoons cornstarch

DUMPLINGS:

1-1/3 cups all-purpose flour
1 tablespoon baking powder
1 tablespoon chopped fresh parsley, optional
1/2 teaspoon salt
1 egg, beaten
1 tablespoon vegetable oil
1/2 cup water

In a 5-qt. Dutch oven, brown beef in oil. Add onions and garlic; continue to cook until onions are tender. Add 3 cups water and all the seasonings. Cover and simmer until the meat is tender, about 2 to 2-1/2 hours. Add carrots and parsnips; cover and simmer for 45 minutes or until vegetables are tender. Stir in browning sauce if desired. Combine cornstarch and remaining water; gradually stir into stew. Bring to a boil, stirring constantly; boil for 1 minute. For dumplings, combine flour, baking powder, parsley if desired and salt. Stir in egg, oil and water. Drop into six mounds onto boiling stew. Cover and cook 10-12 minutes or until done. Do not lift cover. Serve immediately. **Yield:** 6 servings.

SKILLET CHICKEN STEW

Valerie Jordan, Kingmont, West Virginia
(PICTURED AT LEFT)

1/3 cup all-purpose flour
1/2 teaspoon salt
Dash pepper
1-1/2 pounds boneless skinless chicken breasts, cut into 1-inch pieces
3 tablespoons butter *or* margarine
1 medium onion, sliced
3 celery ribs, sliced
2 medium potatoes, peeled and cut into 3/4-inch cubes
3 medium carrots, sliced 1/4 inch thick
1 cup chicken broth
1/2 teaspoon dried thyme
1 tablespoon ketchup
1 tablespoon cornstarch

Combine flour, salt and pepper in a shallow bowl; coat chicken. In a large skillet, melt butter; brown chicken. Add onion and celery; cook for 3 minutes. Stir in potatoes and carrots. Combine broth, thyme, ketchup and cornstarch; stir into skillet. Bring to a boil. Reduce heat; cover and simmer for 15-20 minutes or until the vegetables are tender. **Yield:** 4-6 servings.

PORK AND WINTER SQUASH STEW

Evelyn Plyler, Apple Valley, California
(PICTURED AT LEFT)

✓ This tasty dish uses less sugar, salt and fat. Recipe includes *Diabetic Exchanges*.

2 pounds lean boneless pork, cut into 1-inch cubes
2 tablespoons cooking oil, *divided*
2 cups chopped onion
2 garlic cloves, minced
3 cups sliced fresh mushrooms
2-1/2 cups diagonally sliced carrots
2 cans (14-1/2 ounces *each*) Italian stewed tomatoes
2 teaspoons dried thyme
1/2 teaspoon pepper
1-1/2 teaspoons salt, optional
4 cups cubed peeled butternut squash
Hot cooked noodles, optional

In a 4-qt. Dutch oven, brown pork in 1 tablespoon of oil. Remove from pan; drain and set aside. Heat remaining oil in the same pan over medium heat. Saute onion and garlic for 3 minutes. Return pork to pan. Add mushrooms, carrots, tomatoes and seasonings; bring to a boil. Reduce heat; cover and simmer for 1 hour. Add squash; simmer, uncovered, for 30 minutes or until meat and vegetables are tender. Serve over noodles if desired. **Yield:** 8 servings. **Diabetic Exchanges:** One serving (prepared without added salt and served without noodles) equals 2 meat, 2 vegetable, 1 starch, 1 fat; also, 298 calories, 393 mg sodium, 60 mg cholesterol, 26 gm carbohydrate, 22 gm protein, 14 gm fat.

THICK AND RICH. Like your stew a little thicker? Just before serving, try adding instant potato flakes (about 1/2 cup at a time) until the gravy's the right consistency.

Pasta Meatball Stew

Pat Jelinek, Kitchener, Ontario

(PICTURED ON PAGE 6 AND BACK COVER)

- 1 pound ground beef
- 1 egg, lightly beaten
- 1/4 cup dry bread crumbs
- 1/4 cup milk
- 1/2 teaspoon dry mustard
- 1/2 teaspoon salt
- 1/2 teaspoon pepper
- 1 tablespoon cooking oil

SAUCE:

- 1 cup chopped onion
- 2 garlic cloves, minced
- 1 tablespoon cooking oil
- 2 tablespoons all-purpose flour
- 1-1/2 cups beef broth
- 1 can (14-1/2 ounces) diced tomatoes, undrained
- 2 tablespoons tomato paste
- 1 bay leaf
- 3/4 teaspoon dried thyme
- 1/2 teaspoon salt
- 1-1/2 cups sliced carrots
- 1-1/2 cups chopped zucchini
- 1 cup chopped green pepper
- 1 cup chopped sweet red pepper
- 1 tablespoon minced fresh parsley
- 2 cups cooked pasta

Combine beef, egg, crumbs, milk, mustard, salt and pepper; mix well. Shape into 1-in. balls. In a Dutch oven over medium heat, brown meatballs in oil; drain and set aside. In same pan, saute onion and garlic in oil until onion is tender. Blend in flour. Gradually add broth, stirring constantly; bring to a boil. Cook and stir 1-2 minutes or until thickened. Add tomatoes, paste, bay leaf, thyme and salt; mix well. Add meatballs and carrots; bring to a boil. Reduce heat; cover and simmer 30 minutes. Add zucchini and peppers; bring to a boil. Reduce heat; cover and simmer 10-15 minutes or until vegetables are tender. Add parsley and pasta; heat through. Remove bay leaf. **Yield:** 6-8 servings.

Chili with Potato Dumplings

Shirley Marshall, Michigantown, Indiana

(PICTURED ON PAGE 11)

- 1 pound ground beef
- 1 pound ground turkey
- 1/2 cup chopped onion
- 1 can (15-1/2 ounces) kidney beans, rinsed and drained
- 1 can (15-1/2 ounces) mild chili beans, undrained
- 1/2 cup chopped green pepper
- 4 teaspoons chili powder
- 1 teaspoon salt
- 1 teaspoon paprika
- 1 teaspoon cumin seed
- 1/2 teaspoon garlic salt
- 1/2 teaspoon dried oregano
- 1/4 teaspoon crushed red pepper flakes
- 3 cups tomato-vegetable juice (V-8)

DUMPLINGS:

- 1 cup mashed potato flakes
- 1 cup all-purpose flour
- 1 tablespoon minced fresh parsley
- 2 teaspoons baking powder
- 1/2 teaspoon salt
- 1 cup milk
- 1 egg, beaten

In a 5-qt. Dutch oven, cook beef, turkey and onion until meat is browned; drain. Add the next 11 ingredients; bring to a boil. Reduce heat; cover and simmer for 30 minutes, stirring occasionally. In a medium bowl, combine the first five dumpling ingredients. Add milk and egg; stir just until moistened. Let rest for 3 minutes. Drop by tablespoonfuls into simmering chili. Cover and cook for 15 minutes. **Yield:** 8 servings (2 quarts).

Harvest Stew

Marion Kowalski, Wauwatosa, Wisconsin

HERBED BISCUITS:

- 2 cups cake flour
- 1 tablespoon sugar
- 2 teaspoons baking powder
- 2 teaspoons minced fresh basil *or* 3/4 teaspoon dried basil
- 1 teaspoon minced fresh rosemary *or* 1/4 teaspoon dried rosemary, crushed
- 1/2 teaspoon baking soda
- 1/2 teaspoon salt
- 6 tablespoons cold butter *or* margarine
- 2/3 cup buttermilk

STEW:

- 1-1/2 pounds boneless pork, cut into 1-inch cubes
- 2 tablespoons cooking oil
- 2 cups chicken broth
- 1-1/2 cups chopped onion
- 2 garlic cloves, minced
- 2 teaspoons *each* minced fresh basil and rosemary *or* 3/4 teaspoon *each* dried basil and rosemary, crushed
- 1/2 teaspoon salt
- 1/4 teaspoon pepper
- 1 medium rutabaga (1-1/4 pounds), cut into 1/2-inch cubes
- 2 large carrots, cut into 1/2-inch slices
- 3/4 pound fresh green beans, cut into 1-1/2-inch pieces
- 3 tablespoons cornstarch
- 3 tablespoons cold water

In a medium bowl, combine the first seven ingredients. Cut in butter until mixture resembles coarse crumbs. Stir in buttermilk; mix to form a soft dough (dough will be slightly sticky). Turn onto a floured surface; knead gently 3-4 times. Roll dough to 1/4-in. thickness; cut with a 2-1/2-in. maple leaf or round cutter. Cover and refrigerate. In a 5-qt. Dutch oven, brown pork in oil. Add broth, onion, garlic, basil, rosemary, salt and pepper; cover and simmer for 1 hour. Add rutabaga and carrots; cover and simmer for 30 minutes or until vegetables are crisp-tender. Add beans; cook for 20 minutes. Combine cornstarch and water; stir into stew. Bring to a boil; boil for 2 minutes. Pour into an ungreased shallow 2-1/2- to 3-qt. baking dish. Immediately top with 12 biscuits. Bake, uncovered, at 400° for 15 minutes or until biscuits are golden brown. Bake remaining biscuits on an ungreased baking sheet for 10-12 minutes. **Yield:** 6-8 servings.

Turkey Sausage Stew

Sharon Moon, Hartsville, South Carolina

✓ This tasty dish uses less sugar, salt and fat. Recipe includes *Diabetic Exchanges*.

- 1 package (16 ounces) frozen vegetables for stew
- 1 can (10-3/4 ounces) condensed low-fat tomato soup, undiluted
- 2 cups water
- 1 pound low-fat smoked turkey sausage, sliced 1/4 inch thick
- 1/4 cup ketchup
- 2 garlic cloves, minced
- 1/2 teaspoon dried basil
- 1/4 teaspoon pepper

In a large saucepan, combine vegetables, soup and water; bring to a boil. Reduce heat. Add remaining ingredients; simmer for 35-45 minutes or until the vegetables are tender. **Yield:** 8 servings. **Diabetic Exchanges:** One serving equals 1-1/2 meat, 1 starch; also, 190 calories, 622 mg sodium, 25 mg cholesterol, 17 gm carbohydrate, 11 gm protein, 8 gm fat.

Walk-Along Chili

Joyce vonStempa, Jeffersontown, Kentucky

- 2 pounds ground beef
- 1 small onion, chopped
- 2 garlic cloves, minced
- 1 can (28 ounces) tomatoes with liquid, cut up
- 1 can (8 ounces) tomato sauce
- 1 can (6 ounces) tomato paste

2 to 3 tablespoons chili powder
1 tablespoon paprika
1 tablespoon dried oregano
1-1/2 teaspoons salt
1 teaspoon ground cumin
16 bags (1-1/4 ounces *each*) corn chips
Shredded cheddar cheese

In a large saucepan or Dutch oven over medium heat, brown meat; drain. Add onion and garlic; cook and stir for 5 minutes. Add the next eight ingredients and mix well; bring to a boil. Cover and simmer for 1 hour. To serve, split open bags of chips at the back seam or cut an "x" in the bag; add 1/2 cup of chili to each and top with cheese. **Yield:** 16 servings.

Wiener Stew

Lori Weimer, Somerset, Pennsylvania

2 packages (16 ounces *each*) frozen vegetables for stew
1/2 cup diced celery
1/2 cup diced onion
1-1/2 teaspoons salt
1/2 teaspoon dried thyme
1/4 teaspoon pepper
1/4 teaspoon garlic powder
1/2 cup milk
4 wieners (1/2 pound), cut into 1/2-inch pieces
5 tablespoons all-purpose flour
5 tablespoons butter *or* margarine, softened

In a 3-qt. saucepan, combine the first seven ingredients. Cover with water; bring to a boil. Reduce heat; cover and simmer until the vegetables are tender, about 10-15 minutes. Add milk and wieners; return to a boil. Meanwhile, blend flour and butter. Add to boiling stew, stirring constantly. Cook until thickened. **Yield:** 6-8 servings.

Creamy Pumpkin Soup

Emmi Schneider, Oak Lake, Manitoba

1 medium onion, chopped
2 tablespoons butter *or* margarine
2 cans (14-1/2 ounces *each*) chicken broth
2 cups sliced peeled potatoes
2 cups cooked *or* canned pumpkin
2 to 2-1/2 cups milk
1/2 teaspoon ground nutmeg
1/2 teaspoon salt
1/4 teaspoon pepper
1 cup (8 ounces) sour cream
1 tablespoon chopped fresh parsley
3 bacon strips, cooked and crumbled

In a large saucepan, saute onion in butter until tender. Add the broth, potatoes and pumpkin; cook until the potatoes are tender, about 15 minutes. Remove from the heat; cool. Puree half of the mixture at a time in a blender or food processor until smooth; return all to the pan. Add the milk, nutmeg, salt and pepper; heat through. Meanwhile, combine the sour cream and parsley. Spoon soup into bowls; top each with a dollop of sour cream and sprinkle with bacon. **Yield:** 6 servings (1-1/2 quarts).

Cauliflower Cheese Soup

Rosa Renee McEldowney, Jackson, Michigan

1 medium head cauliflower, broken into florets
1 medium onion, chopped
1 can (14-1/2 ounces) chicken broth
1 chicken bouillon cube
2 tablespoons butter *or* margarine
2 tablespoons all-purpose flour
3 cups milk
2 cups (8 ounces) shredded cheddar cheese
1 tablespoon dried parsley flakes
1 teaspoon salt
1/4 teaspoon ground nutmeg
1/8 teaspoon *each* cayenne pepper, curry powder and white pepper

In a large saucepan, combine the cauliflower, onion, broth and bouillon. Cover and cook over medium heat until the vegetables are tender. Meanwhile, in a medium saucepan, melt butter; stir in flour until smooth. Gradually add milk. Cook and stir until bubbly. Cook and stir for 2-3 minutes longer or until thickened. Reduce heat; add cheese and seasonings. Pour into cauliflower mixture. Simmer slowly for 30 minutes (do not boil). **Yield:** 6-8 servings (2 quarts).

Beef Minestrone

Ann Lape, Richmondville, New York

✓ This tasty dish uses less sugar, salt and fat. Recipe includes *Diabetic Exchanges*.

1 pound ground round
1 cup chopped onion
6 cups water
1 cup cubed peeled potatoes
1 cup chopped tomatoes
1 cup shredded cabbage
1 cup chopped carrots
1/2 cup chopped celery
1/4 cup uncooked long grain rice
1/2 teaspoon dried basil
1/2 teaspoon dried thyme
1 bay leaf
1/4 teaspoon pepper
5 teaspoons grated Parmesan

In a Dutch oven, cook meat and onion until meat is browned and onion is tender; drain. Add next 11 ingredients; bring to a boil. Reduce heat; cover and simmer for 1 hour. Discard bay leaf. Sprinkle each serving with 1/2 teaspoon of Parmesan. **Yield:** 10 servings. **Diabetic Exchanges:** One serving (1 cup) equals 1 meat, 1 vegetable, 1/2 starch; also, 141 calories, 58 mg sodium, 31 mg cholesterol, 10 gm carbohydrate, 11 gm protein, 7 gm fat.

Taco Soup

Roxanne Barone, Billings, Montana

2 pounds ground beef
1 medium onion, finely chopped
1 can (28 ounces) tomatoes
1 can (15 ounces) tomato sauce
1 cup water
1 can (15 ounces) pinto beans, rinsed and drained
1 can (14 to 16 ounces) whole kernel corn, drained
1 envelope taco seasoning mix
Shredded cheddar cheese, sliced avocado, chopped tomato and corn chips, optional

In a large saucepan or a Dutch oven, brown beef and onion; drain. Puree the tomatoes in their liquid; add to pan with tomato sauce, water, beans, corn and taco seasoning. Bring to a boil. Reduce heat and simmer for 5 minutes. If desired, top each serving with cheese, avocado and tomato, and serve with chips. **Yield:** 10 servings (2-1/2 quarts).

Tomato Bisque

Mrs. B.B. Mallory, Irving, Texas

2 cans (14-1/2 ounces *each*) whole tomatoes with liquid, cut up
2 beef bouillon cubes
1 tablespoon sugar
1 to 2 teaspoons salt
1 teaspoon onion powder
1 bay leaf
1/4 teaspoon dried basil
1/4 teaspoon white pepper
1/2 cup butter *or* margarine
1/3 cup all-purpose flour
4 cups milk

In a saucepan, combine the first eight ingredients; bring to a boil. Reduce heat; simmer, uncovered, for 30 minutes. Remove bay leaf; press mixture through sieve and set aside. In a large saucepan, melt butter; blend in flour until smooth and bubbly. Gradually stir in milk. Bring to a boil over medium heat, stirring constantly; cook for 2 minutes. Reduce heat. Gradually stir in tomato mixture until smooth; heat through. **Yield:** 8-10 servings.

TAKE A BREAK from traditional holiday fare with these delightful dishes. They're bound to become newfound favorites in your home. Start your meal with a large tureen of clam chowder and pass a platter of warm corn bread. For a hearty main course, the Hoosier Pork Chop Supper is a special "meat and potatoes" meal in one skillet! For dessert, everyone will love almond brittle dipped in chocolate.

FESTIVE RECIPES. Clockwise from bottom: **Hoosier Pork Chop Supper** (p. 13), **New England Clam Chowder** (p. 23), **Chocolate Almond Brittle** (p. 73) and **Creole Corn Bread** (p. 50).

New England Clam Chowder

Rachel Nydam, Uxbridge, Massachusetts
(PICTURED AT LEFT)

4 medium potatoes, peeled and cubed
2 medium onions, chopped
1/2 cup butter *or* margarine
3/4 cup all-purpose flour
2 quarts milk
3 cans (6-1/2 ounces *each*) chopped clams, undrained
2 to 3 teaspoons salt
1 teaspoon ground sage
1 teaspoon ground thyme
1/2 teaspoon celery salt
1/2 teaspoon pepper
Minced fresh parsley

Place potatoes in a saucepan and cover with water; bring to a boil. Cover and cook until tender. Meanwhile, in a Dutch oven, saute onions in butter until tender. Add flour; mix until smooth. Stir in milk. Cook over medium heat, stirring constantly, until thickened and bubbly. Drain potatoes; add to Dutch oven. Add clams and remaining ingredients; heat through. **Yield:** 10-12 servings (3 quarts).

Quick & Easy

Meatball Stew

Clara Goddard, Orillia, Ontario

1 pound ground beef
1 egg, beaten
1/2 cup dry bread crumbs
1/2 cup finely chopped onion
2 tablespoons dry onion soup mix
1 can (16 ounces) whole potatoes, drained and quartered
1-1/4 cups sliced frozen carrots
1-1/4 cups frozen peas
1 can (10-3/4 ounces) condensed cream of mushroom soup, undiluted
1 can (10-1/2 ounces) condensed beef broth, undiluted
1/2 teaspoon dried savory
1/4 teaspoon dried thyme
2 tablespoons cornstarch
2 tablespoons water
1/4 teaspoon browning sauce, optional

Combine beef, egg, crumbs, onion and soup mix; mix well. Shape into 1-1/2-in. balls. Place in a microwave-safe baking dish. Cover and microwave on high for 5 minutes. Turn meatballs and microwave 5 minutes more; drain. Combine the next seven ingredients. Spoon over meatballs; mix well. Cover and cook at 50% power for 15-20 minutes, stirring once. Combine cornstarch, water and browning sauce; stir into the stew. Microwave on high for 2 minutes or until thickened and bubbly. **Yield:** 4-6 servings.

Beef Vegetable Stew

Donna Nannini, Caledonia, Michigan

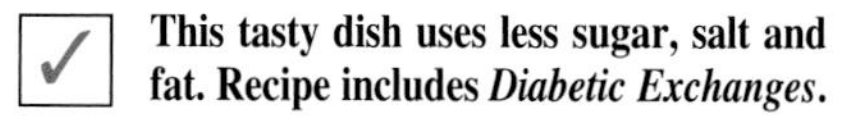

This tasty dish uses less sugar, salt and fat. Recipe includes *Diabetic Exchanges*.

2-1/2 pounds lean beef stew meat, cut into 1-inch cubes
2 large onions, chopped
2 garlic cloves, minced
1/2 cup water
1 low-sodium beef bouillon cube
3 cans (14-1/2 ounces *each*) low-sodium beef broth
4 potatoes, peeled and cubed
3 medium carrots, sliced
2 medium green peppers, cut into 1/2-inch pieces
2 celery ribs, sliced
3 cups cubed rutabaga
1-1/2 cups cubed parsnips
1-1/2 cups cubed turnips
3/4 teaspoon dried marjoram
1/2 teaspoon pepper
1/4 teaspoon dried savory
1/4 teaspoon hot pepper sauce
2 tablespoons cornstarch
3 tablespoons water

In a Dutch oven, combine the beef, onions, garlic, 1/2 cup water, bouillon and enough of the broth to cover. Bring to a boil. Cover and simmer until meat is tender, about 2 hours. Add vegetables, seasonings and remaining broth. Simmer 30-45 minutes or until vegetables are tender. Combine cornstarch and water; gradually add to the boiling mixture. Cook and stir for 2 minutes. **Yield:** 16 servings. **Diabetic Exchanges:** One serving equals 2 vegetable, 1 lean meat, 1/2 starch; also, 143 calories, 59 mg sodium, 21 mg cholesterol, 13 gm carbohydrate, 15 gm protein, 3 gm fat.

Oven Cheese Chowder

Martha Eastham, San Diego, California

1/2 pound zucchini, cut into 1-inch chunks
2 medium onions, chopped
1 can (15 ounces) garbanzo beans, rinsed and drained
1 can (14-1/2 ounces) diced tomatoes with liquid
1 can (11 ounces) Mexican-style corn, drained
1 can (14-1/2 ounces) chicken broth
2 teaspoons salt
1/4 teaspoon pepper
1 garlic clove, minced
1 teaspoon dried basil
1 bay leaf
1 cup (4 ounces) shredded Monterey Jack cheese
1 cup grated Romano cheese
1-1/2 cups half-and-half cream

In a 3-qt. baking dish, combine the first 11 ingredients. Cover and bake at 400° for 1 hour, stirring once. Stir in the cheeses and cream. Bake, uncovered, for 10 minutes. Remove bay leaf. **Yield:** 10-12 servings (3 quarts).

Spicy Stew

Sandra Bradley, Floydada, Texas

1 pound ground beef
3 medium green peppers, chopped
1 medium onion, chopped
1 can (28 ounces) tomatoes with liquid, cut up
1 can (16 to 17 ounces) peas, drained
3 cans (15-1/2 ounces *each*) kidney *or* pinto beans, rinsed and drained
1 tablespoon sugar
2 teaspoons chili powder
1 teaspoon garlic powder
1 teaspoon ground cumin
1/2 teaspoon salt
1/2 teaspoon pepper

In a Dutch oven, cook beef, peppers and onion until meat is browned; drain. Stir in remaining ingredients; bring to a boil. Reduce heat; cover and simmer for 30 minutes. **Yield:** 6-8 servings.

Sausage Stew

Sheila Murphy, Killdeer, North Dakota

1 pound bulk pork sausage
1 package (10 ounces) frozen corn
1 package (10 ounces) frozen peas and carrots
1-1/2 cups diced peeled potatoes
1 cup chopped tomato
1 can (11-1/2 ounces) condensed split pea with ham and bacon soup, undiluted
1-1/4 cups water
1/2 cup chopped celery
1/2 cup chopped onion
1/4 cup chopped green pepper
1-1/2 teaspoons dill weed
1-1/2 teaspoons chili powder

In a Dutch oven, brown and crumble the sausage; drain. Add remaining ingredients; cover and bring to a boil. Reduce heat; cover and simmer for 25-30 minutes or until potatoes are tender. **Yield:** 4-6 servings.

STEWING over what to make for dinner tonight? One look at this spread should give you plenty of answers. They're packed with hearty ingredients like meat, beans, potatoes, pasta, tomatoes and zucchini. So you know they'll please everyone in your family. Now your biggest challenge is deciding which one to make first!

STEWPENDOUS SUPPERS! Clockwise from lower left: **Sausage-Bean Stew**, **Southwestern Meat and Potato Stew**, **Italian Hunters Stew**, **Green Chili Pork Stew**, **Irish Lamb Stew**, **Tangy Beef and Vegetable Stew**, **Easy Oven Stew** and **Tomato Zucchini Stew** (all recipes on pages 26 and 27).

Sausage Bean Stew

Cheryl Nagy, Newark, Ohio

(PICTURED ON PAGE 24)

4 cups chicken broth
3 cans (16 ounces *each*) beans (kidney, butter, pinto *and/or* black-eyed peas, etc.), rinsed and drained
3 medium carrots, diced
3 celery ribs, diced
1 pound smoked sausage, cut into 1/2-inch slices
1 large onion, chopped
1/2 cup pearl barley
1/2 cup dried lentils
1 teaspoon hot pepper sauce
1 cup chopped fresh spinach

In a 4-qt. Dutch oven, place all ingredients except spinach. Cover and cook over medium heat for 45-60 minutes or until the barley and lentils are tender. Stir in spinach and heat through. **Yield:** 6-8 servings.

Southwestern Meat and Potato Stew

Linda Schwarz, Bertrand, Nebraska

(PICTURED ON PAGE 24)

✓ This tasty dish uses less sugar, salt and fat. Recipe includes *Diabetic Exchanges*.

2 pounds ground beef *or* chuck
1 large onion, chopped
1 cup water, *divided*
1 can (28 ounces) tomatoes with liquid, cut up
1 bag (16 ounces) frozen corn
3 medium potatoes, peeled and cubed
1 cup salsa
1 teaspoon salt, optional
1 teaspoon ground cumin
1/2 teaspoon garlic powder
1/2 teaspoon pepper
2 tablespoons all-purpose flour

In a Dutch oven or large kettle, brown beef and onion; drain. Add 3/4 cup water and all remaining ingredients except flour. Bring to a boil; reduce heat. Cover and simmer for 1-1/2 hours. Combine flour and remaining water; stir into stew. Cook and stir until boiling and slightly thickened. **Yield:** 6 servings. **Diabetic Exchanges:** One serving (prepared with ground chuck and low-sodium tomatoes and without added salt) equals 3 meat, 2 starch, 1 vegetable; also, 406 calories, 354 mg sodium, 84 mg cholesterol, 36 gm carbohydrate, 36 gm protein, 13 gm fat.

Italian Hunters Stew

Ann Shorey, Sutherlin, Oregon

(PICTURED ON PAGE 24)

2 pounds lean beef stew meat, cut into 1-1/2-inch cubes
1 tablespoon all-purpose flour
3 tablespoons cooking oil
2 garlic cloves, minced
3 large onions, quartered
1 cup beef broth
2 tablespoons seasoned salt
1 teaspoon chili powder
1 teaspoon dried oregano
1 teaspoon dried rosemary
2 cans (14-1/2 ounces *each*) Italian stewed tomatoes
1 can (6 ounces) tomato paste
1/2 cup minced fresh parsley
3 medium carrots, cut into 1-inch pieces
8 ounces mostaccioli *or* penne pasta, cooked and drained
1/3 cup shredded Parmesan cheese

Toss meat with flour; brown on all sides in oil in a 5-qt. Dutch oven. Add garlic and onions; saute until tender. Stir in broth, seasoned salt, chili powder, oregano and rosemary. Cover and simmer for 1-1/2 hours. Add tomatoes, tomato paste, parsley and carrots. Cover and simmer for 1 hour or until meat and carrots are tender. Stir in macaroni; heat through. Sprinkle with cheese. **Yield:** 8-10 servings.

Green Chili Pork Stew

Pat Henderson, Deer Park, Texas

(PICTURED ON PAGE 24)

✓ This tasty dish uses less sugar, salt and fat. Recipe includes *Diabetic Exchanges*.

2 pounds lean boneless pork, cut into 1-1/2-inch cubes
1 tablespoon cooking oil
4 cups chicken broth, *divided*
3 cans (11 ounces *each*) whole kernel corn, drained
2 celery ribs, diced
2 medium potatoes, peeled and diced
2 medium tomatoes, diced
3 cans (4 ounces *each*) chopped green chilies
2 teaspoons ground cumin
1 teaspoon dried oregano
1 teaspoon salt, optional
3 tablespoons all-purpose flour
Corn bread *or* warmed flour tortillas, optional

In a 5-qt. Dutch oven over medium-high heat, brown pork in oil. Add 3-1/2 cups broth, corn, celery, potatoes, tomatoes, chilies, cumin, oregano and salt if desired; bring to a boil. Reduce heat; cover and simmer for 1 hour or until meat and vegetables are tender. Combine flour and remaining broth; stir into stew. Bring to a boil; cook, stirring constantly, until thickened. Serve with corn bread or tortillas if desired. **Yield:** 8 servings. **Diabetic Exchanges:** One serving (prepared with low-sodium chicken broth and without added salt, and served without corn bread or tortillas) equals 2 meat, 2 vegetable, 1 starch, 1 fat; also, 306 calories, 466 mg sodium, 60 mg cholesterol, 27 gm carbohydrate, 23 gm protein, 12 gm fat.

Irish Lamb Stew

Jeanne Dahling, Elgin, Minnesota

(PICTURED ON PAGE 25)

6 tablespoons all-purpose flour, *divided*
1 teaspoon salt
1/8 teaspoon pepper
1-1/2 pounds lamb stew meat, cut into 1-inch cubes
2 tablespoons cooking oil
1/2 teaspoon dill weed
3 cups water
8 extra-small *or* boiling onions
3 medium carrots, cut into 1-inch pieces
2 large potatoes, peeled and cubed
1/2 cup light cream
Hot biscuits

Combine 4 tablespoons flour, salt and pepper in a plastic bag. Add lamb; shake to coat. In a 4-qt. Dutch oven, heat oil; brown lamb on all sides. Add dill and water; bring to a boil; Reduce heat; cover and simmer for 1-1/2 hours or until meat is almost tender. Add onions, carrots and potatoes. Cover and simmer for 30 minutes or until the meat and vegetables are tender. Combine cream and remaining flour; stir into stew. Cook and stir until boiling and slightly thickened. Serve over biscuits. **Yield:** 6 servings.

YOU SAY TOMATO? When a stew recipe calls for tomato juice, try substituting a can of vegetable juice cocktail instead.

Tangy Beef and Vegetable Stew

Amberleah Holmberg, Calgary, Alberta

(PICTURED ON PAGE 25)

6 cups cubed peeled potatoes (1/2-inch pieces)
8 medium carrots, cut into 1/2-inch pieces
2 medium onions, cubed
4 pounds lean beef stew meat, cut into 1-inch pieces
1/3 cup cooking oil
1/3 cup all-purpose flour
4 beef bouillon cubes
3 cups boiling water
1/3 cup vinegar
1/3 cup ketchup
3 tablespoons prepared horseradish
3 tablespoons prepared mustard
2 tablespoons sugar
2 cups *each* frozen peas and corn
2 cups sliced fresh mushrooms

Place the potatoes, carrots and onions in a large slow cooker. In a large skillet, brown beef in oil, a single layer at a time; place over the vegetables. Sprinkle with flour. Dissolve bouillon cubes in boiling water. Stir in vinegar, ketchup, horseradish, mustard and sugar; pour over meat and vegetables. Cover and cook on high for 5 hours. Add peas, corn and mushrooms. Cover and cook on high for 45 minutes. **Yield:** 12-16 servings. **Editor's Note:** Cooking times may vary with slow cookers.

Easy Oven Stew

Carol Smith, Stuart, Florida

(PICTURED ON PAGE 25)

✓ This tasty dish uses less sugar, salt and fat. Recipe includes *Diabetic Exchanges*.

2 pounds lean beef stew meat, cut into 1-inch cubes
4 large carrots, cut into 1-inch pieces
2 medium onions, cut into 1-inch pieces
2 celery ribs, cut into 1-inch pieces
2 medium parsnips, cut into 1-inch pieces
1 garlic clove, minced
1 can (14-1/2 ounces) Italian stewed tomatoes
1-1/2 cups beef broth
1 can (8 ounces) tomato sauce
1/2 cup quick-cooking tapioca
1 teaspoon instant coffee granules
1/2 teaspoon dried thyme
1/2 teaspoon dried oregano
1/2 teaspoon salt, optional

In a 5-qt. Dutch oven, combine all ingredients. Cover and bake at 300° for 2-1/2 to 3 hours, stirring every hour, or until the meat and vegetables are tender. **Yield:** 8 servings. **Diabetic Exchanges:** One serving (prepared with low-sodium beef broth and tomato sauce and without added salt) equals 2 meat, 2 vegetable, 1 starch; also, 230 calories, 401 mg sodium, 53 mg cholesterol, 27 gm carbohydrate, 23 gm protein, 6 gm fat.

Tomato Zucchini Stew

Helen Miller, Hickory Hills, Illinois

(PICTURED ON PAGE 25)

1-1/4 pounds bulk Italian sausage
1-1/2 cups sliced celery (3/4-inch pieces)
8 medium fresh tomatoes (about 4 pounds), peeled and cut into sixths
1-1/2 cups tomato juice
4 small zucchini, sliced into 1/4-inch pieces
2-1/2 teaspoons Italian seasoning
1-1/2 to 2 teaspoons salt
1 teaspoon sugar
1/2 teaspoon garlic salt
1/2 teaspoon pepper
3 cups canned *or* frozen corn
2 medium green peppers, sliced into 1-inch pieces
1/4 cup cornstarch
1/4 cup water
Shredded mozzarella cheese

In a 4-qt. Dutch oven, brown and crumble sausage. Add celery and cook for 15 minutes; drain. Add tomatoes, tomato juice, zucchini and seasonings; bring to a boil. Reduce heat; cover and simmer for 20 minutes. Add corn and peppers; cover and simmer for 15 minutes. Combine cornstarch and water; stir into stew. Bring to a boil; cook and stir until mixture thickens. Sprinkle with cheese. **Yield:** 6-8 servings. **Editor's Note:** Three 28-ounce cans of tomatoes with liquid (cut up) may be substituted for the fresh tomatoes and tomato juice.

Venison Vegetable Stew

Jennifer Whitaker, Winchendon, Massachusetts

3 bacon strips
2 pounds venison stew meat, cut into 1-inch cubes
2 large onions, chopped
3-1/2 cups water, *divided*
1 can (8 ounces) tomato sauce
1 envelope dry onion soup mix
2 teaspoons salt
1 bay leaf
2 teaspoons Italian seasoning
7 medium carrots, cut into 1-inch pieces
5 medium potatoes, peeled and cut into 1-inch cubes
4 celery ribs, sliced
3 tablespoons all-purpose flour
Cooked noodles

In a 4-qt. Dutch oven, cook bacon until crisp. Remove to a paper towel to drain; reserve drippings in pan. Crumble bacon and set aside. Cook venison and onions in drippings until meat is lightly browned. Add 3 cups water, tomato sauce, soup mix, salt, bay leaf and Italian seasoning; bring to a boil. Reduce heat; cover and simmer for 1-1/2 hours or until meat is almost tender. Add carrots, potatoes and celery; return to a boil. Reduce heat; cover and simmer 30-45 minutes or until meat and vegetables are tender. Combine flour and remaining water; stir into stew. Cook and stir until boiling and slightly thickened. Stir in bacon. Remove bay leaf before serving. Serve over cooked noodles. **Yield:** 8 servings. **Editor's Note:** If desired, beef stew meat or pork can be used in place of the venison.

Shortcut Brunswick Stew

Eva Still, Crescent, Oklahoma

2 bacon strips
1/2 cup chopped onion
1 can (10-3/4 ounces) condensed tomato soup, undiluted
1-1/4 cups plus 1 tablespoon water, *divided*
1 teaspoon Worcestershire sauce
1/4 teaspoon pepper
1 package (10 ounces) frozen lima beans
1 package (10 ounces) frozen whole kernel corn
2 cups cubed cooked chicken
1 tablespoon cornstarch

In a large skillet, cook bacon until crisp; remove to paper towel to drain. In drippings, cook onion until tender. Stir in soup, 1-1/4 cups water, Worcestershire sauce and pepper; bring to a boil. Add beans and corn; return to a boil. Reduce heat; cover and simmer for 20 minutes. Crumble bacon; add to stew with chicken. Combine cornstarch with the remaining water; stir into stew. Bring to a boil, stirring constantly until thickened. **Yield:** 4 servings.

YOU DON'T have to wait for Valentine's Day to show your loved ones how much you care. This marvelous menu features a slightly spicy stew that will surely warm the heart, especially when served with oven-fresh corn bread. No special-occasion supper is complete without dessert, like melt-in-your-mouth butter cookies or rich chocolaty pudding cake.

"HEART"-Y HELPINGS. Clockwise from the top: **Sweetheart Corn Bread** (p. 50), **Texas Beef Stew** (p. 29), **Valentine Butter Cookies** (p. 62) and **Fudge Pudding Cake** (p. 59).

Texas Beef Stew

Wilma James, Ranger, Texas
(PICTURED AT LEFT)

1-1/4 pounds beef stew meat, cut into 1-inch pieces
1 to 2 tablespoons cooking oil, optional
1/4 cup chopped onion
1-1/2 teaspoons garlic powder
1/4 teaspoon pepper
1 cup water
1 can (16 ounces) tomatoes with liquid, cut up
1 tablespoon ground cumin
1 teaspoon salt

In a large kettle or Dutch oven, brown beef, adding oil if desired; drain. Add onion, garlic powder, pepper and water; bring to a boil. Reduce heat; cover and simmer for 45 minutes or until meat is almost tender. Add tomatoes, cumin and salt; return to a boil. Reduce heat; cover and simmer for 15-20 minutes or until meat is tender. **Yield:** 4 servings (1 quart).

Egg Dumpling Soup

Mary Lou Christman, Norwich, New York

6 cups chicken broth
1 cup finely chopped celery
3 tablespoons minced fresh parsley
2 eggs
2/3 cup all-purpose flour
1 to 2 tablespoons milk
Pepper to taste

In a 4-qt. saucepan, bring broth, celery and parsley to a boil. Meanwhile, in a small bowl, beat eggs. Beat in flour and enough milk to form a mixture the consistency of cake batter. Drop by teaspoonfuls into boiling broth. Reduce heat to medium-low; cover and simmer for 10-15 minutes or until dumplings are light and not gummy. Season with pepper. **Yield:** 4-6 servings (1-3/4 quarts).

White Christmas Chili

Angela Biggin, Lyons, Illinois

1 pound dried navy beans
6 cups turkey *or* chicken broth
1 cup chopped onion
4 garlic cloves, minced
1 teaspoon white pepper
1/2 teaspoon crushed red pepper flakes
1/4 to 1/2 teaspoon curry powder
1/4 teaspoon ground cumin
2 pounds turkey *or* chicken breast, cooked and cubed
1 can (15-1/4 ounces) white sweet corn
1 cup heavy cream
Chopped green and sweet red peppers, optional

Place beans in a large saucepan or Dutch oven; cover with water. Bring to a boil for 2 minutes. Remove from the heat and soak for 1 hour. Drain and rinse beans; return to the pan. Add broth, onion, garlic and seasonings. Cover and simmer for 1-1/2 hours or until tender. Add turkey and corn; simmer for 1-1/2 hours or until tender. Add turkey and corn; simmer for 15 minutes. Add cream just before serving; heat through. If desired, garnish individual servings with peppers. **Yield:** 12-14 servings (3 quarts).

Gazpacho

Chris Brooks, Prescott, Arizona

✓ This tasty dish uses less sugar, salt and fat. Recipe includes *Diabetic Exchanges*.

1 can (46 ounces) vegetable juice
1 can (10-1/2 ounces) condensed beef consomme, undiluted
2 cups chopped cucumber
2 cups chopped tomatoes
1 cup chopped green pepper
1/2 cup chopped onion
1/2 cup chopped celery
1/3 cup red wine vinegar
2 tablespoons fresh lemon juice
2 garlic cloves, minced
3 to 4 drops hot pepper sauce

In a large bowl, combine all ingredients; mix well. Cover and chill for 2-3 hours before serving. Serve cold. **Yield:** 12 servings (3 quarts). **Diabetic Exchanges:** One serving equals 2 vegetable; also, 52 calories, 470 mg sodium, 0 cholesterol, 11 gm carbohydrate, 3 gm protein, trace fat.

Savory Pork Stew

Jodi Bierschenk, Newhall, Iowa

✓ This tasty dish uses less sugar, salt and fat. Recipe includes *Diabetic Exchanges*.

1 pound lean boneless pork, cut into 1-inch cubes
1 cup chopped onion
1 teaspoon dried basil
1/2 teaspoon dried rosemary
1/4 teaspoon pepper
1/2 cup water
1 can (16 ounces) low-sodium tomato sauce
2 cups sliced carrots
1 green pepper, chopped
1/2 pound fresh mushrooms, sliced

Place pork in a Dutch oven that has been sprayed with nonstick cooking spray. Cook over medium heat until browned. Add onion, seasonings, water and tomato sauce; bring to a boil. Reduce heat; cover and simmer 1 hour or until meat is tender. Stir in remaining ingredients. Cover and simmer until the vegetables are tender, about 30 minutes. **Yield:** 5 servings. **Diabetic Exchanges:** One serving equals 3 vegetable, 2 lean meat; also, 201 calories, 644 mg sodium, 48 mg cholesterol, 15 gm carbohydrate, 18 gm protein, 7 gm fat.

Southwestern Bean Soup

Grace Nordang, Methow, Washington

4 bacon strips
3/4 cup chopped onion
3/4 cup chopped celery
1/8 teaspoon garlic powder
1 can (16 ounces) refried beans
1/4 cup picante sauce *or* salsa
1 can (14-1/2 ounces) chicken broth
1 tablespoon chopped fresh parsley
Hot pepper sauce, optional
Shredded cheddar cheese
Tortilla chips

In a medium saucepan, cook bacon until crisp; remove to paper towel to drain. Crumble and set aside. In the drippings, saute the onion and celery; sprinkle with the garlic powder. Cover and simmer for 10 minutes or until vegetables are tender. Add beans, picante sauce, broth, parsley and bacon; bring to a boil. Reduce heat and simmer, uncovered, for 5-10 minutes. Season to taste with hot pepper sauce if desired. Ladle into bowls and top with cheese. Serve with tortilla chips. **Yield:** 4 servings.

Cheddar Cheese Soup

La Verne Becker, Mt. Horeb, Wisconsin

1/2 cup chopped onion
1/2 cup butter *or* margarine
2/3 cup all-purpose flour
1 teaspoon dry mustard
1 teaspoon paprika
1 teaspoon salt
4 cups milk
1 can (10-3/4 ounces) condensed cream of chicken soup, undiluted
3 cups (12 ounces) shredded cheddar cheese
3/4 to 1 cup chicken broth

In a large saucepan, saute onion in butter until tender. Combine flour, mustard, paprika and salt; add to saucepan. Stir to make a smooth paste. Gradually add milk and soup; cook and stir until thick, about 10 minutes. Add the cheese and chicken broth; stir until cheese is melted. **Yield:** 6-8 servings.

SOME "trendy" breakfast foods aren't all they're cracked up to be. So it's no surprise that great country cooks continue to rely on a tried-and-true ingredient like eggs. From quiches and french toast to sandwiches and souffles, such back-to-basic dishes will never disappoint you.

SUNNY SELECTIONS. Clockwise from lower left: **Molded Egg Salad** (p. 42), **Egg-Filled Buns**, **Maple Toast and Eggs**, **Salmon Quiche**, **Cinnamon French Toast** and **Three-Cheese Souffles** (recipes on p. 31).

Farmhouse Breakfasts

Give your family's day a scrumptious start with a mouth-watering medley of egg dishes, griddle goodies and sweet breads.

Egg-Filled Buns

Kathy Wells, Brodhead, Wisconsin
(PICTURED AT LEFT)

2 tablespoons butter *or* margarine
4 eggs, beaten
2 packages (2-1/2 ounces each) sliced smoked beef, chopped
1/3 cup mayonnaise
1/4 teaspoon salt
1/4 teaspoon pepper
1 package (16 ounces) hot roll mix
1 tablespoon milk

Melt butter in a medium skillet. Add the eggs; cook and stir gently until set. Remove from the heat. Add beef, mayonnaise, salt and pepper; mix well. Chill. Prepare roll mix according to package directions. Divide dough into six portions; roll each portion into an 8-in. x 3-in. rectangle. Spoon 1/3 cup of egg mixture on half of each rectangle. Fold over and seal edges. Place on a greased baking sheet. Cover and let rise in a warm place until doubled, about 30 minutes. Brush tops with milk. Bake at 350° for 20-25 minutes or until golden brown. Serve warm. **Yield:** 6 servings.

Quick & Easy

Maple Toast and Eggs

Susan Buttel, Plattsburgh, New York
(PICTURED AT LEFT)

12 bacon strips, diced
1/2 cup maple syrup
1/4 cup butter *or* margarine
12 slices firm-textured white bread
12 eggs
Salt and pepper to taste

In a large skillet, cook bacon until crisp; remove to paper towels to drain. In a small saucepan, heat syrup and butter until butter is melted; set aside. Trim crusts from bread; flatten slices with a rolling pin. Brush one side generously with syrup mixture; press each slice into an ungreased muffin cup with syrup side down. Divide bacon among muffin cups. Carefully break one egg into each cup. Sprinkle with salt and pepper. Cover with foil. Bake at 400° for 18-20 minutes or until the eggs reach desired doneness. Serve immediately. **Yield:** 12 servings.

Salmon Quiche

Deanna Baldwin, Bermuda Dunes, California
(PICTURED AT LEFT)

1 unbaked pastry shell (10 inches)
1 medium onion, chopped
1 tablespoon butter *or* margarine
2 cups (8 ounces) shredded Swiss cheese
1 can (14-3/4 ounces) salmon, drained, flaked and cartilage removed
5 eggs
2 cups light cream
1/4 teaspoon salt
Minced fresh parsley, optional

Line unpricked pastry shell with a double thickness of heavy-duty foil. Bake at 425° for 10 minutes or until edges are just beginning to brown. Remove foil and set crust aside. In a small skillet, saute onion in butter until tender. Sprinkle Swiss cheese in the crust; top with the salmon and onion. In a bowl, beat eggs, cream and salt; pour over salmon mixture. Bake at 350° for 45-50 minutes or until a knife inserted near the center comes out clean. Sprinkle with parsley if desired. Let stand 5 minutes before cutting. **Yield:** 6-8 servings.

Cinnamon French Toast

Catherine Buehre, Weeping Water, Nebraska
(PICTURED AT LEFT)

1 loaf (1 pound) unsliced cinnamon-raisin bread
5 eggs
2 egg yolks
1 cup light cream
3/4 cup packed brown sugar
2 teaspoons pumpkin pie spice
1 teaspoon maple flavoring
1 teaspoon vanilla extract
3 cups milk
1/4 cup butter *or* margarine, melted
Fresh strawberries *or* maple syrup, optional

Slice ends from bread and discard or save for another use. Slice remaining loaf into eight 1-in. slices and arrange in the bottom of two greased 8-in. square baking pans. In a large bowl, beat eggs, yolks, cream, brown sugar, pie spice and flavorings. Gradually add milk, beating until well blended; pour over bread. Cover and chill overnight. Remove from the refrigerator 30 minutes before baking. Drizzle with butter. Bake, uncovered, at 350° for 45-60 minutes or until a knife inserted near the center comes out clean. Serve warm; top with strawberries or syrup if desired. **Yield:** 6-8 servings.

Three-Cheese Souffles

Jean Ference, Sherwood Park, Alberta
(PICTURED AT LEFT)

1/3 cup butter *or* margarine
1/3 cup all-purpose flour
2 cups milk
1 teaspoon Dijon mustard
1/4 teaspoon salt
Dash hot pepper sauce
1-1/2 cups (6 ounces) shredded Swiss cheese
1 cup (4 ounces) shredded cheddar cheese
1/4 cup shredded Parmesan cheese
6 eggs, *separated*
1/2 teaspoon cream of tartar

Melt butter in a medium saucepan. Stir in flour; cook for 1 minute or until bubbly. Gradually add milk, mustard, salt and hot pepper sauce; cook and stir until thickened and bubbly. Add cheeses; stir until melted. Remove from the heat and set aside. In a small mixing bowl, beat egg yolks until thick and lemon-colored, about 3-4 minutes. Add 1/3 cup cheese mixture and mix well. Return all to the saucepan; return to the heat and cook for 1-2 minutes. Cool completely, about 30-40 minutes. In another mixing bowl, beat egg whites until soft peaks form. Add cream of tartar; continue beating until stiff peaks form. Fold into cheese mixture. Pour into ungreased 1-cup souffle dishes or custard cups. Place in a shallow pan. Pour warm water into larger pan to a depth of 1 in. Bake, uncovered, at 325° for 40-45 minutes or until tops are golden browned. Serve immediately. **Yield:** 8 servings.

CREATE warm morning memories with hot, fresh Cranberry Doughnuts (recipe below).

Cranberry Doughnuts

Roberta Archer, Passadumkeag, Maine
(PICTURED ABOVE)

1 egg
1/2 cup sugar
1 tablespoon butter *or* margarine, melted
1-1/2 cups all-purpose flour
2 teaspoons baking powder
1/2 teaspoon ground cinnamon
1/2 teaspoon ground nutmeg
1/4 teaspoon salt
1/2 cup milk
1/2 cup chopped fresh *or* frozen cranberries
Oil for deep-fat frying
Additional sugar

In a bowl, beat egg; add sugar and butter. Combine flour, baking powder, cinnamon, nutmeg and salt; add to sugar mixture alternately with milk. Stir in cranberries. Heat oil in an electric skillet or deep-fat fryer to 375°. Drop tablespoonfuls of batter into oil. Fry doughnuts a few at a time, turning with a slotted spoon until golden, about 2 minutes per side. Drain on paper towels; roll in sugar while still warm. **Yield:** 1-1/2 dozen.

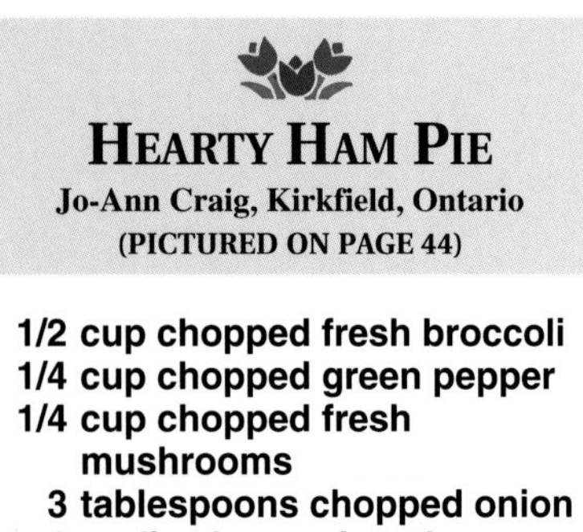

Hearty Ham Pie

Jo-Ann Craig, Kirkfield, Ontario
(PICTURED ON PAGE 44)

1/2 cup chopped fresh broccoli
1/4 cup chopped green pepper
1/4 cup chopped fresh mushrooms
3 tablespoons chopped onion
1 garlic clove, minced
2 teaspoons vegetable oil
2 cups chopped fully cooked ham, *divided*
1-1/2 cups (6 ounces) shredded Swiss cheese, *divided*
1 unbaked pastry shell (9 inches)
4 eggs, beaten
1 cup light cream

In a saucepan, saute the broccoli, green pepper, mushrooms, onion and garlic in oil until tender. Sprinkle half of the ham and cheese into pie crust. Cover with the vegetables and the remaining ham and cheese. Combine eggs and cream; pour over ham and cheese. Bake at 350° for 45-50 minutes or until knife inserted near the center comes out clean. If needed, cover edge of crust with foil to prevent excess browning. **Yield:** 6 servings.

Maple Butter Twists

Marna Krause, Las Vegas, Nevada
(PICTURED ON PAGE 64)

1 package (1/4 ounce) active dry yeast
1/4 cup warm water (110° to 115°)
1/2 cup warm milk (110° to 115°)
1/4 cup butter *or* margarine, melted
2 eggs, beaten
3 tablespoons sugar
1-1/2 teaspoons salt
3-1/4 to 3-1/2 cups all-purpose flour
FILLING:
1/2 cup packed brown sugar
1/2 cup chopped walnuts
1/3 cup sugar
1/4 cup maple syrup
1/4 cup butter *or* margarine, softened
2 tablespoons all-purpose flour
1/2 teaspoon ground cinnamon
1/2 teaspoon maple flavoring

In a large mixing bowl, dissolve yeast in water. Add milk, butter, eggs, sugar, salt and 2 cups flour; beat until smooth. Stir in enough remaining flour to form a soft dough. Turn onto a floured board and knead until smooth and elastic, about 6-8 minutes. Place in a greased bowl, turning once to grease top. Cover and let rise in a warm place until doubled, about 1 hour. Combine all filling ingredients; mix well. Punch dough down and divide in half. Roll each half into a 14-in. x 8-in. rectangle. Spread filling over each rectangle. Starting with the 14-in. edge, roll up and seal edge. Place with seam side down on a greased baking sheet. With a sharp knife, cut roll in half lengthwise; carefully turn cut sides up. Loosely twist strips around each other, keeping cut sides up. Shape into a ring and pinch ends together. Cover and let rise 30 minutes. Bake at 350° for 25-30 minutes or until browned. **Yield:** 2 coffee cakes.

Wild Rice Pancakes

Virginia Byers, Minneapolis, Minnesota

1/2 pound fresh mushrooms, sliced
1/2 cup chopped green onions
2 tablespoons butter *or* margarine
2 cups cooked wild rice*
1/3 cup milk
3 eggs, lightly beaten
1-1/4 cups all-purpose flour
2 teaspoons baking powder
1/2 teaspoon salt
Cooking oil

In a large skillet, saute mushrooms and onions in butter until tender. Place in a large bowl; cool. Add the rice, milk and eggs; mix well. Combine flour, baking powder and salt; stir into rice mixture just until combined. Coat the bottom of the skillet with oil; heat over medium heat. Drop batter by 2 tablespoonfuls into hot oil. Cook about 3 minutes per side or until browned. **Yield:** 1-1/2 dozen. ***Editor's Note:** Two-thirds cup uncooked wild rice yields 2 cups cooked wild rice.

Farmers Breakfast

Jeanette Westphal, Gettysburg, South Dakota

6 bacon strips, diced
2 tablespoons diced onion
3 medium potatoes, cooked and cubed
6 eggs, beaten
Salt and pepper to taste
1/2 cup shredded cheddar cheese

In a skillet, cook bacon until crisp. Remove to paper towel to drain. In drippings, saute onion and potatoes until potatoes are browned, about 5 minutes. Pour eggs into skillet; cook and stir gently until eggs are set and cooked to desired doneness. Season with salt and pepper. Sprinkle with cheese and bacon; let stand for 2-3 minutes or until cheese melts. **Yield:** 4-6 servings.

Breakfast Custard

Arlene Bender, Martin, North Dakota

4 eggs
2 tablespoons butter *or* margarine, melted

- 1 cup milk
- 1 teaspoon cornstarch
- 1/8 teaspoon baking powder
- 1/4 teaspoon salt
- Dash pepper
- 1/2 cup shredded cheddar cheese

In a bowl, beat eggs. Add the next six ingredients. Stir in cheese. Pour into four buttered 4-oz. custard cups. Place cups in a baking pan. Fill pan with boiling water to a depth of 1 in. Bake, uncovered, at 425° for 15-20 minutes or until a knife inserted near the center comes out clean. **Yield:** 4 servings.

Brunch Puffs

Judy Gochenour, Logan, Iowa

- **1 cup water**
- **1/2 cup butter *or* margarine**
- **1/2 teaspoon salt**
- **1 cup all-purpose flour**
- **4 eggs**

FILLING:

- **1/2 cup chopped green pepper**
- **1/2 cup chopped onion**
- **1 tablespoon butter *or* margarine**
- **8 eggs**
- **1/2 teaspoon salt**
- **1/4 teaspoon pepper**
- **1 cup chopped fully cooked ham**
- **1 cup (4 ounces) shredded cheddar cheese**

In a large saucepan, bring water, butter and salt to a boil. Add flour all at once and stir until a smooth ball forms. Remove from the heat; let stand 5 minutes. Add eggs, one at a time, beating well after each addition. Beat until mixture is smooth and shiny. Drop by 1/4 cupfuls 2 in. apart onto a greased baking sheet. Bake at 400° for 35 minutes or until golden brown. Transfer to a wire rack. Immediately split puffs open; remove and discard tops and soft dough from inside. Set aside. In a large skillet, saute green pepper and onion in butter until tender. In a medium bowl, beat eggs, salt and pepper. Add to skillet, stirring over medium heat until almost done. Add ham and cheese; stir until eggs are set. Spoon into puffs. Serve immediately. **Yield:** 8 servings.

Vegetable Frittata

Janet Eckhoff, Woodland, California

- **1/2 cup chopped onion**
- **1/2 cup chopped green pepper**
- **1/2 cup chopped sweet red pepper**
- **1 garlic clove, minced**
- **3 tablespoons olive *or* vegetable oil, *divided***
- **2 medium red potatoes, cooked and cubed**
- **1 small zucchini, cubed**
- **6 eggs**
- **1/2 teaspoon salt**
- **Pinch pepper**

In a 10-in. cast-iron or ovenproof skillet, saute onion, peppers and garlic in 2 tablespoons of oil until the vegetables are tender. Remove vegetables with a slotted spoon; set aside. In the same skillet over medium heat, lightly brown potatoes in remaining oil. Add vegetable mixture and zucchini; simmer for 4 minutes. In a bowl, beat eggs, salt and pepper; pour over vegetables. Cover and cook for 8-10 minutes or until eggs are nearly set. Broil 6 in. from the heat for 2 minutes or until eggs are set on top. Cut into wedges. **Yield:** 4-6 servings.

Bacon and Eggs Casserole

Deanna Durward-Orr, Windsor, Ontario

(PICTURED ON PAGE 52)

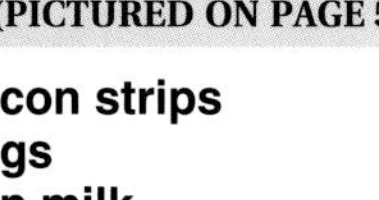

- **4 bacon strips**
- **18 eggs**
- **1 cup milk**
- **1 cup (4 ounces) shredded cheddar cheese**
- **1 cup (8 ounces) sour cream**
- **1/4 cup sliced green onions**
- **1 to 1-1/2 teaspoons salt**
- **1/2 teaspoon pepper**

In a skillet, cook bacon until crisp. Remove to paper towel to drain. In a large bowl, beat eggs. Add milk, cheese, sour cream, onions, salt and pepper. Pour into a greased 13-in. x 9-in. x 2-in. baking dish. Crumble bacon and sprinkle on top. Bake, uncovered, at 325° for 40-45 minutes or until a knife inserted near the center comes out clean. Let stand for 5 minutes. **Yield:** 8-10 servings.

LIGHT AND FLUFFY. To make sure your scrambled eggs come out tender and light, use an electric fry pan. Its controlled heat keeps eggs from becoming tough.

Spiced Doughnut Drops

Ruth Calcagno, Glendale Heights, Illinois

- **1-1/2 cups all-purpose flour**
- **4 teaspoons baking powder**
- **1/4 teaspoon salt**
- **1/4 teaspoon *each* ground cinnamon, nutmeg and ginger**
- **2 eggs**
- **1-1/2 cups sugar**
- **1/4 cup vegetable oil**
- **1 cup canned *or* cooked pumpkin**
- **1/4 cup milk**
- **1 teaspoon vanilla extract**
- **Cooking oil for deep-fat frying**

TOPPING:

- **1 cup sugar**
- **2 teaspoons ground cinnamon**

Combine flour, baking powder, salt and spices; set aside. In a large bowl, beat eggs. Add sugar, oil and pumpkin; mix well. Add dry ingredients alternately with milk. Stir in vanilla. In an electric skillet, heat 1-1/2 in. of oil to 350°. Drop batter by rounded tablespoonfuls into oil; fry about 2 minutes on each side until golden brown. Drain on paper towels. Combine topping ingredients; roll doughnuts in topping while still warm. **Yield:** about 3 dozen.

Dutch Cream Waffles

Barbara Syme, Peoria, Arizona

(PICTURED BELOW)

- **1 cup all-purpose flour**
- **1/4 teaspoon salt**
- **3 eggs, *separated***
- **1 cup heavy cream**

In a large mixing bowl, combine flour and salt. In a small mixing bowl, beat egg yolks on low while adding cream. Beat for 1 minute. Add to flour mixture; blend on low speed, then beat on medium-high until smooth. In another small mixing bowl, beat egg whites on high until stiff but not dry. Gently fold into batter. Bake in a preheated waffle iron according to manufacturer's directions. Serve with warm maple syrup or fresh fruit in season. **Yield:** 2-3 servings.

FEW ingredients are needed to prepare mouth-watering Dutch Cream Waffles (recipe above).

EARLY MORNING entertaining is easy with these two oven entrees. The baked eggs can be prepared the night before for even more convenience. To add a sweet touch to the table, you'll want to serve some of the apple omelet on the side.

EGGCITING EATING. Top to bottom: **Baked Stuffed Eggs** and **Puffy Apple Omelet** (both recipes are on p. 35).

Baked Stuffed Eggs

Lorraine Bylsma, Eustis, Florida
(PICTURED AT LEFT)

STUFFED EGGS:
8 hard-cooked eggs
3 to 4 tablespoons sour cream
2 teaspoons prepared mustard
1/2 teaspoon salt
SAUCE:
1/2 cup chopped onion
2 tablespoons butter *or* margarine
1 can (10-3/4 ounces) condensed cream of mushroom soup, undiluted
1 cup (8 ounces) sour cream
1/2 cup shredded cheddar cheese
1/2 teaspoon paprika

Slice eggs in half lengthwise; remove yolks and set whites aside. In a bowl, mash yolks with a fork. Add sour cream, mustard and salt; mix well. Fill the egg whites; set aside. In a saucepan, saute onion in butter until tender. Add soup and sour cream; mix well. Pour half into an ungreased 11-in. x 7-in. x 2-in. baking pan. Arrange stuffed eggs over the sauce. Spoon remaining sauce on top. Sprinkle with cheese and paprika. Cover and refrigerate overnight. Remove from the refrigerator 30 minutes before baking. Bake, uncovered, at 350° for 25-30 minutes or until heated through. Serve immediately. **Yield:** 6-8 servings.

Puffy Apple Omelet

Melissa Davenport, Campbell, Minnesota
(PICTURED AT LEFT)

✓ This tasty dish uses less sugar, salt and fat. Recipe includes *Diabetic Exchanges*.

3 tablespoons all-purpose flour
1/4 teaspoon baking powder
1/8 teaspoon salt, optional
2 eggs, *separated*
3 tablespoons milk
3 tablespoons sugar
1 tablespoon lemon juice
TOPPING:
1 large baking apple, thinly sliced
1 teaspoon sugar
1/4 teaspoon ground cinnamon

In a small bowl, combine flour, baking powder and salt if desired; mix well. Add egg yolks and milk; mix well and set aside. In a small mixing bowl, beat egg whites until foamy. Gradually add sugar, beating until stiff peaks form. Fold in yolk mixture and lemon juice. Pour into a greased 1-1/2-qt. shallow baking dish. Arrange apple slices on top. Combine sugar and cinnamon; sprinkle over all. Bake, uncovered, at 375° for 18-20 minutes or until a knife inserted near the center comes out clean. Serve immediately. **Yield:** 2 servings. **Diabetic Exchanges:** One serving (prepared with skim milk and without added salt) equals 1 starch, 1 meat, 1/2 fruit; also, 193 calories, 148 mg sodium, 214 mg cholesterol, 26 gm carbohydrate, 9 gm protein, 6 gm fat.

Biscuit Egg Scramble

Jacqueline Boyden, Sparks, Nevada

2 tablespoons butter *or* margarine
8 eggs, beaten
1 can (5 ounces) evaporated milk
1 package (8 ounces) process American cheese, cubed
1 tablespoon prepared mustard
1 cup cubed fully cooked ham
1 tube (10 ounces) refrigerator biscuits

Melt butter in a skillet. Add eggs; cook and stir until set; set aside. In a medium saucepan, combine milk, cheese and mustard; cook over medium-low heat until cheese is melted. Remove from the heat; fold in ham and eggs. Pour into a greased 8-in. square baking dish. Separate biscuits and arrange on top. Bake at 375° for 15-20 minutes or until the biscuits are golden brown. **Yield:** 4-6 servings.

Almond Deviled Eggs

Martha Baechle, Nipomo, California
(PICTURED ON PAGE 52)

6 hard-cooked eggs
1/4 cup mayonnaise
1 teaspoon Dijon mustard
1/4 teaspoon garlic salt
3 tablespoons finely chopped roasted almonds
12 whole roasted almonds
Fresh parsley

Slice eggs in half lengthwise; remove yolks and set whites aside. In a small bowl, mash yolks, mayonnaise, mustard, garlic salt and chopped almonds. Evenly fill the egg whites. Garnish with whole almonds and parsley. Chill until ready to serve. **Yield:** 12 servings.

FOR PERFECT HARD-COOKED EGGS, place them in a saucepan and cover with cold water. Bring to a boil and remove from the heat. Cover and let stand 20 minutes. The eggs will be tender with no gray ring around the yolks!

Overnight French Toast

Sue Marsteller, Gouldsboro, Pennsylvania

9 eggs
3 cups light cream
1/3 cup sugar
1-1/2 teaspoons rum extract, optional
1-1/2 teaspoons vanilla extract
1/2 teaspoon ground nutmeg
24 to 30 slices French bread (3/4 inch thick)
PRALINE SYRUP:
1-1/2 cups packed brown sugar
1/2 cup light corn syrup
1/2 cup water
1/2 cup chopped pecans, toasted
2 tablespoons butter *or* margarine

In a large bowl, lightly beat eggs. Mix in cream, sugar, rum extract if desired, vanilla and nutmeg. Place the bread in a single layer in two well-greased 15-in. x 10-in. x 1-in. baking pans. Pour the egg mixture over bread in each pan. Turn bread over to coat both sides. Cover and refrigerate overnight. Bake, uncovered, at 400° for 20-22 minutes or until golden. Meanwhile, for syrup, bring brown sugar, corn syrup and water to a boil in a saucepan. Reduce heat and simmer for 3 minutes. Add pecans and butter; simmer 2 minutes longer. Serve with the French toast. **Yield:** 10-12 servings.

Herbed Baked Eggs

Sandy Szwarc, Albuquerque, New Mexico

2 tablespoons butter *or* margarine, softened
1/2 teaspoon *each* dried chives, tarragon and parsley flakes
4 eggs
1/4 teaspoon pepper
4 tablespoons light cream
4 tablespoons grated Parmesan cheese

Combine the butter and herbs; divide among four 4-oz. baking dishes. Place dishes in a large baking pan. Place in a 350° oven for 2-4 minutes or until butter has melted. Break one egg into each dish. Sprinkle with pepper. Top with cream and Parmesan cheese. Bake for 12-15 minutes or until eggs reach desired doneness. Serve immediately. **Yield:** 4 servings.

HERE'S AN ARRAY of tasty new recipes for you to sample. Beef, bacon and sauerkraut are all rolled into one main dish. For a change of pace from traditional potato pancakes, try these pleasing parsnip varieties. Pork sausage makes corn-bread stuffing extraordinary. Sauerkraut also stars in the apple cake…it keeps it surprisingly moist.

AUTUMN APPEAL. Clockwise from bottom: **Harvest Roll-Ups** (p. 9), **Deluxe Corn-Bread Stuffing** (p. 37), **Sauerkraut Apple Cake** (p. 62) and **Parsnip Patties** (p. 37).

Side Dishes & Salads

Round out all of your main meals with an interesting new dish that features produce, grains or pasta—or with a cool, refreshing salad.

Deluxe Corn-Bread Stuffing

Pamela Rickman, Valdosta, Georgia

(PICTURED AT LEFT)

6 cups crumbled corn bread
2 cups white bread cubes, toasted
1 cup chopped pecans
1/4 cup minced fresh parsley
1 teaspoon dried thyme
1/2 teaspoon rubbed sage
1/2 teaspoon salt
1/2 teaspoon pepper
1 pound bulk pork sausage
2 tablespoons butter *or* margarine
2 large tart apples, diced
1 cup diced celery
1 medium onion, finely chopped
1-3/4 to 2-1/4 cups chicken broth

In a large bowl, combine bread, pecans and seasonings; set aside. In a large skillet, cook and crumble sausage until browned; remove with a slotted spoon to drain on paper towels. Add butter to drippings; saute apples, celery and onion until tender. Add to bread mixture. Stir in sausage and enough broth to moisten. Spoon into a greased 3-qt. baking dish; cover and bake at 350° for 45 minutes. Uncover and bake for 10 minutes. Or use to stuff a turkey; bake according to recipe. **Yield:** 10-12 servings (about 11 cups).

Quick & Easy

Parsnip Patties

A.L. Hensley, Vancouver, Washington

(PICTURED AT LEFT)

3 cups shredded peeled parsnips (about 1 pound)
1 egg, lightly beaten
1/2 cup all-purpose flour
1/2 teaspoon salt
1/2 cup honey, warmed

In a bowl, combine parsnips, egg, flour and salt. Drop batter by 1/2 cupfuls onto a lightly greased hot griddle. Fry over medium heat for 4-5 minutes per side or until vegetables are tender. Serve with honey. **Yield:** 6 servings.

Sweet Potato Bake

Bernadine Mathewson, Los Angeles, California

4 medium sweet potatoes *or* yams, cooked and peeled
1 cup orange juice
1/2 cup packed brown sugar
1/4 cup raisins
2 tablespoons butter *or* margarine
1 tablespoon cornstarch
1/4 teaspoon salt
3 tablespoons chopped walnuts

Cut potatoes in half lengthwise, then into 2-in. pieces. Place in an ungreased 8-in. square baking dish. In a medium saucepan, combine orange juice, sugar, raisins, butter, cornstarch and salt. Cook over medium heat, stirring constantly, until thickened and bubbly. Cook and stir for 2 minutes longer. Pour over potatoes. Sprinkle with nuts. Bake, uncovered, at 350° for 20 minutes or until bubbly. **Yield:** 4-6 servings.

French Onion Bake

Janice Elder, Charlotte, North Carolina

4 large white *or* yellow onions, thinly sliced
1/4 cup butter *or* margarine, *divided*
3 tablespoons all-purpose flour
1/2 teaspoon salt
1/4 teaspoon pepper
1 can (10-1/2 ounces) condensed beef consomme, undiluted
1/4 cup cooking sherry, optional
4 slices French bread (1 inch thick)
1 cup (4 ounces) shredded Swiss cheese
1/4 cup shredded Parmesan cheese

In a large skillet, saute onions in 2 tablespoons butter until tender. Sprinkle with flour; stir in salt and pepper. Add the consomme and sherry if desired; cook and stir until thickened, about 3 minutes. Pour into a shallow 2-qt. baking dish or individual baking dishes. Spread remaining butter on both sides of bread; place on a baking sheet. Bake at 350° for 10-15 minutes or until golden brown. Place bread on top of onion mixture; sprinkle with cheeses. Bake, uncovered, for 10-15 minutes or until cheese is melted and bubbly. **Yield:** 4 servings.

Pizza Salad

Evelyn Harrington, Glens Falls, New York

1 package (16 ounces) shell macaroni
1 medium sweet red pepper, chopped
1 medium green pepper, chopped
1 large tomato, chopped
4 to 6 green onions, sliced
1 can (4 ounces) sliced mushrooms, drained
1 can (2-1/4 ounces) sliced ripe olives, drained
2-1/2 ounces sliced pepperoni, halved
2 garlic cloves, minced
1 teaspoon dried oregano
1/2 teaspoon salt
1/4 teaspoon pepper
1 bottle (8 ounces) Italian salad dressing
1 cup (4 ounces) shredded mozzarella cheese
2 tablespoons grated Parmesan cheese

Cook macaroni according to package directions; drain and cool. Place in a large bowl; add the next seven ingredients and toss. Add garlic, oregano, salt and pepper; toss. Refrigerate. Just before serving, add dressing and cheeses; toss. **Yield:** 12-16 servings.

PEP UP PARSLEY. If the fresh parsley you were saving for garnish has wilted, here's how to perk it up: Rinse the parsley in very hot tap water, seal in a plastic bag and store in the refrigerator overnight.

GET READY for rave reviews when your menu features colorful chicken salad (recipe below).

Mandarin Chicken Salad

Judy Sloter, Alpharetta, Georgia
(PICTURED ABOVE)

3 cups diced cooked chicken
1 cup diced celery
2 tablespoons lemon juice
1 tablespoon finely chopped onion
3/4 cup mayonnaise
1 can (11 ounces) mandarin oranges, drained
1 cup seedless grapes, halved
1 teaspoon lemon pepper
1/2 cup chopped pecans, toasted

In a medium bowl, combine first eight ingredients; mix well. Cover and chill for 1-2 hours. Fold in pecans just before serving. **Yield:** 4 servings.

Broccoli Tomato Cups

Beatrice Gallo, Richfield Springs, New York
(PICTURED ON PAGE 14)

1-1/2 cups soft bread crumbs, *divided*
1 cup grated Parmesan cheese, *divided*
6 to 8 medium tomatoes
2 cups chopped broccoli
1 cup (4 ounces) shredded cheddar cheese
3/4 cup mayonnaise
Salt and pepper to taste

Combine 1/2 cup of bread crumbs and 1/4 cup Parmesan cheese; set aside. Cut a thin slice off the top of each tomato; scoop out pulp and place in a strainer to drain. Place tomatoes upside down on paper towels. Cook the broccoli until crisp-tender; drain. Chop tomato pulp and place in a large bowl. Add broccoli, cheddar cheese, mayonnaise, salt, pepper and remaining crumbs and Parmesan; mix gently. Stuff tomatoes; place in a greased 11-in. x 7-in. x 2-in. baking dish. Sprinkle with reserved crumb mixture. Bake, uncovered, at 375° for 30-40 minutes. **Yield:** 6-8 servings.

Succotash

Rosa Boone, Mobile, Alabama

1 smoked ham hock (about 1-1/2 pounds)
4 cups water
1 can (28 ounces) diced tomatoes, undrained
1 package (10 ounces) frozen lima beans, thawed
1 package (10 ounces) crowder peas, thawed *or* 1 can (15-1/2 ounces) black-eyed peas, drained
1 package (10 ounces) frozen corn, thawed
1 medium green pepper, chopped
1 medium onion, chopped
1/3 cup ketchup
1-1/2 teaspoons salt
1-1/2 teaspoons dried basil
1 teaspoon rubbed sage
1 teaspoon paprika
1/2 teaspoon pepper
1 bay leaf
1 cup sliced fresh *or* frozen okra

In a Dutch oven or large saucepan, simmer ham hock in water for 1-1/2 hours or until tender. Cool; remove meat from the bone and return to pan. (Discard bone and broth or save for another use.) Add the tomatoes, beans, peas, corn, green pepper, onion, ketchup and seasonings. Simmer, uncovered, for 45 minutes. Add okra; simmer, uncovered, 15 minutes longer. Discard bay leaf before serving. **Yield:** 12-16 servings.

Sour Cream Scalloped Potatoes

Betty Claycomb, Alverton, Pennsylvania

1 bag (32 ounces) frozen hash brown potato cubes
2 cups (16 ounces) sour cream
1 can (10-3/4 ounces) condensed cream of chicken soup, undiluted
1 cup (4 ounces) shredded cheddar cheese
1/2 cup butter *or* margarine, melted
1/2 cup finely chopped onion
1 teaspoon salt
1/2 teaspoon pepper
1 cup french-fried onions

In a bowl, combine the first eight ingredients. Pour into an ungreased 2-1/2-qt. baking dish. Bake, uncovered, at 350° for 1 hour. Sprinkle with onions; return to the oven for 10 minutes. **Yield:** 8 servings.

SUPER-FAST SIDE DISH. For quick and easy potato pancakes, add an egg or two and a little flour to leftover mashed potatoes. Shape into patties and fry until golden brown.

Creamy Corn Casserole

Brenda Wood, Egbert, Ontario

1 cup finely chopped celery
1/4 cup finely chopped onion
1/4 cup finely chopped sweet red pepper
3 tablespoons butter *or* margarine, *divided*
1 can (10-3/4 ounces) condensed cream of chicken soup, undiluted
3 cups fresh, frozen *or* drained canned corn
1 can (8 ounces) sliced water chestnuts, drained
1/3 cup slivered almonds, optional
1/2 cup soft bread crumbs

In a medium skillet, saute celery, onion and red pepper in 2 tablespoons of butter for 2-3 minutes or until vegetables are tender. Remove from the heat; stir in soup, corn, water chestnuts and almonds if desired. Transfer to a 2-qt. baking dish. Melt remaining butter; toss with bread crumbs. Sprinkle on top of casserole. Bake, uncovered, at 350° for 25-30 minutes or until bubbly. **Yield:** 8 servings.

Wilted Lettuce

Rosemary Falls, Austin, Texas

4 cups torn leaf lettuce
1 small onion, sliced
3 radishes, sliced
6 bacon strips, diced
2 tablespoons vinegar
1 teaspoon brown sugar
1/4 teaspoon dry mustard
1/4 to 1/2 teaspoon salt
1/8 teaspoon pepper

In a large salad bowl, toss lettuce, onion and radishes; set aside. In a skillet, cook bacon until crisp; remove with a slotted spoon to drain on paper towel. To the drippings, add vinegar, brown sugar, mustard, salt and pepper; bring to a boil.

Pour over lettuce and toss; sprinkle with bacon. Serve immediately. **Yield:** 4-6 servings.

Maple-Glazed Sweet Potatoes

Joyce Moody, Incline Village, Nevada

2-1/2 to 3 pounds sweet potatoes, peeled
1-3/4 to 2 pounds apples, peeled and cored
3/4 cup maple syrup
1/4 cup apple cider
1/4 cup butter *or* margarine
1/2 teaspoon salt

Cut the sweet potatoes and apples into 1/4-in. slices. Layer in a greased 13-in. x 9-in. x 2-in. baking dish. In a saucepan, bring syrup, cider, butter and salt to a boil. Pour over potatoes and apples. Cover and bake at 350° for 1 hour. Uncover and bake 10-15 minutes more or until tender. **Yield:** 8-10 servings.

Marinated Grilled Vegetables

Marian Platt, Sequim, Washington

(PICTURED ON PAGE 16)

✓ This tasty dish uses less sugar, salt and fat. Recipe includes *Diabetic Exchanges.*

6 small onions, halved
4 carrots, cut into 1-1/2-inch chunks
1/3 cup olive *or* vegetable oil
1/2 teaspoon dried rosemary
1/4 teaspoon dried marjoram
Dash pepper
6 small pattypan *or* sunburst squash
1 medium zucchini, cut into 1-inch chunks
1 medium green pepper, cut into 1-inch pieces
1 medium sweet red pepper, cut into 1-inch pieces

In a saucepan, cook onions and carrots in water for 10 minutes or until crisp-tender; drain. In a large bowl, combine oil and seasonings; add all of the vegetables and mix well. Cover and refrigerate for at least 1 hour. Drain, reserving marinade. Thread vegetables alternately onto skewers. Grill, uncovered, over medium coals for 15-20 minutes or until tender. Turn and baste with the marinade every 5 minutes. **Yield:** 6 servings. **Diabetic Exchanges:** One serving equals 2 vegetable, 1 fat; also, 97 calories, 28 mg sodium, 0 cholesterol, 11 gm carbohydrate, 2 gm protein, 6 gm fat.

Sparkling Rhubarb Salad

Mary Ellen Beachy, Dundee, Ohio

4 cups diced fresh *or* frozen rhubarb
1-1/2 cups water
1/2 cup sugar
1 package (6 ounces) strawberry-flavored gelatin
1 cup fresh orange juice
1 tablespoon grated orange peel
2 cups sliced fresh strawberries

In a saucepan, combine rhubarb, water and sugar. Cook over medium heat until the rhubarb is tender, 5-10 minutes. Remove from the heat. Stir in gelatin until dissolved. Add orange juice and peel. Chill until slightly thickened, 2 to 2-1/2 hours. Add strawberries; pour into a 2-qt. bowl. Chill until firm, about 2-3 hours. **Yield:** 8-10 servings.

Garden State Salad

Mary Jane Ruther, Trenton, New Jersey

1 small bunch romaine, torn
2 medium potatoes, cooked and cubed
2 large tomatoes, cut into wedges
1 cup diced cucumber
1/2 cup chopped celery
1/2 medium green pepper, cut into strips
1 small carrot, shredded
3 hard-cooked eggs, chopped
1/2 cup pitted ripe olives
3 radishes, sliced

DRESSING:

1-1/2 cups mayonnaise *or* salad dressing
2 tablespoons Dijon mustard
2 tablespoons red wine vinegar
1/2 teaspoon sugar
1/4 teaspoon salt
1/8 teaspoon pepper

In a large bowl, toss the first 10 ingredients. In a small bowl, combine dressing ingredients and stir well. Serve with the salad. **Yield:** 6-8 servings.

Shrimp Pasta Salad

Sherri Gentry, Dallas, Oregon

✓ This tasty dish uses less sugar, salt and fat. Recipe includes *Diabetic Exchanges.*

12 ounces spiral pasta, cooked and drained
1 package (10 ounces) frozen cooked shrimp, thawed
1/4 cup sliced green onions
1/4 cup grated Parmesan cheese
1/3 cup vegetable oil
1/3 cup red wine vinegar
2-1/2 teaspoons dill weed
2 teaspoons salt, optional
3/4 teaspoon garlic powder
1/2 teaspoon pepper

In a large bowl, combine pasta, shrimp, onions and Parmesan cheese. In a small bowl, combine remaining ingredients. Pour over pasta mixture and toss. Cover and chill for 1-2 hours. **Yield:** 10 servings. **Diabetic Exchanges:** One serving (without added salt) equals 1-1/2 starch, 1 meat, 1/2 vegetable, 1/2 fat; also, 231 calories, 39 mg sodium, 45 mg cholesterol, 27 gm carbohydrate, 12 gm protein, 8 gm fat.

Banana Split Salad

Shelly Korell, Bayard, Nebraska

(PICTURED BELOW)

1 package (8 ounces) cream cheese, softened
1/2 cup sugar
1 can (20 ounces) crushed pineapple, drained
1 package (10 ounces) frozen sliced strawberries in syrup, thawed
2 medium firm bananas, chopped
1 carton (12 ounces) frozen whipped topping, thawed
1 cup chopped walnuts
Red food coloring, optional

In a large mixing bowl, beat the cream cheese and sugar. Stir in pineapple, strawberries and bananas. Fold in the whipped topping, walnuts and food coloring if desired. Pour into an oiled 13-in. x 9-in. x 2-in. dish. Cover and freeze until firm, at least 3 hours. Remove from the freezer 30 minutes before serving. **Yield:** 12-15 servings.

PLANNING A PARTY? This sweet salad (recipe above) is easily prepared in advance.

REMEMBER WHEN Grandma would lay out a magnificent spread of food at a mid-summer get-together? You can capture those magical memories with this menu. Corned beef sandwiches always make a perfect picnic food. Creamy Coleslaw is made with a "secret" ingredient—*ice cream!*—making it extra creamy with just a touch of sweetness. A light oil-and-vinegar dressing nicely complements summer vegetables. And end the meal with an old-time treat like Banana Cream Dessert.

OLD-FASHIONED FLAVORS. Clockwise from bottom: **Deviled Corned Beef Buns** (p. 8), **Creamy Coleslaw** (p. 41), **Summer Vegetable Salad** (p. 41) and **Banana Cream Dessert** (p. 70).

Creamy Coleslaw

Mattie Green, Ackley, Iowa
(PICTURED AT LEFT)

1/2 cup vanilla ice cream, softened
1/4 cup mayonnaise *or* salad dressing
1 teaspoon prepared mustard
1/4 teaspoon salt
Dash pepper
2 cups shredded green cabbage
1 cup shredded red cabbage
1 medium carrot, shredded

In a large bowl, combine ice cream, mayonnaise, mustard, salt and pepper until smooth. Add cabbage and carrot; mix well. Cover and chill for at least 1 hour. **Yield:** 4 servings.

Summer Vegetable Salad

Rudy Mancini, Calistoga, California
(PICTURED AT LEFT)

1/2 cup red wine vinegar
1/3 cup vegetable oil
3 garlic cloves, minced
1/2 teaspoon salt
1/8 teaspoon pepper
1 teaspoon sugar, optional
1/2 pint cherry tomatoes, halved
1 small cucumber, peeled and thinly sliced
1 small green pepper, julienned
1 small red onion, sliced into rings
1 tablespoon chopped fresh basil *or* 1 teaspoon dried basil

In a large bowl, combine vinegar, oil, garlic, salt, pepper and sugar if desired; mix well. Add remaining ingredients and toss gently. Cover and chill for at least 1 hour. **Yield:** 4-6 servings.

Tomato Mozzarella Salad

Lynn Merendino, Duncannon, Pennsylvania

1/4 cup red wine vinegar
1 garlic clove, minced
1/2 teaspoon salt
Pepper to taste
2/3 cup vegetable *or* olive oil
1 pint cherry tomatoes, halved
1-1/2 cups mozzarella cheese cubes
1/4 cup chopped onion
3 tablespoons minced fresh basil *or* 1 tablespoon dried basil

In a bowl, combine vinegar, garlic, salt and pepper. Whisk in oil until well blended. Add remaining ingredients; toss. Cover and chill at least 1 hour, stirring occasionally. Remove with a slotted spoon to a serving dish. **Yield:** 6 servings.

Red Cabbage With Apples

Peg Schendel, Janesville, Minnesota

1 medium onion, chopped
1/4 cup butter *or* margarine
1 medium head red cabbage (about 2 pounds), shredded
1/2 teaspoon salt
1/4 teaspoon pepper
1/4 cup packed brown sugar
1 cup apple cider
2 tablespoons cider vinegar
2 tart cooking apples, peeled and chopped
2 bacon strips, cooked and crumbled, optional
Snipped fresh parsley, optional

In a large skillet, saute onion in butter until tender but not brown. Add the cabbage, salt, pepper, brown sugar, cider, vinegar and apples. Cover and simmer until the cabbage and apples are tender and the liquid is reduced, about 1 hour. Sprinkle with bacon and parsley if desired. **Yield:** 6-8 servings.

Picnic Potatoes

Lex Ann Eschenbacher, Nine Mile Falls, Wash.

8 to 10 medium potatoes
1-1/2 cups prepared ranch salad dressing
2 cups (8 ounces) shredded sharp cheddar cheese
1/8 teaspoon salt
1/8 teaspoon pepper
1/2 pound sliced bacon, cooked and crumbled, *divided*
Chopped fresh chives

Peel and quarter potatoes; place in a large saucepan or kettle and cover with water. Bring to a boil; cook until tender. Drain and transfer to a large bowl; mash (do not add milk, butter or seasoning). Add salad dressing and mix well. Add cheese, salt, pepper and half of the bacon. Spread evenly into a greased 13-in. x 9-in. x 2-in. baking dish. Sprinkle with chives and remaining bacon. Bake, uncovered, at 350° for 20 minutes. **Yield:** 6-8 servings. **Editor's Note:** If a decorative edge is desired, spread all but 2 cups of the prepared potato mixture into baking dish. Using a pastry bag and large tip, pipe the reserved mixture around the edge of the dish.

Calico Pepper Salad

Jennifer Mottashed, Simcoe, Ontario

✓ This tasty dish uses less sugar, salt and fat. Recipe includes *Diabetic Exchanges*.

1 medium green pepper, julienned
1 medium sweet red pepper, julienned
1 medium sweet yellow pepper, julienned
1 medium purple pepper, julienned
1 small red onion, julienned
1/3 cup vinegar
1/4 cup vegetable oil
1 tablespoon sugar
1 tablespoon minced fresh basil *or* 1 teaspoon dried basil
1/4 teaspoon salt, optional
Dash pepper

In a large bowl, combine peppers and onion. Combine remaining ingredients; mix well and pour over vegetables. Cover and refrigerate 6 hours or overnight. **Yield:** 10 servings. **Diabetic Exchanges:** One serving equals 1 fat, 1 vegetable; also, 68 calories, 1 mg sodium, 0 cholesterol, 5 gm carbohydrate, 1 gm protein, 6 gm fat. **Editor's Note:** This recipe may be easily doubled.

Festive Pineapple Boat

Susan Phelan, Tallahassee, Florida

1 large fresh ripe pineapple
2 medium firm bananas, sliced
2 kiwifruit, peeled and sliced
1/4 cup packed brown sugar
3 tablespoons coarsely chopped pecans
Dash ground cinnamon
Dash ground nutmeg
3 tablespoons flaked coconut
Fresh strawberries, optional

Stand pineapple up and cut about a third off of one side, leaving the top attached. Remove fruit from the piece cut off and discard outer peel. Remove fruit from the remaining pineapple, leaving a 1/2-in. shell intact. Cut pineapple into bite-size pieces; toss with bananas and kiwi. Spoon into "boat". Combine brown sugar, pecans, cinnamon and nutmeg; sprinkle over fruit. Sprinkle with coconut. Garnish with strawberries if desired. Serve immediately. **Yield:** 6-8 servings.

Molded Egg Salad

Lois Chapman, Ridgefield, Washington

(PICTURED ON PAGE 30)

3 packets unflavored gelatin
1 cup water
2 cups mayonnaise
12 hard-cooked eggs, chopped
1/2 cup sweet pickle relish
1/2 cup chopped celery
1/2 cup chopped sweet red pepper
1/2 cup sliced green onions
1 teaspoon salt
1/4 teaspoon pepper
Thinly sliced fully cooked ham, optional

In a medium saucepan, soften gelatin in water for 5 minutes. Stir over low heat until gelatin dissolves. Remove from the heat. Whisk in mayonnaise. Stir in eggs. Add relish, celery, red pepper, onions, salt and pepper; mix well. Pour into an oiled 8-cup mold. Chill overnight. Unmold onto a serving platter. If desired, use ham as a garnish around the sides of the mold, or place several pieces in the center if using a ring mold. **Yield:** 8-10 servings.

Club Sandwich Salad

Karen Dolan, Kunkletown, Pennsylvania

1 cup mayonnaise
1/4 cup ketchup
1 tablespoon chopped green onion
Salt and pepper to taste
1 large head lettuce, torn
2 large tomatoes, cut into wedges
2 hard-cooked eggs, chopped
10 bacon strips, cooked and crumbled
2 cups cubed cooked turkey *or* chicken
Croutons, optional

In a small bowl, combine mayonnaise, ketchup, onion, salt and pepper; mix well. Cover and refrigerate. Just before serving, toss lettuce, tomatoes, eggs, bacon and turkey in a large bowl. Add croutons if desired. Serve with dressing. **Yield:** 8-10 servings.

Spinach Pasta Salad

Kay Odegard, Chicago, Illinois

1 package (7 ounces) macaroni
1 package (10 ounces) fresh spinach, torn
12 ounces fresh mushrooms, sliced
1 medium red onion, sliced
6 bacon strips, chopped
1 tablespoon cornstarch
1 tablespoon sugar
1 teaspoon salt
1/2 teaspoon pepper
3/4 cup mayonnaise
1 cup water
1/3 cup cider vinegar

Cook macaroni according to package directions; drain and cool. In a large bowl, combine macaroni, spinach, mushrooms and onion; set aside. In a medium skillet, cook bacon until crisp. Remove with a slotted spoon to paper towels; discard all but 2 tablespoons of drippings. In a small bowl, combine cornstarch, sugar, salt and pepper; whisk into drippings. Stir in mayonnaise; gradually mix in water and vinegar. Bring to a boil over medium heat, stirring constantly; boil for 1 minute. Pour over salad and toss well. Sprinkle with bacon. Serve immediately or refrigerate. **Yield:** 12-16 servings.

Special Herb Dressing

Trudy Williams, Shannonville, Ontario

1 pound ground beef
1 pound bulk pork sausage
1 pound fresh mushrooms, sliced
1 can (8 ounces) water chestnuts, drained and chopped
2 garlic cloves, minced
2 cups diced peeled apples
1 cup chopped onion
1/4 cup chopped fresh parsley
1/4 cup chopped fresh celery leaves
1-1/2 teaspoons salt
1 teaspoon *each* dried savory and thyme
1 teaspoon rubbed sage
3/4 teaspoon pepper
Pinch nutmeg
1 cup chopped fresh *or* frozen cranberries
12 cups day-old bread cubes
1 cup chicken broth

In a large skillet over medium heat, brown beef and sausage; drain. Add the mushrooms, water chestnuts, garlic, apples, onion, parsley and celery leaves; cook until mushrooms and apples are tender, about 6-8 minutes. Stir in seasonings and cranberries; mix well. Cook for 2 minutes. Place bread cubes in a large bowl. Add meat mixture; stir in broth. Spoon into a greased 13-in. x 9-in. x 2-in. baking dish. Cover and bake at 350° for 35-45 minutes. **Yield:** 14-16 servings.

Blueberry Gelatin Salad

Mildred Livingston, Phoenix, Arizona

1 package (6 ounces) cherry-flavored gelatin
2 cups boiling water
1 can (15 ounces) blueberries in heavy syrup (not pie filling), undrained
1 package (8 ounces) cream cheese, softened
1/2 cup sugar
1 teaspoon vanilla extract
1 cup (8 ounces) sour cream
1/4 cup chopped pecans

In a bowl, dissolve gelatin in boiling water; stir in blueberries. Pour into a 12-in. x 8-in. x 2-in. dish; chill until set. In a mixing bowl, beat cream cheese and sugar until smooth. Add vanilla and sour cream; mix well. Spread over the gelatin layer; sprinkle with pecans. Chill several hours or overnight. **Yield:** 10-12 servings.

Swiss Vegetable Medley

Virginia Shaw, Modesto, California

1 bag (16 ounces) frozen broccoli, carrots and cauliflower medley, thawed and drained
1 can (10-3/4 ounces) condensed cream of mushroom soup, undiluted
1/2 cup sour cream
1/4 teaspoon pepper
1 jar (4 ounces) chopped pimientos, drained
1 cup (4 ounces) shredded Swiss cheese, *divided*
1 can (2.8 ounces) french-fried onions, *divided*

In a bowl, combine vegetables, soup, sour cream, pepper, pimientos and 1/2 cup cheese. Stir in half of the onions; mix well. Pour into an ungreased 1-qt. casserole. Cover and bake at 350° for 30-35 minutes or until bubbly. Uncover; sprinkle with remaining cheese and onions. Return to the oven until cheese is melted, about 5 minutes. **Yield:** 6-8 servings. **Editor's Note:** Fresh broccoli, cauliflower and carrots may be substituted for the frozen vegetables. Parboil and drain before combining with other ingredients.

Potato Dumpling Casserole

Joe Ellen Meskimen, Cedar Rapids, Iowa

DUMPLINGS:

- **2 cups hot mashed potatoes (without milk or seasoning)**
- **1 cup all-purpose flour**
- **2 eggs, beaten**
- **1-1/2 teaspoons salt**
- **1/8 teaspoon white pepper**
- **1/8 teaspoon ground nutmeg**

SAUCE:

- **1 small onion, finely chopped**
- **3 tablespoons butter *or* margarine**
- **2 tablespoons all-purpose flour**
- **1 cup light cream**
- **1 cup chicken broth**
- **1/2 cup shredded Swiss cheese, *divided***
- **1/2 cup grated Parmesan cheese, *divided***
- **Minced fresh parsley, optional**

Combine all dumpling ingredients; spoon into a large pastry bag, half at a time, fitted with a large plain tube (opening should be about 1/2 in. in diameter). Bring 5 qts. of salted water to a boil in a large kettle, then adjust heat so water bubbles very gently. Squeeze out dumplings over water, cutting with scissors at 1-in. intervals and letting drop into water. Simmer, uncovered, until dumplings float, then simmer 1 minute more. Remove with a slotted spoon; drain and keep warm in a 2-qt. baking dish. For the sauce, saute the onion in butter until tender. Blend in flour. Add cream and broth all at once. Cook, stirring constantly, until thickened and bubbly. Remove from the heat; stir in 1/4 cup Swiss cheese and 1/4 cup Parmesan cheese. Pour over dumplings; sprinkle with remaining cheese. Bake at 350° for 45 minutes or until hot and bubbly and golden brown on top. Sprinkle with parsley if desired. **Yield:** 8-10 servings. **Editor's Note:** Dumplings may also be dropped by teaspoonfuls into boiling water instead of using a pastry bag.

Picnic Potato Salad

Louise Kurtti, Fargo, North Dakota

- **4 medium potatoes (about 1-1/2 pounds)**
- **1/2 medium cucumber, diced**
- **3/4 cup chopped fresh broccoli**
- **1/2 cup diced celery**
- **2 hard-cooked eggs, chopped**
- **3/4 cup mayonnaise**
- **2 tablespoons milk**
- **2 tablespoons diced onion**
- **1-1/2 teaspoons chopped fresh parsley**
- **1-1/2 teaspoons prepared mustard**
- **1-1/2 teaspoons vinegar**
- **3/4 teaspoon celery seed**
- **1/2 teaspoon *each* salt, pepper and sugar**

Peel potatoes; place in a saucepan and cover with water. Bring to a boil and cook until tender. Cool; cut into cubes. In a large bowl, combine potatoes with cucumber, broccoli, celery and eggs. In a small bowl, combine remaining ingredients. Pour over salad and mix gently. Cover and chill 1 hour before serving. Store in refrigerator. **Yield:** 4-6 servings.

HOT POTATO TIP. To make your favorite potato salad in a hurry, dice and peel the potatoes *before* cooking.

Potato Wedges

Judy Scholovich, Waukesha, Wisconsin

- **2 tablespoons vegetable oil**
- **1/4 cup Italian-seasoned bread crumbs**
- **2 tablespoons grated Parmesan cheese**
- **1 teaspoon Italian seasoning**
- **1/2 teaspoon paprika**
- **1/2 teaspoon garlic salt**
- **4 medium unpeeled potatoes (about 1-1/2 pounds)**

Spread oil over the bottom of a 13-in. x 9-in. x 2-in. baking pan. Combine the next five ingredients in a large plastic bag. Cut each potato lengthwise into eight wedges. Place half of the potatoes in the bag; shake well to coat. Place in a single layer in pan. Repeat with remaining potatoes. Bake, uncovered, at 350° for 40-45 minutes or until tender, turning once after 25 minutes. **Yield:** 6-8 servings.

Spinach Salad with Honey Dressing

Dee Simpson, Jefferson, Texas

(PICTURED ON PAGE 58)

- **1 bag (10 ounces) fresh spinach, torn**
- **1 small head iceberg lettuce, torn**
- **2 green onions, thinly sliced**
- **3 tablespoons chopped green pepper**
- **1 medium cucumber, quartered and sliced**
- **2 large oranges, cut into bite-size pieces**
- **1/2 cup sunflower seeds**
- **3/4 cup mayonnaise**
- **2 tablespoons honey**
- **1 tablespoon lemon juice**

In a large bowl, combine the first seven ingredients. In a small bowl, stir mayonnaise, honey and lemon juice until smooth. Pour over the salad and toss to coat. Serve immediately. **Yield:** 8-10 servings.

Southwestern Hominy

Clifford Wilson, Raytown, Missouri

(PICTURED BELOW)

- **1/2 cup chopped onion**
- **1/2 cup chopped green pepper**
- **3 tablespoons butter *or* margarine**
- **2 cans (15-1/2 ounces *each*) golden hominy, rinsed and drained**
- **2 to 3 teaspoons chili powder**
- **1/2 teaspoon paprika**
- **1/2 teaspoon salt**
- **1/8 teaspoon pepper**

In a saucepan, saute onion and green pepper in butter until tender. Add the remaining ingredients. Cook, uncovered, over medium-low heat for 5-10 minutes or until heated through, stirring occasionally. **Yield:** 4-6 servings.

BRING a Southwestern flair to your table with this hominy casserole (recipe above).

LOOKING FOR FOODS to serve for an extra-special brunch? Impress family and friends with a traditional, tried-and-true layered salad. The combination of produce and creamy dressing is unforgettable. Loaded with ham and broccoli, the egg pie makes a nice, filling entree. Chocolaty brownies are made extra-moist with the addition of bananas to the batter.

LADIES' LUNCHEON. Clockwise from top right: **Layered Lettuce Salad** (p. 45), **Banana Nut Brownies** (p. 62) and **Hearty Ham Pie** (p. 32).

Layered Lettuce Salad

Julia Burkholder, New Holland, Pennsylvania

(PICTURED AT LEFT)

1 head lettuce, torn
1 cup minced fresh parsley
4 hard-cooked eggs, sliced
2 large tomatoes, chopped
1 package (10 ounces) frozen peas, parboiled
6 bacon strips, cooked and crumbled
1 cup (4 ounces) shredded cheddar cheese
1 small red onion, chopped

DRESSING:

1-1/2 cups mayonnaise
1/2 cup sour cream
1 teaspoon dill weed
3/4 teaspoon dried basil
1/2 teaspoon salt
1/8 teaspoon pepper
Fresh dill sprigs, optional

In a large salad bowl, layer the first eight ingredients in order listed. In a small bowl, combine mayonnaise, sour cream, dill, basil, salt and pepper. Carefully spread on top of salad. Cover and refrigerate for several hours or overnight. Garnish with dill sprigs if desired. **Yield:** 12 servings.

Wild Rice Salad

Kathi Saari, Ames, Iowa

1 cup uncooked wild rice
3 cups water
1 tablespoon instant chicken bouillon granules
1 cup julienned fully cooked ham
1 cup julienned Monterey Jack cheese
1 cup julienned sweet red pepper
1 cup broccoli florets
1/2 cup thinly sliced carrots
1/2 cup thinly sliced green onions with tops

DRESSING:

2 tablespoons lemon juice
2 tablespoons vinegar
1/2 teaspoon dry mustard
1/2 to 1 teaspoon curry powder
Salt and pepper to taste
1/2 cup vegetable oil

In a medium saucepan, bring rice, water and bouillon to a boil. Reduce heat; cover and simmer for 1 hour or until the rice is tender. Drain if necessary; cool. In a large bowl, toss rice with ham, cheese, red pepper, broccoli, carrots and green onions. For dressing, combine lemon juice, vinegar, mustard, curry powder, salt and pepper in a blender or food processor. With machine on high, slowly add oil through the feeder cap until well mixed; dressing will thicken slightly. Pour over salad and toss to coat. Cover and chill several hours or overnight. **Yield:** 6-8 servings.

Beef and Broccoli Salad

Sandra Rohrich, Yakima, Washington

1 pound sirloin steak
8 cups fresh broccoli florets (about 1-1/2 pounds)
8 ounces fresh mushrooms, sliced
1/4 cup vegetable *or* sesame oil
1/4 cup white wine vinegar
1/4 cup soy sauce
1 tablespoon honey
1 garlic clove, minced
1 can (8 ounces) sliced water chestnuts, drained
1-1/2 tablespoons sesame seeds, toasted

Broil steak until it reaches desired doneness. Cool. Thinly slice into bite-size pieces; set aside. In a large skillet, stir-fry broccoli and mushrooms in oil for 3 minutes or until crisp-tender. Transfer to a large bowl. In a jar with a tight-fitting lid, combine vinegar, soy sauce, honey and garlic; shake well. Pour over vegetables. Stir in the beef and water chestnuts; chill for at least 1 hour. Sprinkle with sesame seeds just before serving. **Yield:** 6-8 servings.

Cauliflower with Mushroom-Almond Sauce

Elinor Levine, West Palm Beach, Florida

(PICTURED ON PAGE 72)

1 large head cauliflower (about 2-1/2 pounds)
1/4 pound fresh mushrooms, thinly sliced
1/2 cup sliced almonds
1/3 cup sliced green onions with tops
1/2 cup butter *or* margarine
2 teaspoons instant chicken bouillon granules
1 cup water, *divided*
1 tablespoon cornstarch

In a saucepan containing 1 in. of water, steam whole cauliflower until tender, about 20 minutes. Meanwhile, in a skillet, saute mushrooms, almonds and onions in butter until mushrooms are tender. Dissolve bouillon in 3/4 cup water; add to skillet. Dissolve cornstarch in remaining water; add to skillet. Bring to a boil over medium heat, stirring constantly. Cook and stir for 2 minutes. Place cauliflower in a large bowl; pour sauce over it and serve immediately. **Yield:** 6-8 servings.

Sauerkraut Side Dish

Jane Layo, Waddington, New York

1 medium onion, thinly sliced
2 tablespoons butter *or* margarine
1 can (27 ounces) sauerkraut, rinsed and drained
3 medium tart apples, peeled and sliced
1 large potato, peeled and shredded
1 cup chicken broth
2 tablespoons brown sugar
1 teaspoon caraway seed
1/2 teaspoon salt
Additional brown sugar, optional

In a large saucepan, saute onion in butter until tender. Add the sauerkraut, apples, potato, broth, sugar, caraway and salt; mix well. Cover and simmer for 20 minutes or until the apples are tender. Sprinkle with additional brown sugar if desired. **Yield:** 8 servings.

Paprika Potatoes

Melody Haney, Barberton, Ohio

1/2 cup butter *or* margarine
1/4 cup all-purpose flour
1/4 cup grated Parmesan cheese
1 tablespoon paprika
3/4 teaspoon salt
1/8 teaspoon pepper
Pinch garlic salt *or* onion salt
6 medium potatoes (about 2 pounds), peeled and quartered lengthwise

Melt butter in a 13-in. x 9-in. x 2-in. baking pan. Combine the next six ingredients in a large plastic bag; set aside. Rinse potatoes under cold water; drain well. Place half of the potatoes in the bag; shake well to coat. Place in a single layer in baking pan. Repeat with remaining potatoes. Bake, uncovered, at 350° for 50-60 minutes or until tender, turning once after 30 minutes. **Yield:** 4-6 servings.

WINTER CABBAGE SALAD

Eleanor Shuknecht, Elba, New York

(PICTURED AT RIGHT)

2 cups cider vinegar
1 cup sugar
2 tablespoons salt
1 tablespoon mustard seed
3/4 teaspoon celery seed
1/2 teaspoon ground turmeric
10 cups thinly sliced cabbage (about 2-1/4 pounds)
3 medium onions, thinly sliced
2 medium sweet red peppers, thinly sliced
1 medium green pepper, thinly sliced

In a saucepan, bring the first six ingredients to a boil. Reduce heat; simmer, uncovered, for 5 minutes. Remove from the heat and allow to cool. In a large bowl, combine cabbage, onions and peppers. Pour vinegar mixture over vegetables and stir to coat. Cover and refrigerate overnight. **Yield:** 16-20 servings.

ROASTED RED POTATO SALAD

Ginger Cusano, Sandusky, Ohio

(PICTURED ON FRONT COVER)

2 pounds red potatoes, cut into 1-inch cubes
1 medium onion, chopped
4 hard-cooked eggs, sliced
6 bacon strips, cooked and crumbled
1 cup mayonnaise
1/2 teaspoon salt
1/4 teaspoon pepper
Paprika, optional

Place the potatoes in a greased 15-in. x 10-in. x 1-in. baking pan. Bake, uncovered, at 400° for 25-30 minutes or until tender and golden brown, stirring occasionally. Cool for 15 minutes. Transfer to a large bowl; add onion, eggs, bacon, mayonnaise, salt and pepper. Toss to coat. Cover and refrigerate for several hours or overnight. Sprinkle with paprika if desired. **Yield:** 6-8 servings.

DILLED POTATO SALAD

Cam Cox, Hemet, California

4 to 6 large red potatoes, cooked and cubed
3 green onions with tops, sliced
1/4 cup minced fresh parsley
1/2 cup mayonnaise
3 tablespoons light cream
1/2 teaspoon salt
1/4 teaspoon *each* dill weed, white pepper and garlic powder

In a large bowl, combine potatoes, onions and parsley. Combine remaining ingredients; mix well. Pour over potato mixture and mix gently. Cover and chill for at least 1 hour. **Yield:** 6-8 servings.

GRILLED POTATOES

Kathy Anne Epps, Audubon, Pennsylvania

6 to 8 medium baking potatoes, sliced
1 teaspoon garlic powder
1 teaspoon seasoned salt
1/2 teaspoon paprika
1/4 cup grated Parmesan cheese
6 tablespoons butter *or* margarine

On half of a 24-in. piece of heavy-duty aluminum foil, arrange the potato slices in overlapping rows. Combine garlic powder, seasoned salt, paprika and Parmesan cheese; sprinkle over the potatoes. Dot with butter. Seal foil over potatoes. Grill over medium heat for 30 minutes or until tender, turning once. **Yield:** 6-8 servings.

WESTERN BEANS

Catherine Skelton, Seligman, Missouri

1-1/2 pounds ground beef
1/2 cup chopped onion
2 garlic cloves, minced
2 cans (16 ounces *each*) pork and beans
1/3 cup chopped dill pickle
1/3 cup chili sauce
1 teaspoon Worcestershire sauce
1 teaspoon salt
1/2 teaspoon pepper
1/8 teaspoon hot pepper sauce

Brown beef, onion and garlic in a Dutch oven over medium heat; drain. Add remaining ingredients and heat through. **Yield:** 10-12 servings.

MUSHROOM SPINACH SALAD

Judi Harms, Lithonia, Georgia

6 cups torn fresh spinach
2 cups sliced fresh mushrooms
1/3 cup red wine vinegar
1/2 cup vegetable oil
2 tablespoons finely chopped onion
2 tablespoons sugar
1 tablespoon chopped fresh parsley
1/2 teaspoon seasoned salt
1/2 teaspoon dried oregano
2 garlic cloves, minced
1/8 teaspoon pepper

Combine the spinach and mushrooms in a large salad bowl. Combine remaining ingredients in a jar with tight-fitting lid; shake well. Pour over salad and toss to coat. Serve immediately. **Yield:** 6 servings.

BEST CHILLED BEETS

Dottie Eisiminger, Palm City, Florida

3 cans (16 ounces *each*) sliced beets
2 tablespoons cornstarch
1 cup vinegar
1/2 teaspoon salt
3 tablespoons vegetable oil
3 tablespoons ketchup
1 teaspoon vanilla extract
25 whole cloves, tied in a cheesecloth bag

Drain the beets, reserving 1-1/2 cups of juice in a large saucepan. Add cornstarch to juice and mix well. Add beets and remaining ingredients; bring to a boil. Reduce heat and simmer until the sauce is slightly thickened, stirring often. Remove the spice bag. Cover and refrigerate overnight. **Yield:** 10-12 servings.

CLASSIC COBB SALAD

Patty Kile, Greentown, Pennsylvania

6 cups torn lettuce
2 medium tomatoes, chopped
1 avocado, chopped
3/4 cup diced fully cooked ham
2 hard-cooked eggs, chopped
3/4 cup diced cooked turkey
1-1/4 cups sliced fresh mushrooms
1/2 cup crumbled blue cheese
Red onion rings, lemon wedges and sliced ripe olives, optional
Salad dressing

Arrange lettuce in a large bowl. Place tomatoes across the center, dividing the bowl in half. On one half, arrange the avocado, ham and eggs in sections. On the other half, arrange the turkey, mushrooms and blue cheese. Garnish with onion, lemon and olives if desired. Pass the salad dressing. **Yield:** 12-14 servings.

WORKING AND PLAYING outdoors in winter builds up hearty appetites. So, welcome your family in from the cold with this satisfying meal. Take a break from traditional pizza by serving it on French bread. A refreshing salad featuring cabbage adds a nice touch. And top off the meal with chocolaty brownies.

WINTERTIME TREATS. Clockwise from bottom: **Pizza by the Yard** (p. 15), **Double-Decker Brownies** (p. 60) and **Winter Cabbage Salad** (p. 46).

BREAKFAST, brunch, snacks, potlucks, packed for lunch—you can "make the day" with muffins! From pumpkin-chocolate and cinnamon-lemon to zucchini-carrot and almond-peach, the combination of flavors found in muffins is unbeatable—and nearly unlimited. So why not dive into these delights today?

MELT-IN-YOUR-MOUTH MORSELS. Clockwise from the bottom: **Pumpkin Chip Muffins**, **Lemon Tea Muffins**, **Zucchini Carrot Muffins** and **Almond Peach Muffins** (all recipes on p. 49).

MUFFINS & BREADS

Say "Welcome Home!" with a bonanza of oven-fresh muffins and breads. With so many pleasing possibilities, you'll want to keep plenty on hand.

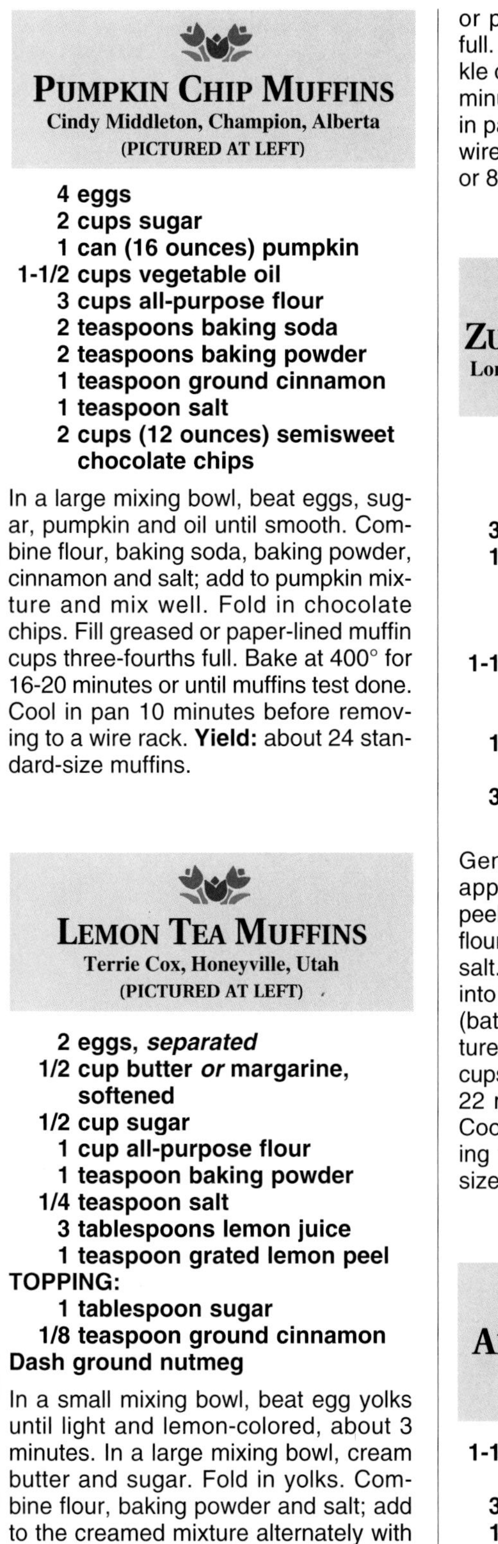

PUMPKIN CHIP MUFFINS

Cindy Middleton, Champion, Alberta
(PICTURED AT LEFT)

4 eggs
2 cups sugar
1 can (16 ounces) pumpkin
1-1/2 cups vegetable oil
3 cups all-purpose flour
2 teaspoons baking soda
2 teaspoons baking powder
1 teaspoon ground cinnamon
1 teaspoon salt
2 cups (12 ounces) semisweet chocolate chips

In a large mixing bowl, beat eggs, sugar, pumpkin and oil until smooth. Combine flour, baking soda, baking powder, cinnamon and salt; add to pumpkin mixture and mix well. Fold in chocolate chips. Fill greased or paper-lined muffin cups three-fourths full. Bake at 400° for 16-20 minutes or until muffins test done. Cool in pan 10 minutes before removing to a wire rack. **Yield:** about 24 standard-size muffins.

LEMON TEA MUFFINS

Terrie Cox, Honeyville, Utah
(PICTURED AT LEFT)

2 eggs, *separated*
1/2 cup butter *or* margarine, softened
1/2 cup sugar
1 cup all-purpose flour
1 teaspoon baking powder
1/4 teaspoon salt
3 tablespoons lemon juice
1 teaspoon grated lemon peel
TOPPING:
1 tablespoon sugar
1/8 teaspoon ground cinnamon
Dash ground nutmeg

In a small mixing bowl, beat egg yolks until light and lemon-colored, about 3 minutes. In a large mixing bowl, cream butter and sugar. Fold in yolks. Combine flour, baking powder and salt; add to the creamed mixture alternately with lemon juice and peel, stirring just until combined. Beat egg whites until stiff peaks form; fold into batter. Fill greased or paper-lined muffin cups two-thirds full. Combine topping ingredients; sprinkle over muffins. Bake at 350° for 20-25 minutes or until muffins test done. Cool in pan 10 minutes before removing to a wire rack. **Yield:** about 24 mini-muffins or 8 standard-size muffins.

ZUCCHINI CARROT MUFFINS

Loretta Blaine, South Burlington, Vermont
(PICTURED AT LEFT)

2 cups shredded carrot
1 cup shredded zucchini
1 cup chopped peeled apple
3/4 cup flaked coconut
1/2 cup chopped almonds
2 teaspoons grated orange peel
2 cups all-purpose flour
1-1/4 cups sugar
1 tablespoon ground cinnamon
2 teaspoons baking soda
1/2 teaspoon salt
3 eggs, lightly beaten
3/4 cup vegetable oil
1 teaspoon vanilla extract

Gently toss together carrot, zucchini, apple, coconut, almonds and orange peel; set aside. In a large bowl, combine flour, sugar, cinnamon, baking soda and salt. Combine eggs, oil and vanilla; stir into dry ingredients just until moistened (batter will be thick). Fold in carrot mixture. Fill greased or paper-lined muffin cups two-thirds full. Bake at 375° for 20-22 minutes or until muffins test done. Cool in pan 10 minutes before removing to a wire rack. **Yield:** 18 standard-size muffins.

ALMOND PEACH MUFFINS

Robin Henry, Sugar Land, Texas
(PICTURED AT LEFT)

1-1/2 cups all-purpose flour
1 cup sugar
3/4 teaspoon salt
1/2 teaspoon baking soda
2 eggs
1/2 cup vegetable oil
1/2 teaspoon vanilla extract
1/8 teaspoon almond extract
1-1/4 cups chopped peeled fresh peaches*
1/2 cup chopped almonds

In a large bowl, combine flour, sugar, salt and baking soda. In another bowl, beat eggs, oil and extracts; stir into dry ingredients just until moistened. Fold in peaches and almonds. Fill greased or paper-lined muffin cups three-fourths full. Bake at 375° for 20-25 minutes or until muffins test done. Cool in pan for 10 minutes before removing to a wire rack. **Yield:** about 12 standard-size muffins. ***Editor's Note:** A 16-ounce can of peaches, drained and chopped, can be substituted for the fresh peaches.

OATMEAL BREAD

Connie Moore, Medway, Ohio

1 cup boiling water
1 cup old-fashioned oats
1 package (1/4 ounce) active dry yeast
1/3 cup warm water (110° to 115°)
1/4 cup honey
1 tablespoon butter *or* margarine
1 teaspoon salt
3 to 3-1/2 cups all-purpose flour
Melted butter *or* margarine
Additional oats

In a large mixing bowl, combine boiling water and oats; let stand until warm (110°-115°). In a small bowl, dissolve yeast in warm water; add to oat mixture. Add honey, butter, salt and 2 cups flour; beat until smooth. Add enough remaining flour to form a soft dough. Turn onto a floured board; knead until smooth and elastic, about 6-8 minutes. Place in a greased bowl, turning once to grease top. Cover and let rise in a warm place until doubled, about 1 hour. Punch the dough down. Shape into a loaf; place in a greased 8-in. x 4-in. x 2-in. loaf pan. Brush with melted butter. Sprinkle with oats. Cover and let rise in a warm place until doubled, about 30 minutes. Bake at 350° for 50-55 minutes or until golden brown. **Yield:** 1 loaf.

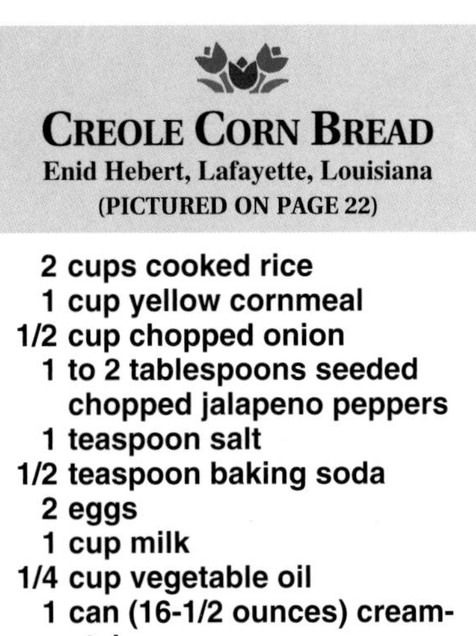

Creole Corn Bread

Enid Hebert, Lafayette, Louisiana

(PICTURED ON PAGE 22)

2 cups cooked rice
1 cup yellow cornmeal
1/2 cup chopped onion
1 to 2 tablespoons seeded chopped jalapeno peppers
1 teaspoon salt
1/2 teaspoon baking soda
2 eggs
1 cup milk
1/4 cup vegetable oil
1 can (16-1/2 ounces) cream-style corn
3 cups (12 ounces) shredded cheddar cheese
Additional cornmeal

In a large bowl, combine rice, cornmeal, onion, peppers, salt and baking soda. In another bowl, beat eggs, milk and oil. Add corn; mix well. Stir into rice mixture until blended. Fold in cheese. Sprinkle a well-greased 10-in. ovenproof skillet with cornmeal. Pour batter into skillet. Bake at 350° for 45-50 minutes or until bread tests done. Cut into wedges and serve warm. **Yield:** 12 servings.

Oatmeal Carrot Muffins

Jane Richter, Pompano Beach, Florida

✓ This tasty dish uses less sugar, salt and fat. Recipe includes *Nutritional Information.*

1 cup old-fashioned oats
1/2 cup raisins
1 cup skim milk
1/2 cup shredded carrot
1/2 cup sugar
1/2 cup packed brown sugar
1/4 cup vegetable oil
2 egg whites
1 teaspoon grated orange peel
1/2 cup all-purpose flour
1/2 cup whole wheat flour
1 tablespoon baking powder
1/2 teaspoon baking soda

In a large bowl, combine oats, raisins and milk; stir well. Cover and refrigerate 2 hours or overnight. Combine carrot, sugars, oil, egg whites and orange peel; stir into oat mixture. Combine dry ingredients; stir into the batter just until moistened. Coat muffin cups with nonstick cooking spray or use paper liners; fill cups two-thirds full. Bake at 400° for 20-25 minutes or until muffins test done. Cool in pan 10 minutes before removing to a wire rack. **Yield:** 10 muffins. **Nutritional Information:** One muffin equals 227 calories, 184 mg sodium, trace cholesterol, 40 gm carbohydrate, 7 gm protein, 6 gm fat.

Low-Fat Banana Muffins

Marcia Lane, Hemet, California

✓ This tasty dish uses less sugar, salt and fat. Recipe includes *Nutritional Information.*

2-1/2 cups all-purpose flour
2 teaspoons baking powder
1 teaspoon baking soda
1 teaspoon ground cinnamon
1/2 cup unsweetened applesauce
1 cup sugar
3 egg whites
3 to 4 medium ripe bananas, mashed (about 2 cups)
1 teaspoon vanilla extract

In a large bowl, combine flour, baking powder, baking soda and cinnamon. Combine remaining ingredients; stir into dry ingredients just until moistened. Coat muffin cups with nonstick cooking spray or use paper liners; fill cups two-thirds full. Bake at 350° for 20-25 minutes or until muffins test done. Cool in pan 10 minutes before removing to a wire rack. **Yield:** 15 muffins. **Nutritional Information:** One muffin equals 163 calories, 125 mg sodium, 0 cholesterol, 38 gm carbohydrate, 3 gm protein, trace fat.

Best-Ever Blueberry Muffins

Elaine Clemens, Birch Run, Michigan

2-1/2 cups all-purpose flour
1 cup sugar
2-1/2 teaspoons baking powder
1/4 teaspoon salt
2 eggs, lightly beaten
1 cup buttermilk
1/4 cup butter *or* margarine, melted
1-1/2 cups fresh blueberries

In a large bowl, combine flour, sugar, baking powder and salt. Combine eggs, buttermilk and butter; stir into dry ingredients just until moistened. Fold in blueberries. Fill greased or paper-lined muffin cups three-fourths full. Bake at 400° for 20-24 minutes or until muffins test done. **Yield:** about 1 dozen.

Cherry Blossom Muffins

Anna Mae Ackerman, Spearville, Kansas

✓ This tasty dish uses less sugar, salt and fat. Recipe includes *Diabetic Exchanges.*

1/4 cup egg substitute
2/3 cup orange juice
2 tablespoons sugar
2 tablespoons vegetable oil
2 cups low-fat buttermilk baking mix
1/2 cup chopped pecans
1/2 cup sugar-free cherry fruit spread

In a bowl, combine egg substitute, orange juice, sugar and oil. Add baking mix; stir for 30 seconds. Fold in pecans. Coat muffin cups with nonstick cooking spray or use paper liners; fill cups one-third full. Top each with 2 teaspoons fruit spread; cover with the remaining batter. Bake at 400° for 20-25 minutes or until muffins test done. Cool in pan 10 minutes before removing to a wire rack. **Yield:** 9 muffins. **Diabetic Exchanges:** One muffin equals 2 starch, 2 fat; also, 241 calories, 330 mg sodium, trace cholesterol, 36 gm carbohydrate, 4 gm protein, 10 gm fat.

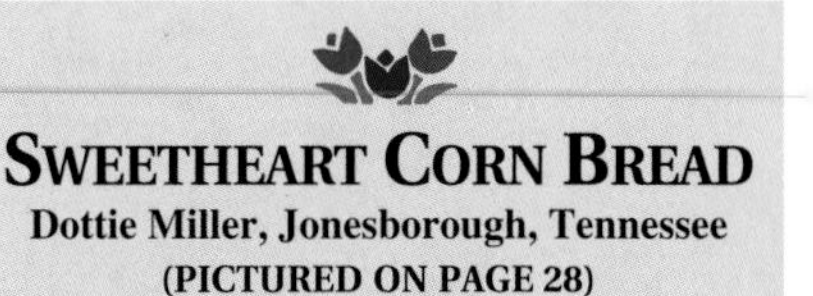

Sweetheart Corn Bread

Dottie Miller, Jonesborough, Tennessee

(PICTURED ON PAGE 28)

2 eggs
1 cup (8 ounces) sour cream
1/2 cup vegetable oil
1 can (8 ounces) cream-style corn
1-1/2 cups self-rising cornmeal

In a large bowl, beat eggs. Add sour cream, oil and corn; mix well. Stir in cornmeal just until combined. Pour into a greased and floured 5-cup heart-shaped baking pan or a 9-in. round pan. Bake at 425° for 20-25 minutes or until bread tests done. Cool 10 minutes in pan before removing to a wire rack. **Yield:** 6-8 servings. **Editor's Note:** For a festive presentation, tie a red ribbon around the edge of the bread before serving.

Butternut Squash Rolls

Bernice Morris, Marshfield, Missouri

1 package (1/4 ounce) active dry yeast
1 cup warm milk (110° to 115°)
1/4 cup warm water (110° to 115°)
3 tablespoons butter *or* margarine, softened
2 teaspoons salt
1/2 cup sugar
1 cup mashed cooked butternut squash
5 to 5-1/2 cups all-purpose flour, *divided*

In a large mixing bowl, dissolve yeast in milk and water. Add butter, salt, sugar, squash and 3 cups flour; beat until smooth. Add enough remaining flour to form a soft dough. Turn onto a floured surface; knead until smooth and elastic, about 6-8 minutes. Place in a greased bowl, turning once to grease top. Cover and let rise in a warm place until doubled, about 1 hour. Punch dough down. Form into rolls; place in two greased 10-in. cast-iron skillets or 9-in. round baking pans. Cover and let rise until doubled, about 30 minutes. Bake at 375° for 20-25 minutes or until golden brown. **Yield:** about 2 dozen.

White Casserole Bread

Lona Sage, Belvidere, Illinois

✓ This tasty dish uses less sugar, salt and fat. Recipe includes *Diabetic Exchanges*.

1 package (1/4 ounce) active dry yeast
1-1/4 cups warm water (110° to 115°)
1 tablespoon sugar
1/2 teaspoon salt
2-1/2 to 3 cups all-purpose flour

In a large mixing bowl, dissolve yeast in water. Add sugar, salt and 1-1/2 cups flour; beat until smooth. Add enough remaining flour to form a soft dough. Turn onto a floured board; knead until smooth and elastic, about 6-8 minutes. Place in a greased bowl, turning once to grease top. Cover and let rise in a warm place until doubled, about 1 hour. Punch dough down. Shape into a round loaf and place in a greased 1-qt. baking dish. Cover and let rise until doubled, about 30 minutes. Using a sharp knife, make three slashes across the top. Bake at 350° for 40-45 minutes. Remove from dish to cool on a wire rack. **Yield:** 1 loaf (16 slices). **Diabetic Exchanges:** One slice equals 1 starch; also, 90 calories, 73 mg sodium, 0 cholesterol, 21 gm carbohydrate, 3 gm protein, trace fat.

Sweet Pineapple Muffins

Tina Hanson, Portage, Wisconsin

2 cups all-purpose flour
2 cups sugar
1 teaspoon baking soda
1 teaspoon baking powder
2 cans (8 ounces *each*) crushed pineapple, undrained
2 eggs
1/2 cup vegetable oil

In a large bowl, combine flour, sugar, baking soda and baking powder. In another bowl, mix pineapple, eggs and oil; stir into the dry ingredients just until moistened. Fill greased or paper-lined muffin cups two-thirds full. Bake at 350° for 20-25 minutes or until muffins test done. Cool in pan for 10 minutes before removing to a wire rack. **Yield:** about 20 muffins.

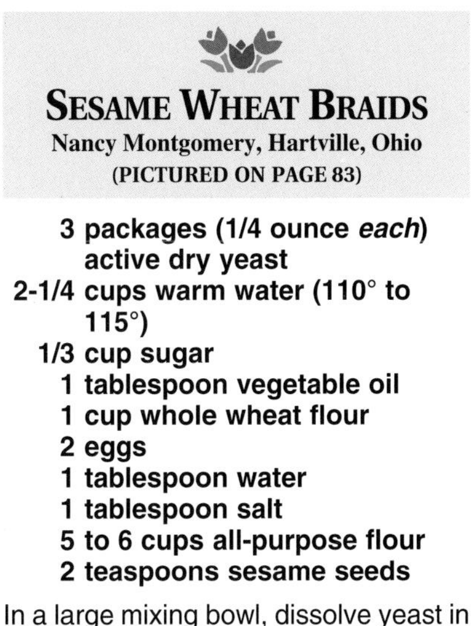

Sesame Wheat Braids

Nancy Montgomery, Hartville, Ohio

(PICTURED ON PAGE 83)

3 packages (1/4 ounce *each*) active dry yeast
2-1/4 cups warm water (110° to 115°)
1/3 cup sugar
1 tablespoon vegetable oil
1 cup whole wheat flour
2 eggs
1 tablespoon water
1 tablespoon salt
5 to 6 cups all-purpose flour
2 teaspoons sesame seeds

In a large mixing bowl, dissolve yeast in water. Add sugar and oil; mix well. Stir in whole wheat flour; let stand until the mixture bubbles, about 5 minutes. In a small bowl, beat eggs and water. Remove 2 tablespoons to a cup or small bowl; cover and refrigerate. Add remaining egg mixture and salt to batter; mix until smooth. Add 4 cups all-purpose flour and beat until smooth. Add enough remaining flour to form a soft dough. Turn onto a floured board and knead until smooth and elastic, about 6-8 minutes. Place in a greased bowl, turning once to grease top. Cover and let rise in a warm place until doubled, about 20 minutes. Punch dough down and divide in half. Divide each half into thirds. Shape each into a rope about 15 in. long. Place three ropes on a greased baking sheet; braid. Pinch ends firmly and tuck under. Brush with the reserved egg mixture; sprinkle with sesame seeds. Repeat, placing second braid on the same baking sheet. Let rise until doubled, about 15-20 minutes. Bake at 350° for 20-25 minutes. Remove from baking sheet to cool on a wire rack. **Yield:** 2 loaves.

Sour Cream Corn Bread

Linda Brown, Sinking Spring, Pennsylvania

1 cup all-purpose flour
1 cup yellow cornmeal
2 tablespoons sugar
2 teaspoons baking powder
1/2 teaspoon salt
1 egg, beaten
1 cup (8 ounces) sour cream
1/3 cup milk
2 tablespoons butter *or* margarine, melted
2 tablespoons chopped pimiento
1 teaspoon minced dried onion

In a bowl, combine dry ingredients; mix well. Add remaining ingredients and stir just until moistened. Pour into a greased 8-in. square baking pan. Bake at 400° for 20-25 minutes or until bread tests done. **Yield:** 9 servings.

Jalapeno Bread

Mary Alice Watt, Upton, Wyoming

2 loaves (1 pound *each*) frozen bread dough, thawed
1 can (8-3/4 ounces) whole kernel corn, drained
1 egg, beaten
1 can (3-1/2 ounces) whole jalapenos, chopped
2 tablespoons taco seasoning mix
1 jar (2 ounces) sliced pimientos, drained
1-1/2 teaspoons vinegar

Cut bread dough into 1-in. pieces. Place all ingredients in a large bowl and toss to mix well. Spoon into two greased 8-in. x 4-in. x 2-in. loaf pans. Cover and let stand for 15 minutes. Bake at 350° for 35-40 minutes. Cool in pan 10 minutes before removing to a wire rack. Serve warm if desired. **Yield:** 2 loaves. **Editor's Note:** Remove the seeds from the jalapenos before chopping for a milder bread.

Honey Raisin Muffins

Joyce Reece, Mena, Arkansas

1-1/4 cups all-purpose flour
1 tablespoon baking powder
1/4 teaspoon salt
2 cups Raisin Bran cereal
1 cup milk
1/4 cup honey
1 egg, lightly beaten
3 tablespoons vegetable oil

Combine flour, baking powder and salt; set aside. In a large bowl, combine cereal, milk and honey; let stand until softened, about 2 minutes. Stir in egg and oil; mix well. Add dry ingredients; stir just until moistened. Fill greased or paper-lined muffin cups two-thirds full. Bake at 400° for 18-20 minutes or until muffins test done. Cool in pan 10 minutes before removing to a wire rack. **Yield:** about 10 muffins.

A USE FOR ZUCCHINI! When zucchini is abundant, shred, drain and freeze some in small amounts for making zucchini bread at a later date.

DON'T LIMIT your use of eggs to just breakfast foods! Of course, no buffet table is complete without deviled eggs and a classic bacon and eggs entree. But credit to the Easter Bread's golden color goes to a number of yolks and whites. Watch the loaf disappear quickly before your eyes! Creamy Caramel Flan is a tasty variation of custard. Best of all, a small slice goes a long way—so it's great to serve a crowd.

GOLDEN MOMENTS. Clockwise from top: **Easter Bread** (p. 53), **Bacon and Eggs Casserole** (p. 33), **Creamy Caramel Flan** (p. 75) and **Almond Deviled Eggs** (p. 35).

Easter Bread

Rose Kostynuik, Calgary, Alberta
(PICTURED AT LEFT)

2 packages (1/4 ounce *each*) active dry yeast
1/2 cup warm water (110° to 115°)
4 eggs
6 egg yolks
1 cup sugar
3/4 cup butter *or* margarine, melted
2 teaspoons salt
1 teaspoon vanilla extract
1 teaspoon lemon juice
2 tablespoons grated lemon peel
2 cups warm milk (110° to 115°)
9-3/4 to 10-1/4 cups all-purpose flour
1 cup golden raisins

In a small bowl, dissolve yeast in water; set aside. In a large mixing bowl, beat the eggs and yolks until lemon-colored; gradually add sugar. Add butter, salt, vanilla, lemon juice and peel; beat well. Blend in milk and yeast mixture. Add 6 cups flour; beat until smooth. By hand, stir in enough remaining flour to form a soft dough. Turn onto a lightly floured surface; knead until smooth and elastic, about 10 minutes. Sprinkle with raisins; knead for 5 minutes more. Place in a greased bowl, turning once to grease top. Cover and let rise in a warm place until doubled, about 1 hour. Punch dough down. Turn onto a lightly floured surface; divide into thirds. Cover and let rest 10 minutes. Shape each portion into a loaf and place in greased 8-in. x 4-in. x 2-in. loaf pans. Cover and let rise in a warm place until almost doubled, about 30 minutes. Bake at 325° for 45 minutes or until golden brown. Remove from pans to cool on wire racks. **Yield:** 3 loaves.

Savory Pull-Apart Bread

Janne Rowe, Wichita, Kansas

1/4 cup grated Parmesan cheese
3 tablespoons sesame seeds
1/2 teaspoon dried basil
1 package (30 ounces) frozen roll dough (24 rolls)
1/4 cup butter *or* margarine, melted
2 tablespoons bacon bits, optional

Combine Parmesan cheese, sesame seeds and basil; sprinkle one-third in the bottom and up the sides of a greased 12-cup fluted tube pan. Place half of the unthawed rolls in pan; drizzle with half of the butter. Sprinkle with half of the remaining cheese mixture and bacon bits if desired. Arrange remaining rolls on top; drizzle with remaining butter. Sprinkle with remaining cheese mixture. Cover and refrigerate overnight. Remove from the refrigerator 30 minutes before baking. Bake at 350° for 20 minutes. Cover loosely with foil; bake 10-15 minutes longer. **Yield:** 10-12 servings.

Virginia Box Bread

Thelma Richardson, La Crosse, Wisconsin

1 package (1/4 ounce) active dry yeast
2/3 cup warm water (110° to 115°)
2 eggs, beaten
2 tablespoons sugar
1 teaspoon salt
5 tablespoons butter *or* margarine, melted and cooled
3-1/4 to 3-3/4 cups all-purpose flour

In a large mixing bowl, dissolve yeast in water. Add eggs, sugar, salt, butter and 2 cups flour. Beat until smooth. Add enough remaining flour to form a soft dough. Turn onto a floured board; knead until smooth and elastic, about 6-8 minutes. Place in a greased bowl, turning once to grease top. Cover and let rise in a warm place until doubled, about 1-1/2 hours. Punch the dough down. On a lightly floured board, roll dough into a 13-in. x 9-in. rectangle. Transfer dough to a greased 13-in. x 9-in. x 2-in. baking pan. Using a sharp knife, cut dough into 16 even squares. Cover and let rise until doubled, about 30 minutes. Bake at 375° for 20 minutes or until golden brown. To serve, separate into rolls. **Yield:** 16 servings.

Quick & Easy

Peanut Butter Muffins

Caroline Sanders, Kansas City, Missouri

2 eggs
1/3 cup sugar
1 cup milk
1/4 cup peanut butter
2 cups buttermilk baking mix
3 tablespoons jam

In a large mixing bowl, beat eggs, sugar, milk and peanut butter until smooth. Stir in baking mix. Fill greased or paper-lined muffin cups two-thirds full. Top each with 1/2 teaspoon jam. Bake at 375° for 15-20 minutes or until muffins test done. Cool in pan 10 minutes before removing to a wire rack. **Yield:** about 12 muffins.

Caraway Rolls

Ruth Hastings, Louisville, Illinois

2 packages (1/4 ounce *each*) active dry yeast
1/2 cup warm water (110° to 115°)
2 tablespoons caraway seeds
2 cups (16 ounces) cottage cheese
1/2 teaspoon baking soda
1/4 cup sugar
2-1/2 teaspoons salt
2 eggs, beaten
4-1/2 to 5 cups all-purpose flour
1 tablespoon butter *or* margarine, melted

In a large mixing bowl, dissolve yeast in water. Add caraway seeds. In a small saucepan, heat cottage cheese until lukewarm; add baking soda and mix well. Stir into yeast mixture. Add sugar, salt and eggs; mix well. Gradually stir in enough flour to form a soft dough. Cover and let rise in a warm place until doubled, about 1 hour. Stir down. Turn onto a lightly floured surface. Divide into 24 pieces. Place in well-greased muffin cups. Cover and let rise until doubled, about 35 minutes. Bake at 350° for 18-20 minutes. Remove to wire racks; brush with melted butter. **Yield:** 2 dozen.

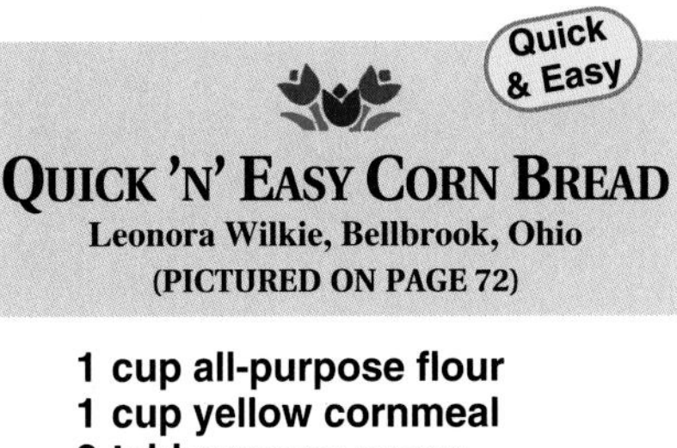

Quick 'n' Easy Corn Bread

Leonora Wilkie, Bellbrook, Ohio
(PICTURED ON PAGE 72)

1 cup all-purpose flour
1 cup yellow cornmeal
2 tablespoons sugar
2 teaspoons baking powder
1 teaspoon crushed dried rosemary
1/2 teaspoon salt
1 egg
1 cup (8 ounces) sour cream
1/3 cup milk
2 tablespoons butter *or* margarine, melted

In a medium bowl, combine dry ingredients. In another bowl, beat egg, sour cream, milk and butter; add to cornmeal mixture and mix just until combined. Pour into a greased 8-in. square baking dish. Bake at 400° for 20-25 minutes or until a toothpick inserted near the center comes out clean. Serve warm. **Yield:** 9 servings.

NOW A HUGE assortment of magnificent muffins is right at your fingertips. From delectable classics like bran, poppy seed and blueberry to exciting new tastes like cheddar-dill, ginger and jam-filled, you're bound to find plenty to please everyone in the family. Why not bake and freeze some today for fast snacking in the future?

MUFFIN MANIA: Clockwise from lower right: **Honey Bran Muffins**, **Cheddar Dill Muffins**, **Apple Butter Muffins**, **Apple Bran Muffins**, **Poppy Seed Muffins**, **Snappy Ginger Muffins**, **Berry Cream Muffins** and **Cinnamon Doughnut Muffins** (all recipes on pages 56 and 57).

Honey Bran Muffins

Pauline Rohloff, Endeavor, Wisconsin

(PICTURED ON PAGE 55)

- **2 cups lukewarm pineapple juice**
- **2 cups golden raisins**
- **1 cup packed brown sugar**
- **1/2 cup vegetable oil**
- **1/2 cup honey**
- **5 eggs, beaten**
- **2 cups all-purpose flour**
- **2 teaspoons baking soda**
- **1 teaspoon salt**
- **4 cups All-Bran cereal**

In a small bowl, combine pineapple juice and raisins; set aside. In a large mixing bowl, combine brown sugar, oil, honey and eggs; mix well. Combine flour, baking soda and salt; stir in cereal. Add to sugar mixture and mix well. Fold in the raisin mixture (batter will be thin). Cover and refrigerate at least 3 hours or overnight. Stir (batter will thicken). Fill greased or paper-lined muffin cups three-fourths full. Bake at 400° for 20-25 minutes or until muffins test done. Cool in pan 10 minutes before removing to a wire rack. **Yield:** about 12 jumbo muffins or 20 standard-size muffins.

Cheddar Dill Muffins

Bernadette Colvin, Houston, Texas

(PICTURED ON PAGE 55)

- **3-1/2 cups all-purpose flour**
- **3 tablespoons sugar**
- **2 tablespoons baking powder**
- **2 teaspoons dill weed**
- **1 teaspoon salt**
- **1 cup (4 ounces) shredded cheddar cheese**
- **1-3/4 cups milk**
- **2 eggs, lightly beaten**
- **1/4 cup butter *or* margarine, melted**

In a bowl, combine the first six ingredients. Combine milk, eggs and butter; stir into dry ingredients just until moistened. Fill greased or paper-lined muffin cups almost full. Bake at 400° for 25-30 minutes or until muffins test done. Cool in pan 10 minutes before removing to a wire rack. **Yield:** about 9 jumbo muffins or 12 standard-size muffins.

MUFFIN MAGIC. Turn an ordinary muffin into a quick and delicious dessert. Just cut a bran muffin in half, add whipped topping and drizzle with your favorite jam or flavored yogurt.

Apple Butter Muffins

Anita Bell, Gallatin, Tennessee

(PICTURED ON PAGE 54)

- **1-3/4 cups all-purpose flour**
- **1/3 cup sugar**
- **2 teaspoons baking powder**
- **1/2 teaspoon ground cinnamon**
- **1/4 teaspoon salt**
- **1/4 teaspoon ground nutmeg**
- **1/8 teaspoon ground allspice**
- **1/8 teaspoon ground ginger**
- **1 egg, lightly beaten**
- **3/4 cup milk**
- **1/4 cup vegetable oil**
- **1/2 cup thick apple butter***

TOPPING:

- **1/2 cup chopped pecans**
- **3 tablespoons sugar**

In a medium bowl, combine the first eight ingredients. Combine egg, milk and oil; stir into dry ingredients just until moistened. Fill greased or paper-lined muffin cups with a rounded tablespoon of batter. Top each with a rounded teaspoon of apple butter and remaining batter. Combine topping ingredients; sprinkle over muffins. Bake at 400° for 15-18 minutes. Cool in pan 10 minutes before removing to a wire rack. **Yield:** about 12 standard-size muffins. ***Editor's Note:** This recipe was tested with commercially prepared apple butter.

Apple Bran Muffins

Nancy Brown, Klamath Falls, Oregon

(PICTURED ON PAGE 54)

- **2 large Golden Delicious apples, peeled and chopped**
- **1/2 cup butter *or* margarine**
- **3 cups All-Bran cereal**
- **1 cup boiling water**
- **2 cups buttermilk**
- **2 eggs, lightly beaten**
- **2/3 cup sugar**
- **1 cup raisins**
- **2-1/2 cups all-purpose flour**
- **2-1/2 teaspoons baking soda**
- **2 teaspoons ground cinnamon**
- **1 teaspoon ground nutmeg**
- **1/2 teaspoon ground cloves**
- **1/2 teaspoon salt**

In a skillet, saute apples in butter until tender, about 10 minutes. Combine cereal and water in a large bowl; stir in the buttermilk, eggs, sugar, raisins and apples with butter. Combine dry ingredients; stir into apple mixture just until moistened. Refrigerate in a tightly covered container for at least 24 hours (batter will be very thick). Fill greased or paper-lined muffin cups three-fourths full. Bake at 400° for 20-25 minutes or until muffins test done. Cool in pan 10 minutes before removing to a wire rack. **Yield:** about 24 standard-size muffins. **Editor's Note:** Batter can be stored in a tightly covered container in the refrigerator for up to 2 weeks.

Poppy Seed Muffins

Kathy Smith, Granger, Indiana

(PICTURED ON PAGE 55)

- **3 cups all-purpose flour**
- **2-1/2 cups sugar**
- **2 tablespoons poppy seeds**
- **1-1/2 teaspoons baking powder**
- **1-1/2 teaspoons salt**
- **3 eggs**
- **1-1/2 cups milk**
- **1 cup vegetable oil**
- **1-1/2 teaspoons vanilla extract**
- **1-1/2 teaspoons almond extract**

In a large bowl, combine flour, sugar, poppy seeds, baking powder and salt. In another bowl, beat eggs, milk, oil and extracts; stir into dry ingredients just until moistened. Fill greased or paper-lined muffin cups two-thirds full. Bake at 350° for 20-25 minutes or until muffins test done. Cool in pan 10 minutes before removing to a wire rack. **Yield:** about 8 dozen mini-muffins or 24 standard-size muffins.

Snappy Ginger Muffins

Marlene Falsetti, Lowbanks, Ontario

(PICTURED ON PAGE 55)

- **1/2 cup vegetable oil**
- **1/4 cup sugar**
- **1/4 cup packed brown sugar**
- **1 cup molasses**
- **1 egg**
- **3 cups all-purpose flour**
- **1-1/2 teaspoons baking soda**
- **1 teaspoon ground cinnamon**
- **1 teaspoon ground ginger**
- **1/2 teaspoon salt**
- **1 cup water**

In a mixing bowl, beat the oil and sugars. Beat in molasses and egg. Combine the flour, baking soda, cinnamon, ginger and salt; stir into molasses mixture alternately with water. Fill greased or paper-lined muffin cups two-thirds full. Bake at 350° for 20-25 minutes or until muffins test done. Cool in pan for 10 minutes before removing to a wire rack. **Yield:** about 20 standard-size muffins.

Berry Cream Muffins

Linda Gilmore, Hampstead, Maryland
(PICTURED ON PAGE 55)

4 cups all-purpose flour
2 cups sugar
2 teaspoons baking powder
1 teaspoon baking soda
1 teaspoon salt
3 cups fresh *or* frozen raspberries *or* blueberries
4 eggs, lightly beaten
2 cups (16 ounces) sour cream
1 cup vegetable oil
1 teaspoon vanilla extract

In a large bowl, combine flour, sugar, baking powder, baking soda and salt; add berries and toss gently. Combine eggs, sour cream, oil and vanilla; mix well. Stir into dry ingredients just until moistened. Fill greased or paper-lined muffin cups two-thirds full. Bake at 400° for 20-25 minutes or until muffins test done. **Yield:** about 24 standard-size muffins.

Banana Praline Muffins

Debbie Fowler, Fort Benton, Montana

1/3 cup chopped pecans
3 tablespoons brown sugar
1 tablespoon sour cream
3 small ripe bananas, mashed (about 1 cup)
1 egg, lightly beaten
1/2 cup sugar
1/4 cup vegetable oil
1-1/2 cups buttermilk baking mix

In a small bowl, combine pecans, brown sugar and sour cream; set aside. In a large bowl, combine bananas, egg, sugar and oil; mix well. Add baking mix and stir just until moistened. Fill greased or paper-lined muffin cups two-thirds full. Place 1 teaspoonful of pecan mixture in center of each muffin. Bake at 400° for 15-18 minutes or until muffins test done. Cool in pan 10 minutes before removing to a wire rack. **Yield:** about 9 muffins.

Cinnamon Doughnut Muffins

Sharon Pullen, Alvinston, Ontario
(PICTURED ON PAGE 55)

1-3/4 cups all-purpose flour
1-1/2 teaspoons baking powder
1/2 teaspoon salt
1/2 teaspoon ground nutmeg
1/4 teaspoon ground cinnamon
3/4 cup sugar
1/3 cup vegetable oil
1 egg, lightly beaten
3/4 cup milk
Jam
TOPPING:
1/4 cup butter *or* margarine, melted
1/3 cup sugar
1 teaspoon ground cinnamon

In a large bowl, combine flour, baking powder, salt, nutmeg and cinnamon. Combine sugar, oil, egg and milk; stir into dry ingredients just until moistened. Fill greased or paper-lined muffin cups half full; place 1 teaspoon jam on top. Cover jam with enough batter to fill muffin cups three-fourths full. Bake at 350° for 20-25 minutes or until muffins test done. Place melted butter in a small bowl; combine sugar and cinnamon in another bowl. Immediately after removing muffins from the oven, dip tops in butter, then in cinnamon-sugar. Serve warm. **Yield:** 10 standard-size muffins.

Onion Cheese Muffins

Judy Johnson, Mundelein, Illinois

1-1/2 cups buttermilk baking mix
3/4 cup shredded Colby *or* cheddar cheese, *divided*
1 egg
1/2 cup milk
1 small onion, finely chopped
1 tablespoon butter *or* margarine
1 tablespoon sesame seeds, toasted

Combine the baking mix and 1/2 cup of cheese in a large bowl; set aside. In a small bowl, beat egg and milk; set aside. In a small skillet, saute onion in butter until tender; add to egg mixture. Stir into cheese mixture just until moistened. Fill greased or paper-lined muffin cups three-fourths full. Top with the sesame seeds and remaining cheese. Bake at 400° for 18-20 minutes or until muffins test done. Cool in pan 10 minutes. Serve warm. **Yield:** about 6 muffins.

Date Nut Bread

Rosemary White, Oneida, New York

1/4 cup shortening
1-1/2 cups sugar
2 eggs
1-1/2 teaspoons vanilla extract
3 cups all-purpose flour
2 teaspoons baking soda
2 teaspoons baking powder
1/4 teaspoon salt
1-1/2 cups orange juice
1-1/2 cups chopped dates
1/2 cup chopped walnuts

In a mixing bowl, cream shortening and sugar. Add eggs and vanilla; beat until fluffy. Combine dry ingredients; add alternately to creamed mixture with orange juice. Blend well. Fold in dates and walnuts. Pour into two greased, floured and waxed paper-lined 8-in. x 4-in. x 2-in. loaf pans. Bake at 350° for 45-50 minutes or until a toothpick inserted near the center comes out clean. Cool in pans 10 minutes before removing to a wire rack. **Yield:** 2 loaves.

Blue Cheese Mini-Muffins

Nancy Bruce, Citrus Heights, California

1/3 cup butter *or* margarine, softened
3/4 cup sugar
2 eggs
2/3 cup milk
1 teaspoon lemon juice
1-1/2 cups all-purpose flour
1/2 cup whole wheat flour
2 teaspoons baking powder
1/2 teaspoon salt
1/4 teaspoon baking soda
1 package (4 ounces) blue cheese, crumbled
3/4 cup finely chopped walnuts
Sesame seeds

In a mixing bowl, cream butter and sugar. Beat in eggs until light and fluffy. Add milk and lemon juice; mix well. Combine dry ingredients; add to creamed mixture along with blue cheese and walnuts. Stir just until moistened. Fill greased mini-muffin cups three-fourths full. Sprinkle with sesame seeds. Bake at 350° for 18-20 minutes or until lightly browned. Serve warm. **Yield:** 3 to 3-1/2 dozen.

Cream Cheese Muffin Puffs

Diane Xavier, Hilmar, California

1/2 cup sugar
1 teaspoon ground cinnamon
1/4 cup butter *or* margarine, melted
1/2 teaspoon vanilla extract
1 tube (10 ounces) refrigerated biscuits
1 package (3 ounces) cream cheese, cut into 10 cubes

In a small bowl, combine sugar and cinnamon. In another bowl, combine butter and vanilla. Separate dough into 10 biscuits; press each into a 3-in. circle. Dip cream cheese cubes in butter and then in cinnamon-sugar. Place one in center of each biscuit. Fold dough over cube; seal and shape into balls. Dip balls in butter and then in cinnamon-sugar. Place seam side down in greased muffin cups. Bake at 375° for 14-18 minutes or until golden brown. Serve warm. **Yield:** 10 muffins.

AFTER WORKING in your garden, you'll appreciate a meal like this one that's not only quick and satisfying, but also refreshing and delicious. Ham and pineapple sandwiches will bring a tropical flair to any table. Tart citrus and sweet honey combine to dress up plain spinach salad. And a hearty slice of Banana Nut Cake is a wonderful way to end the meal.

YOURS FOR THE PICKING. Clockwise from the bottom right: **Hawaiian Ham Sandwiches**, (p. 13), **Banana Nut Cake** (p. 59) and **Spinach Salad with Honey Dressing** (p. 43).

Cakes, Cookies & Bars

No dinner is complete until you pass thick slices of cake, jars brimming with cookies or plates stacked high with a bounty of bars.

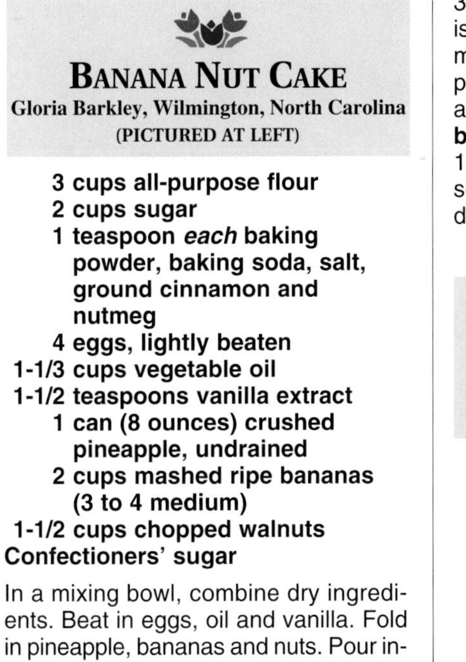

Banana Nut Cake

Gloria Barkley, Wilmington, North Carolina

(PICTURED AT LEFT)

3 cups all-purpose flour
2 cups sugar
1 teaspoon *each* baking powder, baking soda, salt, ground cinnamon and nutmeg
4 eggs, lightly beaten
1-1/3 cups vegetable oil
1-1/2 teaspoons vanilla extract
1 can (8 ounces) crushed pineapple, undrained
2 cups mashed ripe bananas (3 to 4 medium)
1-1/2 cups chopped walnuts
Confectioners' sugar

In a mixing bowl, combine dry ingredients. Beat in eggs, oil and vanilla. Fold in pineapple, bananas and nuts. Pour into a well-greased 10-in. tube pan. Bake at 350° for 60-65 minutes or until cake tests done. Cool in pan 15 minutes before removing to a wire rack. When completely cooled, dust with confectioners' sugar. **Yield:** 12-16 servings.

Angel Food Cake

Sharon Voth, Alexander, Manitoba

✓ This tasty dish uses less sugar, salt and fat. Recipe includes *Diabetic Exchanges*.

1 cup cake flour
1-1/2 cups sugar, *divided*
2 cups egg whites (about 15 large eggs)
1-1/4 teaspoons cream of tartar
1 teaspoon vanilla extract
1/4 teaspoon almond extract
1/4 teaspoon salt

Sift flour and 1/2 cup sugar together four times; set aside. In a mixing bowl, combine egg whites, cream of tartar, extracts and salt; beat on high until soft peaks form but mixture is still moist and glossy. Add remaining sugar, 1/4 cup at a time, beating well after each addition. Sift flour mixture, a fourth at a time, over the egg white mixture; fold in gently, using about 15 strokes for each addition. Spoon batter into an ungreased 10-in. tube pan (pan will be very full). Bake at 375° for 35-40 minutes or until top crust is golden brown and cracks feel dry. Immediately invert cake in pan to cool completely. Loosen sides of cake from pan and remove. **Yield:** 16 servings. **Diabetic Exchanges:** One serving equals 1-1/2 starch; also, 101 calories, 106 mg sodium, 0 cholesterol, 24 gm carbohydrate, 2 gm protein, trace fat.

Fudge Pudding Cake

Roxanne Bender, Waymart, Pennsylvania

(PICTURED ON PAGE 28)

3/4 cup sugar
1 tablespoon butter *or* margarine, softened
1/2 cup milk
1 cup all-purpose flour
2 tablespoons baking cocoa
1 teaspoon baking powder
1/4 teaspoon salt
1/2 cup chopped walnuts
TOPPING:
1/2 cup sugar
1/2 cup packed brown sugar
1/4 cup baking cocoa
1-1/4 cups boiling water
Ice cream, optional

In a mixing bowl, beat sugar, butter and milk. Combine flour, cocoa, baking powder and salt; stir into the sugar mixture. Add walnuts. Pour into a greased 9-in. square baking pan. For topping, combine sugars and cocoa; sprinkle over batter. Pour water over all. *Do not stir.* Bake at 350° for 30 minutes. Cool for 10 minutes. Spoon some of the fudge sauce over each serving; top with ice cream if desired. **Yield:** 9 servings.

Almond Bars

Astrid Miller, Farmington, Minnesota

1-1/2 cups all-purpose flour
3/4 cup sugar
1/2 cup butter *or* margarine, softened
1/2 teaspoon salt
FILLING:
2 packages (one 8 ounces, one 3 ounces) cream cheese, softened
3 eggs
1/2 teaspoon almond extract
FROSTING:
2-1/2 cups confectioners' sugar
1/3 cup butter *or* margarine, softened
2 tablespoons plus 1 teaspoon milk
1 teaspoon almond extract
Sliced almonds, toasted

Combine the first four ingredients; mix well. Pat into an ungreased 13-in. x 9-in. x 2-in. baking pan. Bake at 350° for 15 minutes. In a mixing bowl, combine filling ingredients; beat until smooth. Pour over crust. Bake for 15-20 minutes or until edges are lightly browned. Cool completely. For frosting, in a bowl, combine sugar, butter, milk and extract; stir until smooth. Frost bars and sprinkle with almonds. Store in the refrigerator. **Yield:** 3 dozen.

Chewy Chocolate Brownies

Carol Ann Humphries, Lindrith, New Mexico

1/2 cup shortening
2 squares (1 ounce *each*) unsweetened chocolate
3/4 cup all-purpose flour
3/4 teaspoon salt
1/2 teaspoon baking powder
2 eggs
1 cup sugar
1 teaspoon vanilla extract
2 tablespoons dark corn syrup
1 cup chopped nuts
1 cup vanilla-flavored chips
FROSTING:
1/4 cup butter *or* margarine, melted
3 tablespoons baking cocoa
3 cups confectioners' sugar
3 to 4 tablespoons milk

In a microwave or saucepan, melt shortening and chocolate; cool. Combine flour, salt and baking powder; set aside. In a mixing bowl, beat eggs; add sugar, vanilla, corn syrup and chocolate mixture. Add flour mixture; mix well. Fold in nuts and chips. Spread into a greased 11-in. x 7-in. x 2-in. baking pan. Bake at 350° for 30-35 minutes. Cool. In a small bowl, combine frosting ingredients; stir until smooth. Spread over brownies. **Yield:** 4 dozen.

Double-Decker Brownies

Heather Hooker, Belmont, Ontario

(PICTURED ON PAGE 47)

CHOCOLATE LAYER:
2 eggs, lightly beaten
1 cup sugar
3/4 cup all-purpose flour
1/2 cup chopped walnuts
Pinch salt
1/2 cup butter *or* margarine, melted
1/4 cup baking cocoa
BUTTERSCOTCH LAYER:
1-1/2 cups packed brown sugar
1/2 cup butter *or* margarine, softened
2 eggs
2 teaspoons vanilla extract
1-1/2 cups all-purpose flour
1/4 teaspoon salt
1/2 cup chopped walnuts
FROSTING:
1/2 cup packed brown sugar
1/4 cup butter *or* margarine
3 tablespoons milk
1-1/2 cups confectioners' sugar, sifted
1/3 cup semisweet chocolate chips
1/3 cup butterscotch chips
1 tablespoon shortening

In a bowl, combine eggs, sugar, flour, walnuts and salt. In another bowl, stir butter and cocoa until smooth; add to egg mixture and blend well with a wooden spoon. Pour into a greased 13-in. x 9-in. x 2-in. baking pan; set aside. For butterscotch layer, cream brown sugar and butter in a mixing bowl. Beat in eggs and vanilla. Stir in flour, salt and walnuts. Spoon over the chocolate layer. Bake at 350° for 30-35 minutes or until brownies begin to pull away from sides of pan; cool. For frosting, combine brown sugar, butter and milk in a small saucepan; bring to a boil and boil for 2 minutes. Remove from the heat; stir in confectioners' sugar until smooth. Quickly spread over brownies. In a small saucepan over low heat, melt chocolate chips, butterscotch chips and shortening, stirring frequently. Drizzle over frosting. **Yield:** 3 dozen.

Lemon Sugar Cookies

Eula Forbes, Wagoner, Oklahoma

1 cup butter *or* margarine, softened
1 cup sugar
1 cup confectioners' sugar
1 cup vegetable oil
2 eggs
1 teaspoon lemon extract
4-1/2 cups all-purpose flour
1 teaspoon baking soda
1 teaspoon cream of tartar
Additional sugar

In a large mixing bowl, cream butter, sugars and oil. Beat in eggs and extract. Combine flour, baking soda and cream of tartar; stir into creamed mixture (dough will be stiff). Roll into 1-in. balls; place 2 in. apart on ungreased baking sheets. Press with the bottom of a glass dipped in water, then in sugar. Bake at 350° for 10 minutes or until edges are lightly browned. **Yield:** about 11 dozen.

After-School Gingersnaps

Alice Thomas, Phoenix, Maryland

3/4 cup butter *or* margarine, softened
1/2 cup sugar
1/2 cup packed brown sugar
1/4 cup dark molasses
1 egg, beaten
2-1/4 cups all-purpose flour
1-1/2 teaspoons baking soda
1/4 teaspoon salt
2 to 3 teaspoons ground cinnamon
2 to 3 teaspoons ground ginger

In a mixing bowl, cream butter, sugars, molasses and egg. Combine flour, baking soda, salt, cinnamon and ginger; add to creamed mixture and mix well. Cover and refrigerate for 1 hour. Roll out the dough on a lightly floured surface to 1/8-in. thickness and cut into desired shapes. Place on ungreased baking sheets. Bake at 375° for 5-6 minutes or until set (do not overbake). Remove from pan to cool on wire racks. **Yield:** about 6 dozen (2-1/2-inch cookies).

Snowflake Bar Cookies

Barbara Neuschwanger, Olympia, Washington

1 cup butter *or* margarine, softened
3/4 cup packed brown sugar
1/4 cup sugar
1 package (3.9 ounces) instant chocolate pudding mix
2 eggs
1-1/2 teaspoons vanilla extract
1-3/4 cups quick-cooking oats
1-1/2 cups all-purpose flour
1 teaspoon baking soda
1 cup vanilla-flavored baking chips
1/2 cup semisweet chocolate chips

In a mixing bowl, cream the butter and sugars. Add pudding mix, eggs and vanilla; mix well. Combine oats, flour and baking soda; gradually add to creamed mixture. Mix until smooth. Stir in chips. Spread into a greased 15-in. x 10-in. x 1-in. baking pan. Bake at 350° for 15-20 minutes or until bars test done. Cool. **Yield:** 3-4 dozen.

Peppermint Snowballs

Judy Scholovich, Waukesha, Wisconsin

1 cup butter *or* margarine, softened
1/2 cup confectioners' sugar
1 teaspoon vanilla extract
2-1/2 cups all-purpose flour
FILLING:
2 tablespoons cream cheese, softened
1 tablespoon milk
1/2 cup confectioners' sugar
2 tablespoons finely crushed peppermint candy *or* candy canes
1 drop red food coloring
TOPPING:
1/4 cup confectioners' sugar
6 tablespoons finely crushed peppermint candy *or* candy canes

In a mixing bowl, cream butter and sugar; add vanilla. Stir in flour; knead until well mixed. Reserve 1/2 cup of dough; shape remaining dough into 1-in. balls. For filling, combine cream cheese and milk in a small bowl. Stir in sugar, candy and food coloring; mix well. Make a deep well in the center of each ball; fill with 1/4 teaspoon filling. Use reserved dough to cover filling. Reshape if necessary into smooth balls. Place on ungreased baking sheets. Bake at 350° for 12-14 minutes. Combine topping ingredients; roll cookies in mixture while still warm. Cool on wire racks. **Yield:** about 4 dozen.

Pumpkin Pound Cake

Leah Grooms, Rockingham, North Carolina

1 cup butter *or* margarine, softened
3 cups sugar
5 eggs, room temperature
3 cups all-purpose flour
2 teaspoons baking powder
2 teaspoons ground cinnamon
1/2 teaspoon baking soda
1/2 teaspoon salt
1/4 teaspoon ground cloves
1/8 teaspoon apple pie spice
1 cup solid-pack pumpkin
2 tablespoons rum flavoring
Confectioners' sugar

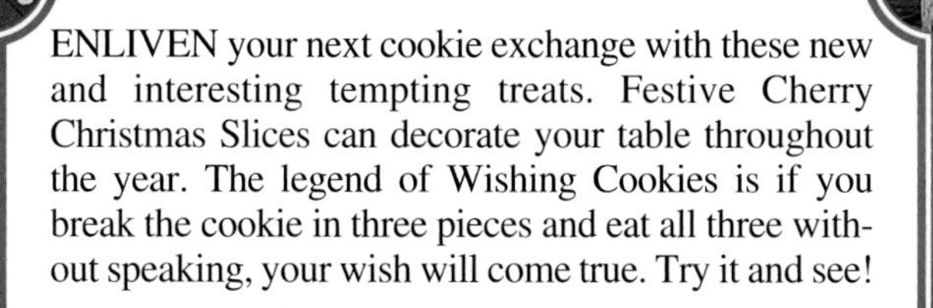

ENLIVEN your next cookie exchange with these new and interesting tempting treats. Festive Cherry Christmas Slices can decorate your table throughout the year. The legend of Wishing Cookies is if you break the cookie in three pieces and eat all three without speaking, your wish will come true. Try it and see!

MAGICAL MORSELS. Top to bottom: **Wishing Cookies** and **Christmas Cherry Slices** (both recipes below).

In a mixing bowl, beat butter on medium speed for 2 minutes or until soft and creamy. Gradually add sugar, beating for 5-7 minutes. Add eggs, one at a time, beating well after each addition. Combine flour, baking powder, cinnamon, soda, salt, cloves and pie spice. In a small bowl, combine pumpkin and rum flavoring. Add dry ingredients to egg mixture alternately with pumpkin mixture, beginning and ending with dry ingredients. Pour into a greased and floured 12-cup fluted tube pan. Bake at 325° for 80-90 minutes or until cake tests done. Cool in pan 10 minutes before removing to a wire rack to cool completely. Dust with confectioners' sugar. **Yield:** 12-16 servings.

Wishing Cookies

Katie Koziolek, Hartland, Minnesota
(PICTURED ABOVE)

- **1 cup butter *or* margarine, softened**
- **1-1/2 cups sugar**
- **1 egg**
- **2 tablespoons molasses**
- **1 tablespoon water**
- **1/2 to 1 teaspoon grated orange peel**
- **3-1/4 cups all-purpose flour**
- **1 teaspoon baking soda**
- **1 teaspoon ground cinnamon**
- **1/2 teaspoon ground ginger**
- **1/4 teaspoon ground nutmeg**

ICING:

- **1 cup confectioners' sugar**
- **1/2 teaspoon vanilla extract**
- **1 to 2 tablespoons milk**

In a mixing bowl, cream butter and sugar until fluffy. Add egg, molasses, water and orange peel; mix well. Combine flour, baking soda, cinnamon, ginger and nutmeg; gradually add to creamed mixture, beating well after each addition. Cover and chill at least 2 hours. On a lightly floured surface, roll dough to 1/8-in. thickness. Cut into stars or desired shapes and place on ungreased baking sheets. Bake at 375° for 6-8 minutes or until edges are lightly browned. Cool on wire racks. For icing, combine sugar, vanilla and enough milk to achieve a drizzling consistency. Ice cookies as desired. **Yield:** about 6 dozen.

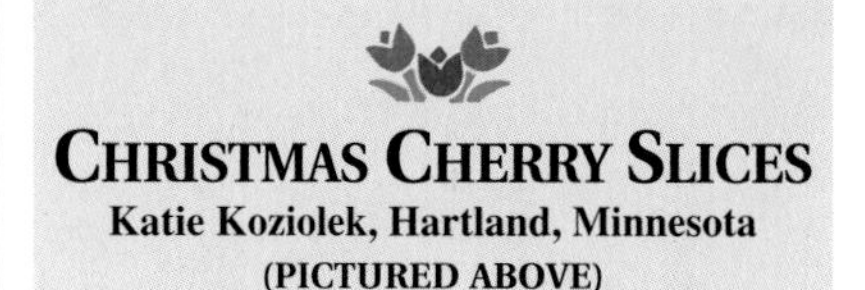

Christmas Cherry Slices

Katie Koziolek, Hartland, Minnesota
(PICTURED ABOVE)

- **1 cup butter *or* margarine, softened**
- **1 cup confectioners' sugar**
- **1 egg**
- **1 teaspoon vanilla extract**
- **2-1/4 cups all-purpose flour**
- **2 cups red and green candied cherries, halved**
- **1 cup pecan halves**

In a mixing bowl, cream the butter and sugar. Add egg and vanilla; beat until fluffy. Add flour; mix well. Stir in cherries and pecans. Chill for 1 hour. Shape dough into three 10-in. rolls; wrap in plastic wrap and place in a freezer bag. Freeze up to 2 months or until ready to bake. To bake, cut frozen rolls into 1/8-in. slices. Place on ungreased baking sheets. Bake at 325° for 10-12 minutes or until edges are golden brown. Cool on wire racks. **Yield:** about 11 dozen.

SPICING UP standard sugar cookies is easy with hint of cinnamon (recipe below).

Cinnamon Sugar Cookies

Leah Costigan, Otto, North Carolina
(PICTURED ABOVE)

1 cup butter *or* margarine, softened
1 cup sugar
1 cup confectioners' sugar
1 cup vegetable oil
2 eggs
1 teaspoon vanilla extract
4-1/3 cups all-purpose flour
1 teaspoon salt
1 teaspoon baking soda
1 teaspoon ground cinnamon
1 teaspoon cream of tartar
1 cup finely chopped pecans, optional
Colored sugar, optional

In a large mixing bowl, cream the butter, sugars and oil. Add eggs and vanilla; mix well. Add flour, salt, baking soda, cinnamon and cream of tartar. Stir in the pecans if desired. Roll into 1-in. balls. Place on greased baking sheets; flatten with the bottom of a glass dipped in sugar. Sprinkle with colored sugar if desired. Bake at 375° for 10-12 minutes. **Yield:** about 8 dozen.

Valentine Butter Cookies

Eleanor Slimak, Chicago, Illinois
(PICTURED ON PAGE 28)

2 cups butter (no substitutes), softened
2 cups sugar
3 eggs
1 tablespoon vanilla extract
6 cups all-purpose flour
2 teaspoons baking powder
Red decorators' sugar, optional

In a mixing bowl, cream butter and sugar. Add eggs and vanilla; mix well. Combine flour and baking powder; gradually add to creamed mixture and mix well. Shape with a cookie press. Place on ungreased cookie sheets. Decorate with sugar if desired. Bake at 350° for 10-12 minutes or until edges are light brown. **Yield:** 18-19 dozen (1-inch cookies).

Pistachio Coconut Cake

Arlene Bontrager, Haven, Kansas

1 package (14-1/2 ounces) white cake mix without pudding
3/4 cup vegetable oil
3 eggs
1 cup lemon-lime *or* club soda
1 package (3.4 ounces) instant pistachio pudding mix
1 cup chopped pecans
1/2 cup flaked coconut
ICING:
2 envelopes whipped topping mix
1-1/2 cups milk
1 package (3.4 ounces) instant pistachio pudding mix
3/4 cup chopped pecans
1/2 cup coconut

In a mixing bowl, combine the first five ingredients and mix well. Stir in pecans and coconut. Pour into a greased and floured 13-in. x 9-in. x 2-in. baking pan. Bake at 350° for 45 minutes or until cake tests done. Cool. Combine the first three icing ingredients in a mixing bowl; beat until thickened, about 4 minutes. Spread over cake. Sprinkle with pecans and coconut. **Yield:** 12-15 servings.

Sauerkraut Apple Cake

Eleanor Lais, Lafayette, New Jersey
(PICTURED ON PAGE 36)

4 eggs
1 cup sugar
1/2 cup packed brown sugar
1 can (14 ounces) sauerkraut, rinsed and drained
1 large tart apple
1 cup vegetable oil
1 cup chopped walnuts
2 cups all-purpose flour
2 teaspoons baking powder
2 teaspoons ground cinnamon
1 teaspoon baking soda
1 teaspoon salt
1/2 teaspoon ground nutmeg
CREAM CHEESE FROSTING:
1 package (8 ounces) cream cheese, softened
2 to 3 tablespoons whipping cream, *divided*
4-1/2 cups confectioners' sugar
1 tablespoon grated orange peel
1/2 teaspoon ground cinnamon
1 teaspoon vanilla extract
Chopped walnuts, optional

In a large bowl, beat eggs and sugars; set aside. Squeeze sauerkraut until dry; finely chop and add to egg mixture. Peel and finely grate apple; squeeze dry. Stir into egg mixture. Add oil and walnuts. Combine flour, baking powder, cinnamon, baking soda, salt and nutmeg; stir into egg mixture. Line the bottom of two 8-in. round cake pans with waxed paper; grease and flour paper and sides of pan. Pour batter into pans. Bake at 350° for 35-40 minutes or until a toothpick inserted near the center comes out clean. Cool in pans for 10 minutes before inverting onto a wire rack to cool completely. For frosting, beat cream cheese and 2 tablespoons cream in a small mixing bowl. Add sugar; beat until fluffy. Add orange peel, cinnamon and vanilla; mix well. Add remaining cream if needed. Spread between layers and over entire cake. Garnish with chopped walnuts if desired. Store in the refrigerator. **Yield:** 10-12 servings.

EXTRA-SPECIAL BROWNIES. Melt raspberry-flavored semisweet chocolate chips and add to your favorite recipe in place of standard semisweet chips.

Banana Nut Brownies

Christine Mol, Grand Rapids, Michigan
(PICTURED ON PAGE 44)

1/2 cup butter *or* margarine, melted and cooled
1 cup sugar
3 tablespoons baking cocoa
2 eggs, lightly beaten
1 tablespoon milk
1 teaspoon vanilla extract
1/2 cup all-purpose flour
1 teaspoon baking powder
1/4 teaspoon salt
1 cup mashed ripe bananas (2-1/2 to 3 medium)
1/2 cup chopped walnuts
Confectioners' sugar, optional

In a bowl, combine butter, sugar and cocoa. Stir in eggs, milk and vanilla. Blend in flour, baking powder and salt. Stir in bananas and nuts. Pour into a greased 9-in. square baking pan. Bake at 350°

for 40-45 minutes or until brownies test done. Cool on a wire rack. Just before serving, dust with confectioners' sugar if desired. **Yield:** 16 servings.

Eggnog Cake

Edith Disch, Fairview Park, Ohio

(PICTURED ON PAGE 76)

1/2 cup butter, softened
1 cup sugar, *divided*
2 eggs, *separated*
3/4 cup orange juice
1-1/2 teaspoons grated orange peel
1 teaspoon vanilla extract
2 cups sifted cake flour
2 teaspoons baking powder
1/2 teaspoon ground nutmeg
1/4 teaspoon baking soda
1/4 teaspoon salt

EGGNOG FILLING:

5 tablespoons all-purpose flour
1-1/4 cups store-bought eggnog
1 cup butter, softened
3/4 cup sugar
1 teaspoon vanilla extract
1/4 teaspoon ground nutmeg

CHOCOLATE FROSTING:

2 ounces unsweetened chocolate, melted
2/3 cup confectioners' sugar
1/4 teaspoon ground cinnamon
1/8 teaspoon ground nutmeg
3 tablespoons butter, softened
2 tablespoons whipping cream
2 to 3 tablespoons hot water

Cream butter and 3/4 cup sugar. Add yolks, one at a time, beating well after each. Combine orange juice, peel and vanilla. Combine dry ingredients; add to creamed mixture alternately with juice mixture, beating well. In another bowl, beat whites until foamy; gradually add remaining sugar, beating until soft peaks form. Fold into batter. Line two greased 9-in. round cake pans with waxed paper; grease paper. Pour batter into pans. Bake at 350° for 20 minutes or until cake tests done. Cool 5 minutes; remove to wire rack. Peel off paper; cool. For filling, combine flour and a small amount of eggnog in a pan; stir until smooth. Stir in remaining eggnog; bring to a boil, stirring constantly. Cook and stir 2 minutes. Cool completely. Cream butter and sugar; add vanilla and nutmeg. Gradually beat in eggnog mixture. For frosting, mix chocolate, sugar, cinnamon and nutmeg. Beat in butter and cream. Add water until frosting drizzles slightly. Split cakes in half; spread filling on three layers. Stack with plain layer on top; frost the top. **Yield:** 14 servings.

ADDING A RIPE BANANA to a chocolate cake not only keeps the cake moist but also gives it good flavor.

Apricot Fruitcake

Clare Brooks, Juneau, Alaska

(PICTURED ON PAGE 77)

2 cups golden raisins
2 cups *each* coarsely chopped dried apricots and dates
1 cup *each* red and green candied cherries, halved
2 cups *each* coarsely chopped pecans, walnuts and Brazil nuts
1/2 cup honey
1/4 cup water
1 teaspoon lemon juice
1 cup butter *or* margarine, softened
1-1/4 cups packed brown sugar
4 eggs
2 cups all-purpose flour
1 teaspoon ground cinnamon
1/2 teaspoon *each* ground cloves, mace and nutmeg
1/2 teaspoon salt
1/4 teaspoon baking soda

In a large bowl, combine the fruits, nuts, honey, water and lemon juice; set aside. In a mixing bowl, cream butter and sugar. Add eggs and mix well. Fold into fruit mixture. Combine dry ingredients; gradually fold into the fruit mixture until evenly coated. Pour into two greased and waxed paper-lined 9-in. x 5-in. x 3-in. loaf pans. With a shallow pan of water in the bottom of the oven, bake at 275° for 2-1/2 hours or until cake tests done. Cover with foil during the last 30 minutes. Cool 10 minutes; remove to wire rack to cool completely. Remove waxed paper and wrap each cake in foil. Place in plastic bags and store in a cool dry place. **Yield:** 2 loaves.

Banana Coconut Cake

Deanna Carruthers, Mossley, Ontario

(PICTURED ON PAGE 83)

3/4 cup shortening
1-1/2 cups sugar
2 eggs
1 cup mashed ripe bananas
1 teaspoon vanilla extract
2 cups cake flour
1 teaspoon baking soda
1 teaspoon baking powder
1/2 teaspoon salt
1/2 cup buttermilk
1/2 cup chopped pecans, optional
1 cup flaked coconut

BUTTER CREAM FROSTING:

1/2 cup shortening
1/2 cup butter *or* margarine, softened
2 cups confectioners' sugar
1/2 teaspoon vanilla extract
1/2 teaspoon coconut extract
Pinch salt
1/4 cup cold evaporated milk

In a mixing bowl, cream shortening and sugar until fluffy. Add eggs; beat for 2 minutes. Add bananas and vanilla; beat for 2 minutes. Combine dry ingredients; add to creamed mixture alternately with buttermilk. Mix well. Stir in pecans if desired. Pour into two greased and floured 9-in. cake pans. Sprinkle each with coconut. Bake at 375° for 25-30 minutes or until cake tests done; loosely cover with foil during the last 10 minutes of baking. Cool in pans 15 minutes before removing to a wire rack, coconut side up. In a mixing bowl, cream shortening and butter. Add remaining frosting ingredients. Mix on low until combined; beat on high for 5 minutes. Place one cake layer, coconut side down, on a cake plate; spread with some of the frosting. Top with second layer, coconut side up; frost sides and 1 in. around top edge of cake, leaving coconut center showing. **Yield:** 12 servings.

Chewy Oatmeal Cookies

Janis Plageman, Lynden, Washington

1 cup butter *or* margarine, softened
1 cup sugar
1 cup packed brown sugar
2 eggs
1 tablespoon molasses
2 teaspoons vanilla extract
2 cups all-purpose flour
2 cups quick-cooking oats
1-1/2 teaspoons baking soda
1 teaspoon ground cinnamon
1/2 teaspoon salt
1 cup *each* raisins and chopped pecans
1 cup (6 ounces) semisweet chocolate chips

In a mixing bowl, cream butter and sugars. Add eggs, molasses and vanilla. Combine flour, oats, baking soda, cinnamon and salt; add to creamed mixture. Stir in raisins, pecans and chocolate chips. Drop by tablespoonfuls 2 in. apart onto greased baking sheets. Bake at 350° for 9-10 minutes or until lightly browned. Cool 2 minutes before removing to a wire rack. **Yield:** about 5 dozen.

RECIPE FOR: MAPLE BUTTER TWISTS
1 PACKAGE (1/4 OZ.) ACTIVE DRY
1/4 CUP WARM WATER (110° TO
1/2 CUP WARM MILK (110° TO
1/4 CUP BUTTER OR MARGARINE,
2 EGGS
3 T SUGAR
1 1/2 t SALT
3 1/4-3 1/2 CUPS ALL-PURPOSE
1st
PLACE
RECIPE FOR: Strawberry Lemonade
4 quarts
1st
1st

IF ONLY YOU COULD, wouldn't it be great to take your family "fair hopping"—stopping at fairs cross-country to sample the best local fare? Well, now you can with this roundup of winning recipes…all without leaving the comforts of home. You can nibble on cookies, sample a slice of cake, sip a cool refreshment, dip into a zesty relish and so much more!

COUNTRY FAIR FAVORITES. Clockwise from lower left: **Frosted Cashew Cookies** (p. 66), **Strawberry Lemonade** (p. 82), **Maple Butter Twists** (p. 32), **Zucchini Relish** (p. 82), **Orange Chiffon Cake** (p. 66), **Five-Star Brownies** (p. 66), **Raspberry Peach Jam** (p. 82) and **Scottish Shortbread** (p. 66).

Frosted Cashew Cookies

Sheila Wyum, Rutland, North Dakota

(PICTURED ON PAGE 64)

1/2 cup butter *or* margarine
1 cup packed brown sugar
1 egg
1/3 cup sour cream
1/2 teaspoon vanilla extract
2 cups all-purpose flour
3/4 teaspoon *each* baking powder, baking soda and salt
1-3/4 cups salted cashew halves

BROWNED BUTTER FROSTING:

1/2 cup butter (no substitutes)
3 tablespoons light cream
1/4 teaspoon vanilla extract
2 cups confectioners' sugar
Additional cashew halves, optional

In a mixing bowl, cream the butter and brown sugar. Beat in egg, sour cream and vanilla; mix well. Combine dry ingredients; add to creamed mixture and mix well. Fold in the cashews. Drop by rounded teaspoonfuls onto greased baking sheets. Bake at 375° for 8-10 minutes or until lightly browned. Cool on a wire rack. For the frosting, lightly brown butter in a small saucepan. Remove from the heat; add cream and vanilla. Beat in confectioners' sugar until smooth and thick. Frost cookies. Top each with a cashew half if desired. **Yield:** about 3 dozen.

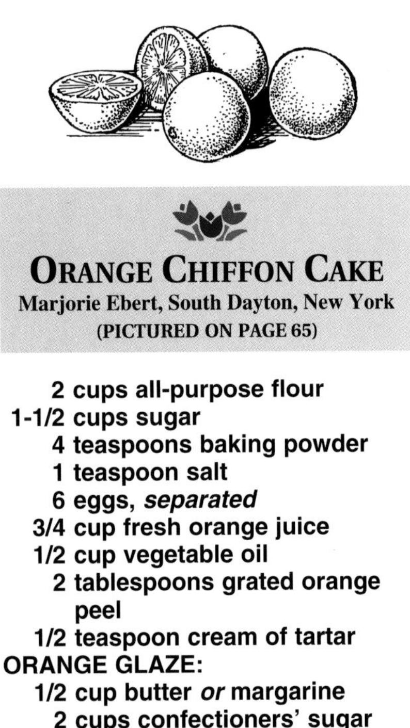

Orange Chiffon Cake

Marjorie Ebert, South Dayton, New York

(PICTURED ON PAGE 65)

2 cups all-purpose flour
1-1/2 cups sugar
4 teaspoons baking powder
1 teaspoon salt
6 eggs, *separated*
3/4 cup fresh orange juice
1/2 cup vegetable oil
2 tablespoons grated orange peel
1/2 teaspoon cream of tartar

ORANGE GLAZE:

1/2 cup butter *or* margarine
2 cups confectioners' sugar
2 to 4 tablespoons fresh orange juice
1/2 teaspoon grated orange peel

In a large mixing bowl, combine the first four ingredients. Add egg yolks, orange juice, oil and peel; beat until smooth, about 5 minutes. In another mixing bowl, beat egg whites and cream of tartar until stiff but not dry. Fold into orange mixture. Spoon into an ungreased 10-in. tube pan. Bake at 350° for 45-50 minutes or until cake tests done with a wooden pick. Immediately invert pan to cool. When cool, remove cake from the pan. For glaze, melt butter in a small saucepan; add remaining ingredients. Stir until smooth. Pour over top of cake, allowing it to drizzle down sides. **Yield:** 16 servings.

Five Star Brownies

Pam Buerki Rogers, Victoria, Kansas

(PICTURED ON PAGE 65)

3 eggs
2 cups sugar
1-1/2 teaspoons vanilla extract
1/2 cup butter *or* margarine, melted
1/4 cup shortening, melted
1-1/2 cups all-purpose flour
3/4 cup baking cocoa
1-1/4 teaspoons salt
1 cup chopped nuts, optional

In a mixing bowl, beat eggs, sugar and vanilla until well mixed. Add butter and shortening. Combine flour, cocoa and salt; stir into egg mixture and mix well. Add nuts if desired. Line a 13-in. x 9-in. x 2-in. baking pan with foil and grease the foil; pour batter into pan. Bake at 350° for 30 minutes or until brownies test done with a wooden pick. Cool in pan. Turn brownies out of pan onto a cookie sheet; remove foil. Place a wire rack over brownies; turn over and remove cookie sheet. Cut with a star cutter or into bars. **Yield:** about 3 dozen.

Quick & Easy

Scottish Shortbread

Rose Mabee, Selkirk, Manitoba

(PICTURED ON PAGE 65)

1 pound butter (no substitutes), softened
1 cup packed brown sugar
4 to 4-1/2 cups all-purpose flour

In a mixing bowl, cream the butter and brown sugar. Add 3-3/4 cups flour; mix well. Sprinkle a board with some of the remaining flour. Knead for 5 minutes, adding enough remaining flour to make a soft, non-sticky dough. Roll to 1/2-in. thickness. Cut into 3-in. x 1-in. strips. Place 1 in. apart on ungreased baking sheets. Prick with a fork. Bake at 325° for 20-25 minutes or until cookies are lightly browned. **Yield:** about 4 dozen.

Chocolate Angel Food Cake

Margaret Zickert, Deerfield, Wisconsin

1 cup cake flour
1/2 cup baking cocoa
2 cups egg whites (12 to 16 large eggs)
2 teaspoons cream of tartar
2 cups sugar
1 teaspoon vanilla extract

Sift flour and cocoa together three times; set aside. In a large mixing bowl, beat the egg whites until foamy. Sprinkle with cream of tartar and beat until soft peaks form. Gradually add sugar, about 2 tablespoons at a time, beating until stiff peaks form. Blend in vanilla. Sift about a fourth of the flour mixture over egg white mixture; fold in gently. Repeat, folding in remaining flour mixture by fourths. Pour into an ungreased 10-in. tube pan. Bake at 325° for 1 hour. Turn off the oven, but let cake sit in the oven for 5 minutes. Remove from the oven and immediately invert pan; cool. Loosen sides of cake from pan and remove. **Yield:** 12 servings.

Grandparents' Birthday Cake

Alberta McKay, Bartlesville, Oklahoma

2 cups all-purpose flour
1-1/3 cups sugar
3/4 teaspoon baking soda
3/4 teaspoon salt
1/2 teaspoon ground cinnamon
1 cup vegetable oil
2 eggs, lightly beaten
1-1/2 teaspoons vanilla extract
2 cups chopped peeled baking apples
2/3 cup chopped walnuts

FROSTING:

5 tablespoons all-purpose flour
1 cup milk
1 cup butter *or* margarine, softened
2 cups confectioners' sugar
1 teaspoon vanilla extract
1/4 teaspoon salt
1 to 1-1/4 cups chopped walnuts
Red food coloring, optional

In a mixing bowl, combine flour, sugar, baking soda, salt and cinnamon. Combine oil, eggs and vanilla; add to dry ingredients and beat well. Fold in apples and walnuts (batter will be thick). Spread into two greased 8-in. round cake pans. Bake at 350° for 35-40 minutes or until cake tests done; cool. For frosting, combine flour and milk in a saucepan. Bring to a boil; cook and stir for 1 minute. Set aside, uncovered, at room temperature for 20 minutes. In a mixing bowl, cream butter, sugar and vanilla. Add salt and cooked flour mixture; beat until smooth. If you wish to "write" on the cake with frosting, reserve 1/4 cup and tint with red food coloring; set aside. Use remaining frosting to frost between layers and on top and sides of cake. If desired, use the red frosting and a round decorator's tip to add "Happy Birthday" on top. Carefully press walnuts around sides. Store in the refrigerator. **Yield:** 12-16 servings.

Apricot Walnut Balls

Phyl Budreau, Westfield, Massachusetts

2 cups finely chopped dried apricots
2-1/2 cups flaked coconut
1 can (14 ounces) sweetened condensed milk
1-1/4 cups chopped walnuts
Confectioners' sugar

In a bowl, combine apricots and coconut. Add milk; mix well. Stir in walnuts. Chill for 30 minutes (the mixture will be sticky). Shape into 1-in. balls and roll in confectioners' sugar. Cover and refrigerate at least 2 hours before serving. Store in refrigerator. **Yield:** 5-6 dozen.

Holiday Fig Torte

Judy Trott, Goldsboro, North Carolina

(PICTURED ON PAGE 77)

30 to 35 fig newton cookies (about 1 pound)
1 package (8 ounces) cream cheese, softened
1 cup confectioners' sugar
2 large bananas, sliced
2 tablespoons lemon juice
1 package (5.1 ounces) instant vanilla pudding mix
3 cups cold milk
1 carton (12 ounces) frozen whipped topping, thawed, *divided*
1/2 cup chopped pecans
Red and green maraschino cherries, well drained

Cover the bottom of a 13-in. x 9-in. x 2-in. baking pan with cookies. In a mixing bowl, beat the cream cheese and sugar until fluffy; spread over cookies. Toss bananas with lemon juice; arrange over the cream cheese layer. In another bowl, beat pudding mix and milk according to package directions. Fold in half of the whipped topping; spread over bananas. Spread remaining topping over pudding layer. Sprinkle with pecans. Decorate with cherries. Cover and chill overnight. **Yield:** 12-16 servings.

Pecan Stars

Denise Goedeken, Platte Center, Nebraska

1/4 cup butter *or* margarine, softened
1/4 cup sugar
1 egg, beaten
1 teaspoon *each* vanilla and almond extract
1-1/3 cups all-purpose flour
1-1/2 teaspoons baking powder
1/8 teaspoon salt

FILLING:

1-1/4 cups ground pecans
1/3 cup sugar
1 tablespoon butter *or* margarine, melted
2 tablespoons water
1 teaspoon salt

In a mixing bowl, cream butter and sugar. Add egg and extracts; mix well. Combine dry ingredients; gradually add to creamed mixture. Cover and chill for 1 hour. Roll out onto a lightly floured surface to 1/8-in. thickness. Cut into 3-in. stars. Combine filling ingredients; place 1/2 teaspoonful in center of each star. Bring the five points upright; starting at base, pinch sides together so points of star stand up, allowing filling to show. Place on ungreased baking sheets. Bake at 375° for 6-8 minutes or until golden brown. Cool for 2 minutes before removing to wire racks. **Yield:** about 3-1/2 dozen.

Holiday Shortbread

Wendy Masters, Grand Valley, Ontario

2 cups butter (no substitutes), softened
1 cup sugar
1 teaspoon vanilla extract
4 cups all-purpose flour
Colored sugar

In a mixing bowl, cream butter; gradually add sugar and beat well. Add vanilla and mix well. Gradually add flour; mix until dough forms a ball. Roll out on a lightly floured surface to 1/2-in. thickness. Cut into 1-1/2-in. squares, diamonds and triangles. Place on ungreased baking sheets; sprinkle with colored sugar. Bake at 325° for 14-18 minutes or until edges are lightly browned. Cool on wire racks. **Yield:** about 6-1/2 dozen.

Chocolate Snappers

Sally Parker, Idalia, Colorado

3/4 cup shortening
1 cup sugar
1 egg
1-3/4 cups all-purpose flour
1/3 cup baking cocoa
1/4 cup light corn syrup
2 tablespoons vegetable oil
2 teaspoons baking soda
1 teaspoon ground cinnamon
1/4 teaspoon salt
Additional sugar

In a mixing bowl, cream shortening and sugar. Add egg; beat well. Add flour, cocoa, corn syrup, oil, baking soda, cinnamon and salt; mix well. Shape by rounded teaspoonfuls into balls; roll in sugar. Place on greased cookie sheets. Bake at 350° for 12-15 minutes. Cool on wire racks. **Yield:** 5 dozen.

Cinnamon Apple Cake

Mrs. William Hiltz, Clearwater, Florida

(PICTURED ON FRONT COVER)

2 cups all-purpose flour
2 teaspoons ground cinnamon
1-1/2 teaspoons baking soda
1 teaspoon salt
3/4 cup vegetable oil
2 eggs
1 teaspoon vanilla extract
3 cups finely chopped peeled baking apples
2 cups sugar

TOPPING:

2 tablespoons butter *or* margarine, softened
1/3 cup packed brown sugar
1/3 cup sugar
1/2 teaspoon ground cinnamon
1/2 cup flaked coconut
1/3 cup chopped walnuts

In a mixing bowl, combine flour, cinnamon, baking soda and salt. Add oil, eggs and vanilla; mix well (batter will be thick). Toss apples with sugar; fold into batter. Spread into a greased and floured 13-in. x 9-in. x 2-in. baking pan. For topping, beat the butter, sugars and cinnamon in a small mixing bowl. Stir in coconut and walnuts; mix well. Sprinkle over the batter. Bake at 350° for 40-45 minutes or until the cake tests done. **Yield:** 16-20 servings.

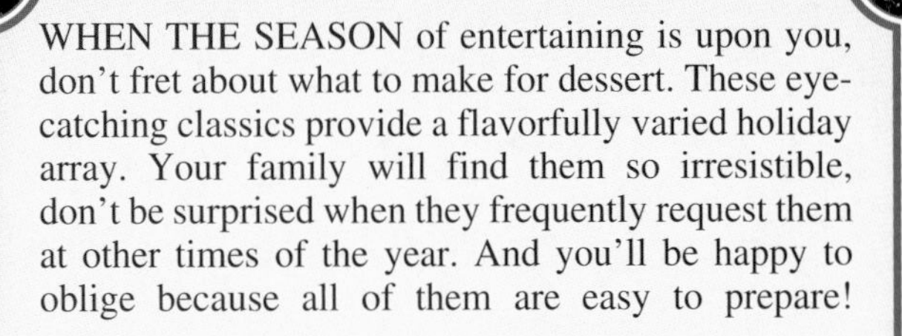

WHEN THE SEASON of entertaining is upon you, don't fret about what to make for dessert. These eye-catching classics provide a flavorfully varied holiday array. Your family will find them so irresistible, don't be surprised when they frequently request them at other times of the year. And you'll be happy to oblige because all of them are easy to prepare!

DAZZLING DESSERTS. Clockwise from the top: **Raspberry Trifle**, **Pecan Cake Roll**, **Crimson Devonshire Cream** and **Apple Cranberry Tart** (all recipes on p. 69).

Pies & Desserts

Unforgettable endings to down-home dinners are in sight with tantalizing fruit and cream pies, ice cream, puddings, candies and more!

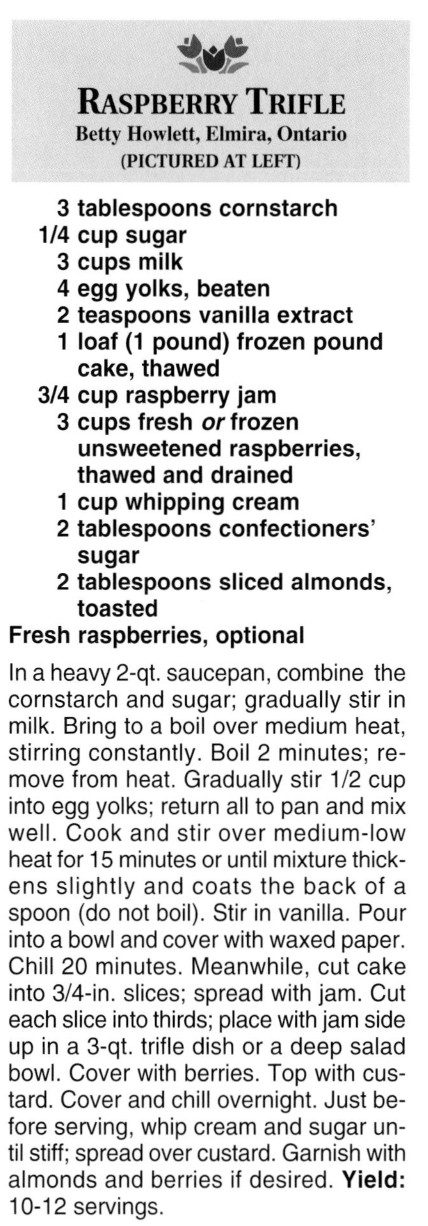

Raspberry Trifle

Betty Howlett, Elmira, Ontario
(PICTURED AT LEFT)

3 tablespoons cornstarch
1/4 cup sugar
3 cups milk
4 egg yolks, beaten
2 teaspoons vanilla extract
1 loaf (1 pound) frozen pound cake, thawed
3/4 cup raspberry jam
3 cups fresh *or* frozen unsweetened raspberries, thawed and drained
1 cup whipping cream
2 tablespoons confectioners' sugar
2 tablespoons sliced almonds, toasted
Fresh raspberries, optional

In a heavy 2-qt. saucepan, combine the cornstarch and sugar; gradually stir in milk. Bring to a boil over medium heat, stirring constantly. Boil 2 minutes; remove from heat. Gradually stir 1/2 cup into egg yolks; return all to pan and mix well. Cook and stir over medium-low heat for 15 minutes or until mixture thickens slightly and coats the back of a spoon (do not boil). Stir in vanilla. Pour into a bowl and cover with waxed paper. Chill 20 minutes. Meanwhile, cut cake into 3/4-in. slices; spread with jam. Cut each slice into thirds; place with jam side up in a 3-qt. trifle dish or a deep salad bowl. Cover with berries. Top with custard. Cover and chill overnight. Just before serving, whip cream and sugar until stiff; spread over custard. Garnish with almonds and berries if desired. **Yield:** 10-12 servings.

Pecan Cake Roll

Shirley Awald, Walkerton, Indiana
(PICTURED AT LEFT)

4 eggs, *separated*
1 cup confectioners' sugar
2 cups ground pecans
1 cup whipping cream
3 tablespoons sugar
2 teaspoons baking cocoa
1/2 teaspoon vanilla extract
Chocolate shavings and additional confectioners' sugar, optional

In a mixing bowl, beat egg yolks and confectioners' sugar until thick, about 5 minutes. In another bowl, beat whites until soft peaks form; fold into yolk mixture. Fold in pecans until well blended (batter will be thin). Grease a 15-in. x 10-in. x 1-in. baking pan; line with waxed paper and grease and flour paper. Spread batter into pan. Bake at 375° for 10-15 minutes or until cake springs back when lightly touched. Turn onto a linen towel dusted with confectioners' sugar. Peel off paper and roll cake up in towel, starting with short end. Cool on wire rack 1 hour. Meanwhile, beat the cream, sugar, cocoa and vanilla in a mixing bowl until soft peaks form. Carefully unroll cake. Spread filling over cake; roll up again. Refrigerate. If desired, garnish with chocolate shavings and confectioners' sugar. **Yield:** 10-12 servings. **Editor's Note:** This cake does not contain flour.

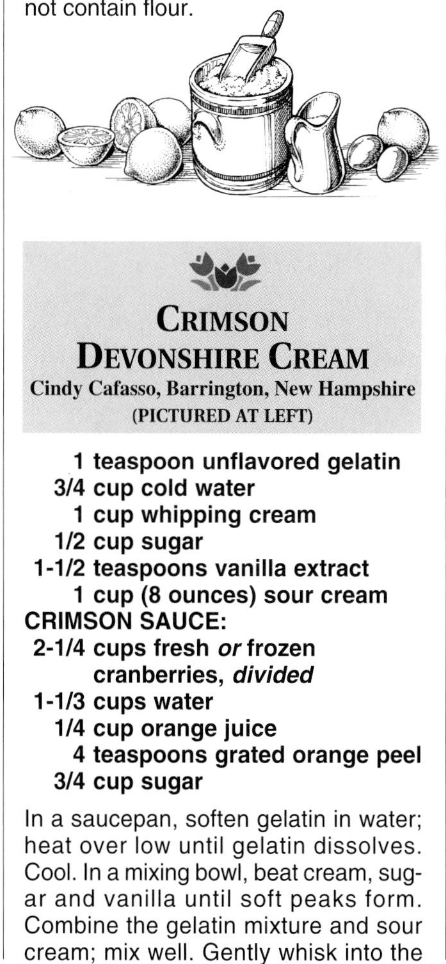

Crimson Devonshire Cream

Cindy Cafasso, Barrington, New Hampshire
(PICTURED AT LEFT)

1 teaspoon unflavored gelatin
3/4 cup cold water
1 cup whipping cream
1/2 cup sugar
1-1/2 teaspoons vanilla extract
1 cup (8 ounces) sour cream
CRIMSON SAUCE:
2-1/4 cups fresh *or* frozen cranberries, *divided*
1-1/3 cups water
1/4 cup orange juice
4 teaspoons grated orange peel
3/4 cup sugar

In a saucepan, soften gelatin in water; heat over low until gelatin dissolves. Cool. In a mixing bowl, beat cream, sugar and vanilla until soft peaks form. Combine the gelatin mixture and sour cream; mix well. Gently whisk into the cream mixture. Pour into small bowls or parfait glasses. Chill until set, about 1 hour. For sauce, combine 1-1/2 cups cranberries, water, orange juice and peel in a saucepan; bring to a boil. Reduce heat; simmer, uncovered, for 15 minutes. Sieve sauce, discarding skins. Return sauce to pan; add sugar and remaining cranberries. Cook over medium heat until berries pop, about 8 minutes. Chill. Spoon over each serving of cream. **Yield:** 8 servings.

Apple Cranberry Tart

Jo Ann Fisher, Huntington Beach, California
(PICTURED AT LEFT)

1-1/4 cups unsweetened apple juice *or* cider, *divided*
1-1/3 cups sugar
3 medium tart apples, peeled and cubed
1 package (12 ounces) fresh *or* frozen cranberries
1/2 cup all-purpose flour
Pastry for single-crust pie (10 inches)
TOPPING:
1/3 cup chopped pecans
1/3 cup all-purpose flour
3 tablespoons butter *or* margarine, melted
1/4 cup packed brown sugar
12 pecan halves

In a saucepan over medium heat, bring 3/4 cup apple juice and sugar to a boil, stirring occasionally. Add apples and cranberries; return to a boil. Reduce heat; simmer, uncovered, until apples are tender and berries pop, 5-8 minutes. Whisk flour and remaining juice until smooth; stir into cranberry mixture. Bring to a boil; cook and stir for 2 minutes. Cool to room temperature. Fit pastry into an 11-in. fluted tart pan with removable bottom, or press into the bottom and 1 in. up the sides of a 10-in. springform pan. Line pastry with double thickness of heavy-duty foil. Bake at 450° for 5 minutes. Remove foil; bake 7-10 minutes or until pastry is nearly done. Cool. Add apple mixture. Combine first four topping ingredients; sprinkle over filling. Arrange pecan halves on top. Bake at 375° for 30-35 minutes or until golden brown. **Yield:** 12 servings.

Banana Cream Dessert

Nancy Walters, Ft. Myers, Florida

(PICTURED ON PAGE 40)

1 cup heavy cream
1 teaspoon vanilla extract
1 cup crushed peanut brittle, *divided*
2 ripe bananas, sliced
4 to 6 maraschino cherries

In a mixing bowl, beat cream until soft peaks form. Add vanilla and continue beating just until stiff peaks form. Fold in 3/4 cup peanut brittle and the bananas. Spoon into individual dessert dishes. Chill for 1 hour. Sprinkle with remaining peanut brittle and top each with a cherry. **Yield:** 4-6 servings.

Icebox Apple Pie

Johanna King, Sparta, Wisconsin

(PICTURED ON PAGE 14)

4-1/2 cups sliced peeled baking apples
1-1/2 cups water
1 tablespoon butter *or* margarine
1/4 teaspoon ground cinnamon
1/4 teaspoon ground nutmeg
1 package (3 ounces) peach-flavored gelatin
1 package (3 ounces) cook and serve vanilla pudding mix
1 pastry shell (9 inches), baked
TOPPING:
1/4 cup graham cracker crumbs
1 tablespoon butter *or* margarine, melted
1-1/2 teaspoons sugar

In a large saucepan, combine apples, water, butter, cinnamon and nutmeg; bring to a boil. Reduce heat; simmer, uncovered, for 5 minutes or until the apples are tender. Gradually stir in gelatin and pudding; bring to a boil. Remove from the heat; let stand 5 minutes. Pour into pie shell. Combine topping ingredients; sprinkle over filling. Chill 3-4 hours or until firm. **Yield:** 6-8 servings.

Chocolate Souffle

Carol Ice, Burlingham, New York

2 squares (1 ounce *each*) unsweetened chocolate
1/4 cup butter *or* margarine
5 tablespoons all-purpose flour
1/3 cup plus 1 teaspoon sugar, *divided*
1/4 teaspoon salt
1 cup milk
3 eggs, *separated*
1 teaspoon vanilla extract
1/4 teaspoon almond extract
SAUCE:
1 cup heavy cream
1/4 cup confectioners' sugar
1/4 teaspoon vanilla extract
Baking cocoa *or* ground cinnamon, optional

In the top of a double boiler over simmering water, melt chocolate and butter. In a bowl, combine flour, 1/3 cup sugar and salt. Add milk; stir into the melted chocolate. Cook and stir until thickened, about 7 minutes. In a small bowl, beat egg yolks; add a small amount of hot mixture. Return all to pan. Remove from the heat; add extracts. In a small mixing bowl, beat egg whites and remaining sugar until stiff peaks form. Fold into chocolate mixture. Grease the bottom of a 1-1/2-qt. baking dish; add chocolate mixture. Place dish in a larger pan; add 1 in. of hot water to pan. Bake at 325° for 1 hour or until a knife inserted near the center comes out clean. Combine the first three sauce ingredients in a small mixing bowl; beat until soft peaks form. Serve souffle warm with a dollop of sauce. Sprinkle with cocoa or cinnamon if desired. **Yield:** 4-6 servings.

Frosty Cherry Dessert

Diane Hays, Morris, Minnesota

2 cans (8 ounces *each*) crushed pineapple, undrained
1 can (21 ounces) cherry pie filling
1 can (14 ounces) sweetened condensed milk
1 carton (8 ounces) frozen whipped topping, thawed
Green maraschino cherries and additional whipped topping, optional

In a bowl, combine pineapple, pie filling and milk; fold in the whipped topping. Spread into a 13-in. x 9-in. x 2-in. baking dish that has been sprayed with nonstick cooking spray. Cover and freeze until firm. Garnish with cherries and whipped topping if desired. **Yield:** 12-16 servings.

Green Tomato Pie

Violet Thompson, Port Ludlow, Washington

1-1/2 cups sugar
5 tablespoons all-purpose flour
1 teaspoon ground cinnamon
Pinch salt
3 cups thinly sliced green tomatoes (about 4 to 5 medium)
1 tablespoon cider vinegar
Pastry for double-crust pie (9 inches)
1 tablespoon butter *or* margarine

In a bowl, combine sugar, flour, cinnamon and salt. Add tomatoes and vinegar; toss to mix. Line a pie plate with bottom crust. Add filling; dot with butter. Top with a lattice crust. Bake at 350° for 1 hour or until tomatoes are tender. **Yield:** 6-8 servings.

Butter Brickle Dessert

Leila Flavell, Bulyea, Saskatchewan

1 cup butter *or* margarine, melted
2 cups all-purpose flour
1/2 cup packed brown sugar
1/2 cup quick-cooking oats
1 cup chopped pecans
1 jar (12-1/2 ounces) caramel topping *or* sauce
1/2 gallon (rectangular) vanilla ice cream

In a bowl, combine butter, flour, sugar, oats and pecans; spread into a greased 15-in. x 10-in. x 1-in. baking pan. Bake at 350° for 15 minutes. Cool 5 minutes; break into pieces while still warm. Pat half of the crumbs into a 13-in. x 9-in. x 2-in. baking pan. Drizzle with half of the caramel topping. Cut ice cream into 1-in. slices; place in a single layer in pan. Sprinkle with remaining crumbs. Drizzle with remaining topping. Freeze until firm, about 2-3 hours. Remove from freezer 10 minutes before cutting. **Yield:** 16-20 servings.

Caramel Apples

Karen Ann Bland, Gove, Kansas

1 cup butter (no substitutes)
2 cups packed brown sugar
1 cup light corn syrup
1 can (14 ounces) sweetened condensed milk
1 teaspoon vanilla extract
8 to 10 wooden sticks
8 to 10 medium tart apples

In a heavy 3-qt. saucepan, combine butter, brown sugar, corn syrup and milk; bring to a boil over medium-high heat. Cook and stir until mixture reaches 248° (firm-ball stage) on a candy thermometer, about 30-40 minutes. Remove from the heat; stir in vanilla. Insert wooden sticks into apples. Dip each apple into hot caramel mixture; turn to coat. Set on waxed paper to cool. **Yield:** 8-10 apples.

Special Chocolate Ice Cream

Alice Taylor, Swansboro, North Carolina

(PICTURED ON PAGE 16)

✓ This tasty dish uses less sugar, salt and fat. Recipe includes *Diabetic Exchanges.*

1 package (1.5 ounces) sugar-free instant chocolate pudding mix
6 packets aspartame sweetener (equivalent to 1/4 cup sugar)
2 tablespoons baking cocoa
4 cups evaporated skim milk
1 teaspoon vanilla extract
4 ounces light frozen whipped topping, thawed

In a blender, combine the pudding mix, sweetener, cocoa, milk and vanilla; process on low until smooth. Fold in the whipped topping until smooth. Pour into a shallow 2-qt. freezer container. Cover and freeze for 30 minutes. Stir with a wire whisk; return to freezer until ready to serve. **Yield:** 12 servings. **Diabetic Exchanges:** One 1/2-cup serving equals 1 skim milk, 1/2 starch, 1/2 fat; also, 140 calories, 257 mg sodium, 4 mg cholesterol, 20 gm carbohydrate, 10 gm protein, 3 gm fat.

Peppermint Stick Pie

Mildred Peachey, Wooster, Ohio

4-1/2 cups crisp rice cereal
1 cup (6 ounces) semisweet chocolate chips, melted
2 quarts peppermint stick ice cream, softened
Chocolate syrup *or* chocolate fudge topping
Crushed peppermint candies

Combine cereal and chocolate; mix well. Press into the bottom and up the sides of an ungreased 10-in. pie plate. Freeze for 5 minutes. Spoon ice cream into the crust. Freeze until ready to serve. Garnish with chocolate syrup and peppermint candies. **Yield:** 6-8 servings. **Editor's Note:** Pie may be made ahead and frozen. Remove from freezer 15 minutes before serving.

Peach Pizza Pie

Ann Kidd, Lewes, Delaware

1/2 cup butter *or* margarine, softened
1/4 cup confectioners' sugar
1 cup all-purpose flour
4 to 5 cups sliced fresh peaches
GLAZE:
2 tablespoons sugar
1 tablespoon cornstarch
1/8 to 1/4 teaspoon ground mace, optional
1/2 cup orange juice
1/2 cup red currant jelly
Whipped cream, optional

In a mixing bowl, cream butter and sugar. Add flour and mix well. Pat into a greased 12-in. pizza pan; prick with a fork. Bake at 350° for 10-15 minutes or until golden. Cool completely. Arrange peach slices on crust. In a saucepan, mix sugar, cornstarch and mace if desired. Add orange juice and jelly; cook and stir over medium heat until smooth. Bring to a boil; boil for 2 minutes. Remove from the heat and cool slightly, about 5 minutes. Spoon over peaches. Chill for 1 hour or until set. Garnish with whipped cream if desired and serve immediately. **Yield:** 12-15 servings.

Black Walnut Pie

Helen Holbrook, De Soto, Missouri

1/2 cup plus 1 tablespoon sugar, *divided*
1 tablespoon all-purpose flour
1 unbaked pastry shell (9 inches)
1 cup light corn syrup
1/2 cup packed brown sugar
3 tablespoons butter *or* margarine
3 eggs, lightly beaten
1 cup chopped black walnuts*

Combine 1 tablespoon sugar and flour; sprinkle over bottom of pie shell and set aside. In a medium saucepan, bring corn syrup, brown sugar and remaining sugar just to a boil. Remove from the heat; stir in butter until melted. Let cool for 3 minutes. Gradually stir eggs into hot mixture. Add walnuts and mix well. Pour into pie shell. Preheat the oven to 350°. Place pie in oven; immediately reduce heat to 325°. Bake for 55 minutes or until top is browned. **Yield:** 8 servings. ***Editor's Note:** Regular walnuts can be substituted for the black walnuts.

Anniversary Cheesecake

Kathy Anderson, Brookfield, Wisconsin

1 cup graham cracker crumbs
1 tablespoon sugar
1/4 cup butter *or* margarine, melted
FILLING:
4 packages (8 ounces *each*) cream cheese, softened
1 cup sugar
2 eggs
1 tablespoon cornstarch
1-1/2 teaspoons vanilla extract
1 tablespoon lemon juice
1 cup (8 ounces) sour cream
Red, yellow and green food coloring, optional
2 teaspoons grated lemon peel

Combine the first three ingredients; press into the bottom of a 9-in. springform pan. Bake at 325° for 6 minutes. Cool. In a large mixing bowl, beat cream cheese until smooth. Gradually add sugar; mix well. Add eggs, one at a time, beating well after each addition. In a small bowl, mix cornstarch, vanilla and lemon juice until smooth. Add to cream cheese mixture. Fold in sour cream. To make decorations if desired: Take 3 tablespoons filling and place 1 tablespoon each into three small bowls; using food coloring, tint filling in one bowl pink, one yellow and one green. Add lemon peel to remaining filling; pour into crust. Using a small spoon or a pastry bag, use colored filling to draw decorations on top of cheesecake (a toothpick will help define shapes). Bake at 325° for 45-50 minutes or until center still jiggles. *Do not overbake.* The center should not be completely set when removed from oven. Cool thoroughly on a wire rack. Chill overnight. **Yield:** 12-16 servings.

Strawberry Dessert

Marcille Meyer, Battle Creek, Nebraska

✓ This tasty dish uses less sugar, salt and fat. Recipe includes *Diabetic Exchanges.*

1 loaf (10-1/2 ounces) angel food cake, cubed
1 package (1 ounce) sugar-free instant vanilla pudding mix
1 cup cold skim milk
2 cups sugar-free low-fat vanilla ice cream, softened
1 package (.3 ounce) sugar-free strawberry-flavored gelatin
1 cup boiling water
1 cup cold water
1 bag (20 ounces) frozen unsweetened strawberries, partially thawed and sliced

Place cake in the bottom of a 13-in. x 9-in. x 2-in. baking dish. In a mixing bowl, beat pudding mix and milk on low 1-1/2 minutes. Add ice cream; beat on low 1 minute. Pour over cake; chill. Dissolve gelatin in boiling water. Add cold water and strawberries; mix until partially set. Spoon over pudding layer. Cover and chill overnight. **Yield:** 24 servings. **Diabetic Exchanges:** One serving equals 1 starch; also, 62 calories, 142 mg sodium, 0 cholesterol, 14 gm carbohydrate, 3 gm protein, trace fat.

WHAT'S the best way to top off Father's Day? With a hearty dinner, of course! The recipes here will make one that's fit for a king. The herbs that top the pork roast add flavor everyone will savor. A creamy mushroom sauce turns plain cauliflower into an extra-special side dish. A hint of rosemary makes corn bread stand out from all the rest. And blueberry pie will remind Dad of the pies his mother used to prepare.

DINNER FOR DAD. Clockwise from bottom: **Fresh Blueberry Pie** (p. 73), **Herbed Pork Roast** (p. 9), **Quick 'n' Easy Corn Bread** (p. 53) and **Cauliflower with Mushroom-Almond Sauce** (p. 45).

Fresh Blueberry Pie

Nellie VanSickle, Silver Bay, New York
(PICTURED AT LEFT)

4 cups fresh blueberries, *divided*
3/4 cup water
1 tablespoon butter *or* margarine
3/4 cup sugar
3 tablespoons cornstarch
1/8 teaspoon ground cinnamon
Dash salt
1 teaspoon lemon juice
1 pastry shell (9 inches), baked
Ice cream *or* whipped cream
Shredded lemon peel, optional

In a saucepan, combine 1 cup of blueberries, water and butter; simmer for 4 minutes. Combine sugar, cornstarch, cinnamon and salt; add to saucepan. Bring to a boil over medium heat, stirring constantly. Cook and stir for 2 minutes. Stir in lemon juice and remaining blueberries. Pour into pie shell. Chill for 2-3 hours. Serve with ice cream or whipped cream. Garnish with lemon peel if desired. Refrigerate any leftovers. **Yield:** 6-8 servings.

Strawberry Cloud

Patricia Kile, Greentown, Pennsylvania

1 package (3 ounces) strawberry-flavored gelatin
1 package (3 ounces) cook and serve vanilla pudding mix
2-1/2 cups water
1 carton (8 ounces) frozen whipped topping, thawed

In a saucepan over medium heat, cook and stir gelatin, pudding mix and water until mixture boils, about 15 minutes. Cool until partially set; fold in whipped topping. Spoon into a bowl or individual dishes or parfait glasses. Chill until ready to serve. **Yield:** 6-8 servings.

Peaches 'n' Cream Tart

Mary Ann Kosmas, Minneapolis, Minnesota

1 cup finely chopped pecans
2/3 cup all-purpose flour
1/2 cup butter *or* margarine, melted
1/2 cup heavy cream
1 package (8 ounces) cream cheese, softened
1/3 cup sugar
1 teaspoon vanilla extract
1/2 teaspoon almond extract
1 teaspoon grated orange peel
1 can (16 ounces) sliced peaches, drained
1/2 cup fresh raspberries
1/4 cup apricot preserves
2 tablespoons honey

Combine pecans, flour and butter; press into the bottom and up the sides of an ungreased 9-in. tart pan with removable bottom. Bake at 350° for 25-30 minutes or until golden brown. Cool completely. Whip cream until soft peaks form; set aside. In a mixing bowl, beat the cream cheese and sugar until fluffy. Add extracts and orange peel; mix well. Mix in the whipped cream on low speed. Spoon into crust. Chill for 2-4 hours. Just before serving, arrange peaches and raspberries over filling. In the microwave or on the stovetop, melt preserves and honey; mix well. Carefully spoon or brush over fruit. Cut into wedges to serve. **Yield:** 6-8 servings.

Chocolate Almond Brittle

Pat Parsons, Bakersfield, California
(PICTURED ON PAGE 22)

1 cup sugar
1/2 cup light corn syrup
1/8 teaspoon salt
1 cup coarsely chopped almonds
1 tablespoon butter *or* margarine
1 teaspoon vanilla extract
1-1/2 teaspoons baking soda
3/4 pound dark *or* milk chocolate confectionery coating

In a 1-1/2-qt. microwave-safe bowl, combine sugar, corn syrup and salt; mix well. Microwave on high for 4 minutes. Stir in almonds; microwave on high for 4 minutes. Add the butter and vanilla; microwave on high for 1-1/2 minutes. Stir in baking soda. As soon as the mixture foams, quickly pour onto a greased metal baking sheet. Cool completely. Break into 2-in. pieces. Melt chocolate coating in a double boiler or microwave. Dip one side of brittle in chocolate and place on waxed paper to harden. Store in an airtight container. **Yield:** about 1 pound. **Editor's Note:** This recipe was tested using a 700-watt microwave.

Raisin Pudding

Margaret Vieth, Norwalk, Wisconsin

1 package (3 ounces) cook and serve vanilla pudding mix
1 cup milk
1/2 cup water
1 cup raisins
1/2 teaspoon vanilla extract
1-1/4 cups plain yogurt
Whipped topping and ground nutmeg, optional

In a saucepan, combine pudding mix, milk and water; cook over medium heat until thickened. Remove from the heat; stir in the raisins and vanilla. Cool for 15 minutes; stir in yogurt. Spoon into individual dessert dishes. Chill for 2-3 hours. If desired, garnish with whipped topping and sprinkle with nutmeg. **Yield:** 6 servings. **Editor's Note:** Sugar-free vanilla pudding mix can be substituted for the regular pudding.

Apple Butter Pie

Marjorie Fowler, Summerfield, Florida

1/2 cup apple butter
1 egg, lightly beaten
1/2 cup sugar
1 tablespoon all-purpose flour
2 cups evaporated milk
Ground cinnamon
1 unbaked pastry shell (9 inches)

In a bowl, combine apple butter, egg, sugar, flour and milk; mix well. Pour into the pie shell; sprinkle with cinnamon. Bake at 425° for 10 minutes. Reduce temperature to 350°; bake 35 minutes more or until a knife inserted near the center comes out clean. Cool on a wire rack. Store in the refrigerator. **Yield:** 6-8 servings.

Bread Pudding

Evette Rios, Westfield, Massachusetts

3 eggs
3 cans (12 ounces *each*) evaporated milk
1-1/4 cups sugar
1/4 cup butter *or* margarine, melted
1/2 to 1 cup raisins
1 teaspoon ground cinnamon
2 teaspoons vanilla extract
1/2 teaspoon salt
1 loaf (1 pound) bread, cut into cubes

In a large bowl, beat eggs. Add milk, sugar, butter, raisins, cinnamon, vanilla and salt; mix well. Add bread cubes; stir gently. Pour into a greased 13-in. x 9-in. x 2-in. baking dish. Bake at 325° for 50-60 minutes or until a knife inserted near the center comes out clean. Serve warm or cold. Store in the refrigerator. **Yield:** 12-16 servings.

WHEN SHORTCAKE (recipe below) appears on table, every day becomes special.

SENSATIONAL STRAWBERRY SHORTCAKE

Sarah Martin, Ridgeland, Mississippi
(PICTURED ABOVE)

1 quart strawberries, sliced
1 cup sugar, *divided*
2 cups all-purpose flour
1 tablespoon plus 1 teaspoon baking powder
1/4 teaspoon salt
Dash ground nutmeg
1/2 cup butter *or* margarine
1/2 cup milk
2 eggs, *separated*
2 to 3 cups sweetened whipped cream
Fresh mint, optional

In a bowl, gently stir strawberries and 1/2 cup sugar; chill. Meanwhile, in another bowl, combine flour, 1/4 cup sugar, baking powder, salt and nutmeg; cut in butter until crumbly. Combine milk and egg yolks; mix well. Add to crumb mixture, stirring just until moistened. Divide and pat into two greased 9-in. round cake pans. In a small mixing bowl, beat egg whites until stiff peaks form; spread over dough. Sprinkle with remaining sugar. Bake at 300° for 40-45 minutes or until golden. Cool 10 minutes before removing from pan to a wire rack. (Layers will be thin.) Cool completely. Place one cake layer on a large serving plate; spread with half of the whipped cream. Spoon half of the strawberries over cream. Repeat layers. Garnish with mint if desired. **Yield:** 8-10 servings. **Editor's Note:** This dessert is best when served the same day as prepared.

PICTURE PERFECT. To have your cheesecake look its best, place a shallow pan of water in the oven while baking. The moisture helps prevent cracking.

CRUNCHY BAKED APPLES

Jayne King, Liberty, South Carolina

1/2 cup chopped walnuts
1/4 cup sugar
1/2 teaspoon ground cinnamon
1/4 cup packed brown sugar
1/4 cup raisins
6 tablespoons butter *or* margarine, melted, *divided*
4 medium baking apples
1 lemon, halved
4 short cinnamon sticks
3/4 cup apple juice

In a blender or food processor, grind walnuts and sugar. Add cinnamon and set aside. Combine the brown sugar, raisins and 2 tablespoons of butter; set aside. Core apples and peel the top two-thirds of each. Rub tops and sides with lemon; squeeze juice into centers. Brush apples with 2 tablespoons butter; press nut mixture evenly over peeled sides. Place in an ungreased 9-in. square baking dish. Fill apples with raisin mixture. Place a cinnamon stick in each apple; drizzle with remaining butter. Pour apple juice around apples. Bake, uncovered, at 375° for 40-50 minutes or until apples are tender. Cool 15 minutes before serving. **Yield:** 4 servings.

FUDGY CHRISTMAS WREATH

Nancy Maguire, Stony Plain, Alberta

1 can (14 ounces) sweetened condensed milk
2 cups (12 ounces) semisweet chocolate chips
1 cup chopped walnuts
1/2 teaspoon vanilla extract
Red and green maraschino cherries

In a saucepan over low heat, cook and stir milk and chocolate chips until chocolate melts and mixture is slightly thickened, about 6 minutes. Remove from heat; stir in nuts and vanilla. Cool until it starts to set, about 15 minutes. Line a baking sheet with waxed paper. Spoon chocolate mixture by 2 tablespoonfuls into small mounds to form a wreath. Decorate with cherries. Chill until firm; serve chilled. **Yield:** about 24 servings.

PINEAPPLE SHERBET

Martha Sue Stroud, Clarksville, Texas

2 quarts milk
3 cups sugar, *divided*
3 tablespoons all-purpose flour
1 can (20 ounces) crushed pineapple, undrained
1/2 cup lemon juice

In a saucepan, combine milk and 1 cup sugar; bring to a boil over medium heat, stirring constantly. Combine flour and remaining sugar; stir into milk mixture. Bring to a boil, stirring constantly; boil 15 minutes or until slightly thickened. Remove from the heat; cool. Add pineapple and lemon juice; mix well. Freeze in an ice cream freezer according to manufacturer's directions. **Yield:** about 2 quarts.

LIGHT 'N' LUSCIOUS TRIFLE

Paula Marchesi, Rocky Point, New York

✓ This tasty dish uses less sugar, salt and fat. Recipe includes *Nutritional Information.*

6 cups cubed honeydew melon
6 cups sliced fresh strawberries
1/2 cup strawberry all-fruit spread
2 packages (8 ounces *each*) fat-free cream cheese, softened
1-1/2 cups confectioners' sugar
1 cup (8 ounces) fat-free sour cream
2 cups frozen light whipped topping, thawed
1 loaf (10-1/2 ounces) angel food cake, cubed
1/3 cup grated semisweet chocolate

In a large bowl, toss the honeydew and strawberries with fruit spread; set aside. In a mixing bowl, beat cream cheese and sugar until smooth. Add sour cream; mix well. Fold in whipped topping and cake. Drain juice from fruit mixture. In a trifle dish or deep salad bowl, layer a third of the fruit, a third of the cake mixture and a third of the chocolate. Repeat layers twice. Serve immediately. **Yield:** 16 servings. **Nutritional Information:** One 1-cup serving equals 214 calories, 272 mg sodium, 0 cholesterol, 42 gm carbohydrate, 6 gm protein, 2 gm fat.

CHOCOLATE-COVERED CHERRIES

Linda Hammerich, Bonanza, Oregon

2-1/2 cups confectioners' sugar
1/4 cup butter *or* margarine, softened
1 tablespoon milk
1/2 teaspoon almond extract
2 jars (8 ounces *each*) maraschino cherries with stems, well drained
2 cups (12 ounces) semisweet chocolate chips
2 tablespoons shortening

In a mixing bowl, combine sugar, butter, milk and extract; mix well. Knead into a large ball. Roll into 1-in. balls and flatten each into a 2-in. circle. Wrap around cherries and lightly roll in hands. Place with stems up on waxed paper-lined baking sheet. Cover loosely and refrigerate 4 hours or overnight. Melt the chocolate chips and shortening in a double boiler or microwave-safe bowl. Holding on to stem, dip cherries into chocolate; set on waxed paper to harden. Store in a covered container. Refrigerate 1-2 weeks before serving. **Yield:** about 3 dozen.

Creamy Caramel Flan

Pat Forte, Miami, Florida

(PICTURED ON PAGE 52)

3/4 cup sugar
1 package (8 ounces) cream cheese, softened
5 eggs
1 can (14 ounces) sweetened condensed milk
1 can (12 ounces) evaporated milk
1 teaspoon vanilla extract

In a heavy saucepan over medium-low heat, cook and stir sugar until melted and golden, about 15 minutes. Quickly pour into an ungreased 2-qt. round baking or souffle dish, tilting to coat the bottom; let stand for 10 minutes. In a mixing bowl, beat the cream cheese until smooth. Beat in eggs, one at a time, until thoroughly combined. Add remaining ingredients; mix well. Pour over caramelized sugar. Place the dish in a larger baking pan. Pour boiling water into larger pan to a depth of 1 in. Bake at 350° for 50-60 minutes or until center is just set (mixture will jiggle). Remove dish from larger pan to a wire rack; cool for 1 hour. Refrigerate overnight. To unmold, run a knife around edges and invert onto a large rimmed serving platter. Cut into wedges or spoon onto dessert plates; spoon sauce over each serving. **Yield:** 8-10 servings.

Quick & Easy

Maple Walnut Cream

Ida Hartnett, Sparta, New Jersey

1 cup real maple syrup
2 cups milk, *divided*
2 tablespoons cornstarch
1/4 teaspoon salt
2 eggs, lightly beaten
1 cup finely chopped walnuts

In the top of a double boiler over boiling water, scald syrup and 1-3/4 cups milk. Combine cornstarch, salt and remaining milk; gradually add to the syrup mixture. Cook and stir until thickened, about 25 minutes. Add a small amount to eggs. Return all to pan; cook for 5 minutes. Pour into serving dishes. Sprinkle with walnuts; cool. **Yield:** 6 servings.

Sugar-Free Pineapple Pie

Ethel Lou Haley, Mayfield, Kentucky

✓ **This tasty dish uses less sugar, salt and fat. Recipe includes *Diabetic Exchanges.***

1 cup crushed graham cracker crumbs
1/4 cup margarine, melted
1 package (1 ounce) sugar-free instant vanilla pudding mix
1 cup (8 ounces) fat-free sour cream
1 can (20 ounces) crushed pineapple in natural juices, drained
1 packet artificial sweetener

Combine crumbs and margarine; press into bottom and up the sides of a 9-in. pie plate. Bake at 350° for 8-10 minutes; cool. In a bowl, combine pudding mix and sour cream; mix well. Stir in pineapple and sweetener. Spread into crust. Chill at least 3 hours. **Yield:** 8 servings. **Diabetic Exchanges:** One serving equals 2 fat, 1 starch, 1/2 fruit; also, 212 calories, 322 mg sodium, 0 cholesterol, 24 gm carbohydrate, 3 gm protein, 9 gm fat.

Golden Apple Pie

Theresa Brazil, Petaluma, California

(PICTURED ON PAGE 83)

6 cups sliced peeled Golden Delicious apples
3/4 cup plus 2 tablespoons apple juice, *divided*
3/4 cup sugar
1 teaspoon ground cinnamon
1/2 teaspoon apple pie spice
1/4 teaspoon vanilla extract
2 tablespoons cornstarch

CRUST:
2-1/2 cups all-purpose flour
1 teaspoon salt
1 cup cold butter *or* margarine
6 to 8 tablespoons ice water

In a large saucepan, combine apples, 3/4 cup apple juice, sugar, cinnamon, apple pie spice and vanilla; bring to a boil over medium heat, stirring occasionally. Combine cornstarch and remaining apple juice; add to saucepan. Return to a boil, stirring constantly. Cook and stir 1 minute more or until thickened. Remove from the heat and cool to room temperature, stirring occasionally. Meanwhile, in a bowl, combine flour and salt; cut in the butter until crumbly. Sprinkle with water, 1 tablespoon at a time; stir with a fork until dough can be formed into a ball. Divide in half. On a lightly floured surface, roll one half to fit a 9-in. pie plate. Place in plate and add filling. Roll remaining pastry to fit top of pie. Place over filling and seal edges; cut vents in the top. If desired, decorate top of pie with pastry scraps cut into small apple shapes. Bake at 400° for 40-45 minutes or until crust is lightly browned and apples are tender. **Yield:** 6-8 servings.

Strawberry Cream Pie

Michele Battles, Runnells, Iowa

(PICTURED ON PAGE 3)

1 pastry shell (9 inches), baked
1/2 cup slivered almonds, optional

FILLING:
1/2 cup sugar
3 tablespoons cornstarch
3 tablespoons all-purpose flour
1/2 teaspoon salt
2 cups milk
1 egg, lightly beaten
1/2 teaspoon vanilla extract
1/2 teaspoon almond extract, optional
1/2 cup heavy cream

GLAZE:
1/2 cup crushed strawberries
1/2 cup water
1/4 cup sugar
2 teaspoons cornstarch
3 cups fresh strawberries, halved
Whipped cream, optional

Cover bottom of pie shell with nuts if desired; set aside. In a saucepan, combine sugar, cornstarch, flour and salt; gradually stir in milk. Cook and stir over medium-high heat until thickened and bubbly. Reduce heat; cook and stir 2 minutes more. Remove from the heat and stir a small amount into egg; return all to the saucepan. Cook and stir until almost bubbly. Reduce heat; cook and stir 1-2 minutes more (do not boil). Remove from the heat; stir in vanilla and almond extract if desired. Cool to room temperature. Whip cream; fold into filling. Pour into pie shell. Chill for at least 2 hours. About 2 hours before serving, prepare glaze. Combine crushed strawberries and water in a saucepan; cook for 2 minutes. Combine sugar and cornstarch; gradually stir into the berries. Cook until thick and clear, stirring constantly. Strain. Cool for 20 minutes. Meanwhile, arrange berry halves over filling; pour glaze evenly over berries. Refrigerate for at least 1 hour. Garnish with whipped cream if desired. **Yield:** 6-8 servings.

FRIENDS AND FAMILY will surely save room for dessert when they know you're preparing one of these delicious recipes. Some are old-fashioned...some light and refreshing...some home-style...some festive and fancy... and all are perfect for any gathering. One taste and you'll agree they're the fantastic finale to your favorite meals.

SWEET SUCCESS. Clockwise from top: **Gingerbread Yule Log** (p. 78), **Raspberry Ribbon Pie** (p. 78), **Praline Pumpkin Pie** (p. 78), **Apricot Fruitcake** (p. 63), **Holiday Fig Torte** (p. 67), **Walnut Mincemeat Pie** (p. 78), **Christmas Carrot Pudding** (p. 78) and **Eggnog Cake** (p. 63).

Gingerbread Yule Log

Bernadette Colvin, Houston, Texas
(PICTURED ON PAGE 76)

- 3 eggs, *separated*
- 1/2 cup molasses
- 1 tablespoon butter *or* margarine, melted
- 1/4 cup sugar
- 1 cup all-purpose flour
- 3/4 teaspoon *each* baking powder and baking soda
- 1/2 teaspoon *each* ground cinnamon, ginger and cloves
- 1/8 teaspoon salt

SPICED CREAM FILLING:

- 1-1/2 cups whipping cream
- 1/3 cup confectioners' sugar
- 1 teaspoon ground cinnamon
- 1 teaspoon vanilla extract
- 1/4 teaspoon ground cloves
- Additional ground cinnamon, optional

In a mixing bowl, beat yolks on high until thickened, about 3 minutes. Beat in molasses and butter. In another bowl, beat whites until foamy; gradually add sugar, beating until soft peaks form. Fold into yolk mixture. Combine dry ingredients; gently fold into egg mixture until well mixed. Line a greased 15-in. x 10-in. x 1-in. baking pan with waxed paper; grease and flour paper. Spread batter into pan. Bake at 375° for 9-12 minutes or until cake springs back when lightly touched. Turn onto a linen towel dusted with confectioners' sugar. Peel off paper and roll cake up in towel, starting with short end. Cool on a wire rack. Meanwhile, beat the first five filling ingredients in a mixing bowl until soft peaks form. Unroll cake; spread with half the filling. Roll up. Spread remaining filling over cake. Sprinkle with cinnamon if desired. **Yield:** 10 servings.

Raspberry Ribbon Pie

Victoria Newman, Antelope, California
(PICTURED ON PAGE 77)

- 2 packages (3 ounces *each*) cream cheese, softened
- 1/2 cup confectioners' sugar
- Dash salt
- 1 cup whipping cream, whipped
- 1 pastry shell with high fluted edge (9 inches), baked
- 1 package (3 ounces) raspberry-flavored gelatin
- 1-1/4 cups boiling water
- 1 tablespoon lemon juice
- 1 package (10 ounces) frozen raspberries in syrup, thawed

In a mixing bowl, beat the cream cheese, sugar and salt until light and fluffy. Fold in cream. Spread half into pie shell. Chill 30 minutes. Meanwhile, dissolve gelatin in water; add lemon juice and raspberries. Carefully spoon half over cream cheese layer. Chill until set, about 30 minutes. Set aside the remaining gelatin mixture at room temperature. Carefully spread remaining cream cheese mixture over top of pie. Chill 30 minutes. Top with remaining gelatin. Chill until firm. **Yield:** 6-8 servings.

Praline Pumpkin Pie

Sandra Haase, Baltimore, Maryland
(PICTURED ON PAGE 77)

- 1/3 cup finely chopped pecans
- 1/3 cup packed brown sugar
- 3 tablespoons butter *or* margarine, softened
- 1 unbaked pastry shell (10 inches)

FILLING:

- 3 eggs, lightly beaten
- 1/2 cup packed brown sugar
- 1/2 cup sugar
- 2 tablespoons all-purpose flour
- 3/4 teaspoon ground cinnamon
- 1/2 teaspoon salt
- 1/2 teaspoon ground ginger
- 1/4 teaspoon ground cloves
- 1 can (16 ounces) pumpkin
- 1-1/2 cups half-and-half cream
- Additional chopped pecans, optional

Combine the pecans, sugar and butter; press into the bottom of pie shell. Prick sides of pastry with a fork. Bake at 450° for 10 minutes; cool for 5 minutes. Combine first eight filling ingredients; stir in pumpkin. Gradually add cream. Pour into pie shell. If desired, sprinkle chopped pecans on top. Bake at 350° for 45-50 minutes or until a knife inserted near the center comes out clean. Cool completely. Store in the refrigerator. **Yield:** 8-10 servings.

Walnut Mincemeat Pie

Laverne Kamp, Kutztown, Pennsylvania
(PICTURED ON PAGE 76)

- 2 eggs
- 1 cup sugar
- 2 tablespoons all-purpose flour
- 1/8 teaspoon salt
- 2 cups prepared mincemeat
- 1/2 cup chopped walnuts
- 1/4 cup butter *or* margarine, melted
- 1 unbaked pastry shell (9 inches)

In a mixing bowl, lightly beat eggs. Combine sugar, flour and salt; gradually add to eggs. Stir in mincemeat, nuts and butter; pour into pie shell. Bake at 400° for 15 minutes. Reduce heat to 325°; bake 35-40 minutes or until a knife inserted near the center comes out clean. Cool completely. Store in refrigerator. **Yield:** 6-8 servings.

Christmas Carrot Pudding

RaNae Cleverly, Bountiful, Utah
(PICTURED ON PAGE 76)

- 1 cup all-purpose flour
- 1/2 cup sugar
- 1/2 cup packed brown sugar
- 1 teaspoon baking soda
- 1 teaspoon ground cinnamon
- 1 teaspoon ground nutmeg
- 1/4 teaspoon ground cloves
- 1/4 teaspoon salt
- 1 cup dry bread crumbs
- 1/2 cup vegetable oil
- 1 cup *each* grated peeled carrot, apple and potato
- 1 cup raisins
- 1 cup chopped walnuts

CARAMEL SAUCE:

- 1/2 cup packed brown sugar
- 2 tablespoons cornstarch
- 1-3/4 cups water
- 2 tablespoons butter *or* margarine
- 1 teaspoon vanilla extract

In a large bowl, combine the first nine ingredients; stir in oil. Add carrot, apple, potato, raisins and nuts; mix well. Spoon into two greased 13-oz. coffee cans; cover tightly with foil and secure with string. Place cans on a rack in a large kettle. Add boiling water to depth of 1-1/2 in. Cover and simmer for 3-1/4 hours or until cake tests done. Cool, covered, for 30 minutes; unmold. For sauce, combine brown sugar and cornstarch in a saucepan; gradually stir in water until smooth. Add butter and vanilla; bring to a boil over medium heat, stirring constantly. Boil 1-2 minutes. Serve hot over warm pudding. **Yield:** 10-12 servings.

Orange Rhubarb Pie

Mrs. M.E. Kaufman, Haines City, Florida

- 1-1/4 cups sugar, *divided*
- 1/4 cup all-purpose flour
- 1/4 teaspoon salt
- 3 tablespoons orange juice concentrate

1/4 cup butter *or* margarine, melted
3 eggs, *separated*
2-1/2 cups diced rhubarb (1/2-inch pieces)
1 unbaked pie shell (9 inches)
1/3 cup chopped walnuts

In a large bowl, combine 1 cup sugar, flour and salt. Stir in orange juice and butter. In a small bowl, lightly beat egg yolks; stir into the orange juice mixture. Add rhubarb. In a mixing bowl, beat egg whites until soft peaks begin to form; gradually beat in remaining sugar until stiff peaks form. Fold into rhubarb mixture. Pour into pie shell. Top with nuts. Bake at 375° for 15 minutes. Reduce heat to 325°; bake for 40 minutes or until golden. If needed, cover pie loosely with foil during the last 10 minutes to prevent excess browning. Cool on a wire rack. Store in the refrigerator. **Yield:** 6-8 servings.

Raspberry/Cherry Pie

Fern Buffington, Traer, Iowa

2 cups fresh *or* frozen unsweetened raspberries
1 cup pitted fresh, frozen *or* canned tart cherries
1-1/2 cups sugar
3 tablespoons quick-cooking tapioca
1 teaspoon lemon juice
Pastry for double-crust pie (9 inches)
1 to 2 tablespoons butter *or* margarine

In a large bowl, combine the raspberries and cherries. Add sugar, tapioca and lemon juice; mix well. Let stand for 1 hour. Line pie plate with bottom crust; add the filling. Dot with butter. Top with a lattice crust. Bake at 450° for 10 minutes; reduce heat to 350° and bake for 30 minutes more. Cool to room temperature. **Yield:** 6-8 servings.

Christmas Rice Pudding

Barbara Garfield, Jamestown, New York

1-3/4 cups uncooked long grain rice
2 cups water
4 cups milk
1-1/2 cups sugar
1 teaspoon salt
1/4 cup butter *or* margarine
Sliced almonds and ground cinnamon, optional

In a saucepan, combine the rice and water. Simmer for 10 minutes; add milk and bring to a boil. Reduce heat and simmer, uncovered, for 60-70 minutes or until rice is tender. Add sugar, salt and butter; mix well. Spoon into small bowls or dessert dishes. Garnish with almonds and sprinkle with cinnamon if desired. **Yield:** 6-8 servings.

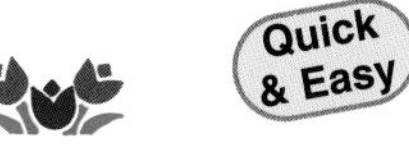

Cranberry-Chocolate Ice Cream

Marilou Robinson, Portland, Oregon

2 cups fresh *or* frozen cranberries
1/2 cup orange juice
1/2 teaspoon almond extract
1 quart vanilla ice cream, softened
4 squares (1 ounce *each*) semisweet chocolate, coarsely chopped *or* 3/4 cup semisweet mini chocolate chips

In a saucepan over medium heat, cook cranberries and orange juice until cranberries pop, about 8 minutes. Place in food processor or blender; add extract and pulse for about 5 minutes or until coarsely chopped. Freeze 10 minutes. Place ice cream in a large bowl; fold in cranberry mixture and chocolate. Serve immediately or cover and freeze. **Yield:** 6-8 servings.

Caramel Fudge Sundaes

Auton Miller, Piney Flats, Tennessee

1 can (12 ounces) evaporated milk
1 cup sugar
Dash salt
1 cup butter *or* margarine
3 tablespoons dark corn syrup
1 cup (6 ounces) semisweet chocolate chips
24 caramels
1/2 teaspoon vanilla extract
Vanilla ice cream
Chopped pecans *or* peanuts, optional

In a saucepan, combine the first seven ingredients in order given. Cook, stirring constantly, over medium heat until the caramels are melted and mixture is smooth (do not boil). Reduce heat to low. With an electric hand mixer on medium speed, beat in vanilla; continue beating for 5 minutes. Beat on high for 2 minutes. Remove from the heat and cool for 30 minutes (sauce will thicken as it cools). Serve over ice cream; sprinkle with nuts if desired. Store in the refrigerator. Reheat in the top of a double boiler over simmering water. **Yield:** 1 quart sauce.

Cran-Apple Pie

Janet Morgan-Cavallaro, Pincourt, Quebec

2-1/2 pounds baking apples, peeled and sliced
1 cup fresh *or* frozen cranberries
3/4 cup packed brown sugar
1/4 cup all-purpose flour
1/2 teaspoon ground cinnamon
1/2 teaspoon aniseed, crushed
1/4 teaspoon ground nutmeg
Pastry for double-crust pie (9 inches)
1 egg white
1 tablespoon water
1/4 teaspoon sugar

In a large bowl, combine the first seven ingredients; toss well. Line a deep 9-in. pie plate with the bottom pastry. Add filling. Top with a lattice crust; flute edges. Lightly beat egg white and water; brush over crust. Sprinkle with sugar. Bake at 375° for 50-55 minutes or until apples are tender. **Yield:** 6-8 servings.

> **GARNISH WITH FLAIR.** Here's a quick decorating tip for chocolate desserts. Try grating a chocolate candy bar over the top of whipped cream.

Brownie Ice Cream Pie

Mrs. Travis Baker, Litchfield, Illinois

1 cup (6 ounces) semisweet chocolate chips
1/2 cup butter *or* margarine, softened
1 cup sugar
2 eggs
1/2 cup all-purpose flour
1/4 teaspoon salt
1/2 teaspoon vanilla extract
1 cup chopped nuts
2 to 3 pints ice cream
Chocolate sauce, optional

In a double boiler over simmering water, melt chocolate chips; remove from the heat and set aside. In a mixing bowl, cream butter and sugar. Add eggs, one at a time, beating well after each addition. Beat in flour and salt; add vanilla and melted chocolate. Stir in nuts. Spoon into a greased 10-in. springform pan; place pan on a jelly roll pan. Bake at 350° for 30 minutes or until brownie tests done with a wooden pick. Cool on a wire rack for at least 1 hour. Fill with scoops of ice cream. Cover and freeze at least 4 hours or overnight. Remove outer ring of pan. Let stand 10 minutes before serving. Top with chocolate sauce if desired. **Yield:** 10-12 servings.

WHAT COUNTRY COOK doesn't take advantage of summer's bountiful harvest? With these relishes and preserves, you can feed your family for months to come. Plus, they provide you with a perfect opportunity to prepare some holiday presents in advance! So you can bring a taste of summer to the table long after winter has set in.

GARDEN-FRESH GIFTS. Clockwise from top: **Spicy Garden Salsa**, **Pepper Jelly**, **Raspberry Apple Butter** and **Golden Corn Relish** (all recipes on p. 81).

Canned Goods & Condiments

It's time to stock up on fruit-cellar favorites and country condiments like sauces, dressings, preserves, relishes...even canned lemonade!

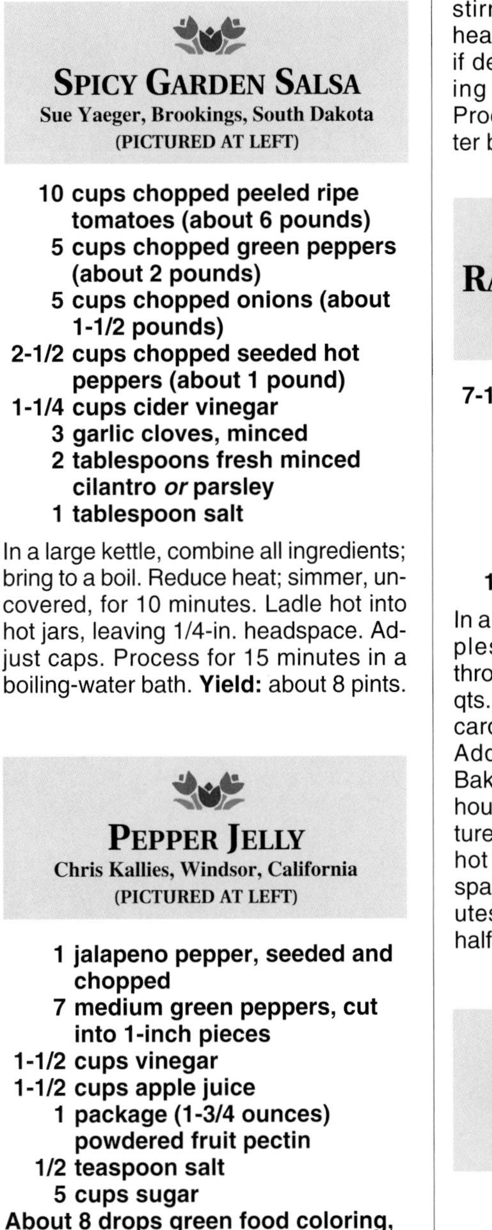

Spicy Garden Salsa

Sue Yaeger, Brookings, South Dakota
(PICTURED AT LEFT)

10 cups chopped peeled ripe tomatoes (about 6 pounds)
5 cups chopped green peppers (about 2 pounds)
5 cups chopped onions (about 1-1/2 pounds)
2-1/2 cups chopped seeded hot peppers (about 1 pound)
1-1/4 cups cider vinegar
3 garlic cloves, minced
2 tablespoons fresh minced cilantro *or* parsley
1 tablespoon salt

In a large kettle, combine all ingredients; bring to a boil. Reduce heat; simmer, uncovered, for 10 minutes. Ladle hot into hot jars, leaving 1/4-in. headspace. Adjust caps. Process for 15 minutes in a boiling-water bath. **Yield:** about 8 pints.

Pepper Jelly

Chris Kallies, Windsor, California
(PICTURED AT LEFT)

1 jalapeno pepper, seeded and chopped
7 medium green peppers, cut into 1-inch pieces
1-1/2 cups vinegar
1-1/2 cups apple juice
1 package (1-3/4 ounces) powdered fruit pectin
1/2 teaspoon salt
5 cups sugar
About 8 drops green food coloring, optional

Place the jalapeno, half of the green peppers and half of the vinegar in a blender or food processor; puree. Pour into a large bowl. Puree remaining green peppers and vinegar; add to the bowl. Add apple juice; mix well. Cover and chill overnight. Strain through several layers of damp cheesecloth. Measure 4 cups juice into a large kettle (add water if needed to make 4 cups). Stir in pectin and salt; bring to a rolling boil over high heat, stirring constantly. Add sugar; return to a rolling boil. Boil for 1 minute, stirring constantly. Remove from the heat; skim off foam. Add food coloring if desired. Pour hot into hot jars, leaving 1/4-in. headspace. Adjust caps. Process for 5 minutes in a boiling-water bath. **Yield:** about 6 half-pints.

Raspberry Apple Butter

Karla Hall, Prairie City, Iowa
(PICTURED AT LEFT)

7-1/2 pounds large unpeeled apples (about 20), quartered and cored
1 cup water
4 cups sugar
3 cups fresh raspberries
1 teaspoon ground cinnamon
1/4 teaspoon ground cloves

In a large covered kettle, simmer the apples and water until tender. Press through a sieve or food mill. Measure 2 qts. of pulp; place in a large roaster (discard the rest or save for another use). Add remaining ingredients; mix well. Bake, uncovered, at 300° for 2 to 2-1/2 hours, stirring occasionally, or until mixture reaches desired consistency. Pour hot into hot jars, leaving 1/4-in. headspace. Adjust caps. Process for 10 minutes in a boiling-water bath. **Yield:** 10 half-pints.

Golden Corn Relish

Rachel Davison, Stinnett, Kentucky
(PICTURED AT LEFT)

2 quarts cut corn (about 16 medium ears)
1 quart chopped cabbage (about 1 small head)
1-1/4 cups chopped onion
1 cup chopped green pepper
1 cup chopped sweet red pepper
1 cup chopped celery
4 cups vinegar
1-1/2 cups sugar
1 cup water
2 tablespoons mustard seed
1 tablespoon salt
1 tablespoon ground turmeric
1 teaspoon celery seed

In a large kettle, combine all ingredients; simmer, uncovered, for 20 minutes, stirring occasionally. Ladle hot into hot jars, leaving 1/4-in. headspace. Adjust caps. Process for 15 minutes in a boiling-water bath. **Yield:** about 7 pints.

Mincemeat-Cranberry Sauce

Mavis Hauser, Wallaceburg, Ontario

1 can (16 ounces) whole-berry cranberry sauce
1 jar (20-1/2 ounces) mincemeat
1/4 cup orange juice
Vanilla ice cream

In a saucepan over medium heat, stir cranberry sauce, mincemeat and orange juice until heated through. Serve warm over ice cream. Store leftovers in refrigerator. **Yield:** about 3-1/2 cups.

Dilled Onions

Donna Torres, Grand Rapids, Minnesota

2 large sweet onions, cut into 1/4-inch slices
1 teaspoon dill seed
1/2 cup sugar
1/2 cup vinegar
1/4 cup water
2 teaspoons salt

Sprinkle onions with dill seed. Layer in a wide-mouth pint jar. In a saucepan, combine remaining ingredients; cook and stir over medium heat until sugar is dissolved. Pour over onions. Cover and refrigerate for 36 hours. Serve as a relish or on sandwiches. **Yield:** 2 cups.

Raspberry Vinaigrette

Debbie Jones, California, Maryland

1/2 cup vegetable oil
1/4 cup raspberry vinegar
4 teaspoons sugar
2 teaspoons Dijon mustard

In a small bowl or jar with tight-fitting lid, combine all ingredients. Mix or shake well. Store in the refrigerator. **Yield:** about 3/4 cup.

Bread 'n' Butter Pickles

Muriel Looney, Eugene, Oregon

(PICTURED AT RIGHT)

- **8 pounds large cucumbers (about 12), cut into 1/4-inch slices**
- **8 large onions, cut into 1/8-inch slices**
- **4 large green peppers, sliced**
- **2/3 cup canning salt**
- **6 cups vinegar**
- **6 cups sugar**
- **2 teaspoons celery seed**
- **2 teaspoons mustard seed**
- **1 teaspoon ground turmeric**

In a large container, combine cucumbers, onions, green peppers and salt. Add enough cold water to cover. Chill for 2 hours. Drain and rinse. In a large kettle, combine remaining ingredients; bring to a boil. Add cucumber mixture; return to a boil. Ladle hot into hot jars, leaving 1/4-in. headspace. Adjust lids. Process for 10 minutes in a boiling-water bath. **Yield:** 10 pints.

Strawberry Lemonade

Cindy DePue, Saylorsburg, Pennsylvania

(PICTURED ON PAGE 64)

- **4 quarts strawberries, hulled**
- **4 cups fresh lemon juice (about 16 lemons)**
- **3 quarts water**
- **6 cups sugar**
- **Lemon-lime soda *or* ginger ale**

In a blender or food processor, puree the strawberries. Place in a large kettle; add lemon juice, water and sugar. Bring to 165° over medium heat, stirring occasionally (do not boil). Remove from the heat; skim off foam. Pour hot into hot jars, leaving 1/4-in. headspace. Adjust caps. Process for 15 minutes in a boiling-water bath. To serve, mix about one-third concentrate with two-thirds soda or ginger ale. **Yield:** about 6 quarts concentrate.

Zucchini Relish

Claire Fitzgaireld, Willow, Alaska

(PICTURED ON PAGE 64)

- **10 cups chopped unpeeled zucchini (about 7 medium)**
- **4 cups chopped onion (about 4 large)**
- **1 large sweet red pepper, chopped**
- **1 can (4 ounces) chopped green chilies**
- **3 tablespoons canning salt**
- **3-1/2 cups sugar**
- **3 cups vinegar**
- **1 tablespoon ground turmeric**
- **4 teaspoons celery seed**
- **1 teaspoon pepper**
- **1/2 teaspoon ground nutmeg**

In a large container, combine zucchini, onion, pepper, chilies and salt; stir well. Chill overnight. Rinse thoroughly; drain. In a large kettle, combine the remaining ingredients; bring to a boil. Add the zucchini mixture; simmer for 10 minutes. Ladle hot into hot jars, leaving 1/4-in. headspace. Adjust lids. Process for 10 minutes in a boiling-water bath. **Yield:** 5 pints.

Raspberry Peach Jam

Patricia Larsen, Leslieville, Alberta

(PICTURED ON PAGE 65)

- **2-2/3 cups finely chopped peeled peaches**
- **1-1/2 cups crushed fresh *or* frozen raspberries**
- **3 cups sugar**
- **1-1/2 teaspoons lemon juice**

In a large kettle, combine all ingredients. Cook over low heat, stirring occasionally, until sugar is dissolved and mixture is bubbly, about 10 minutes. Bring to a full rolling boil; boil for 15 minutes, stirring constantly. Remove from the heat; skim off foam. Pour hot into hot jars, leaving 1/4-in. headspace. Adjust caps. Process for 15 minutes in a boiling-water bath. **Yield:** 5 half-pints.

Creamy Celery Seed Dressing

Patricia Dougherty, Dunkirk, New York

- **1/2 cup butter *or* margarine**
- **1 cup vinegar**
- **3 eggs, lightly beaten**
- **1-1/2 teaspoons celery seed**
- **1 teaspoon salt**
- **1/4 teaspoon white pepper**
- **2 cups mayonnaise**
- **3/4 cup prepared Italian salad dressing**
- **1/2 cup sugar**

In a saucepan, melt butter. Meanwhile, combine vinegar, eggs, celery seed, salt and pepper. Gradually add to butter, stirring constantly. Cook and stir over medium heat until slightly thickened, about 5 minutes. Remove from the heat and allow to cool. Mix in mayonnaise, Italian dressing and sugar. Cover and chill for at least 1 hour. Serve over coleslaw, vegetables or pasta. **Yield:** 4-1/2 cups.

Spiced Honey Butter

Mary Bates, Cleveland, Ohio

- **1/2 cup butter *or* margarine, room temperature**
- **1/4 cup honey**
- **1 teaspoon grated orange peel**
- **1/2 teaspoon ground cinnamon**

In a small bowl, combine all ingredients; mix well. Refrigerate, covered, until ready to serve. Recipe may be doubled or tripled and packed into small jars or plastic containers for gifts. **Yield:** 3/4 cup.

Delicious Chocolate Sauce

Dorothy Anderson, Ottawa, Kansas

- **1/2 cup butter *or* margarine**
- **4 squares (1 ounce *each*) unsweetened chocolate**
- **3 cups sugar**
- **1/2 teaspoon salt**
- **1 can (12 ounces) evaporated milk**
- **1 teaspoon vanilla extract**

In a double boiler over simmering water, melt butter and chocolate; stir in sugar and salt. Gradually add milk; mix well. Cover and simmer for 5-7 minutes or until sugar is dissolved. Stir in vanilla. Serve warm or at room temperature (sauce will thicken as it cools). Store in the refrigerator. **Yield:** 4 cups.

Buttermilk Salad Dressing

Mary Gehl, Victor, Montana

- **1 garlic clove, minced**
- **3/4 cup mayonnaise**
- **1/2 cup buttermilk**
- **1 teaspoon dried parsley flakes**
- **1/2 teaspoon dried minced onion**
- **1/4 to 1/2 teaspoon salt**
- **1/8 teaspoon pepper**

Combine all ingredients in a jar with a tight-fitting lid; shake until smooth. Chill for 30 minutes. **Yield:** 1-1/4 cups.

BLUE-RIBBON recipes are as close as the nearest county fair. Each of the recipes featured here has been awarded foremost honors at a different local competition. So you know they're guaranteed to be good. Why not try the pickles, apple pie, yeast bread and layered cake featured here soon?

TABLE TOPPERS. Clockwise from top right: **Bread 'n' Butter Pickles** (p. 82), **Golden Apple Pie** (p. 75), **Sesame Wheat Braids** (p. 51) and **Banana Coconut Cake** (p. 63).

Meals in Minutes

Give a whole new meaning to "fast food" with six complete meals that go from start to serving in under 30 minutes!

Flavorful Fare Features Fowl

A FEW YEARS AGO, Nancy Tafoya quickly came to depend upon fast and flavorful meals for her family. Explains the Fort Collins, Colorado cook, "Back then, I was not only working full-time, I was attending school two nights a week and volunteering time to the Girl Scouts!"

Understandably, that hectic schedule left Nancy little chance for leisurely cooking. So she put together this meal and soon was serving it weekly.

"I especially like the convenience of the chicken dish," she relates. "It takes just minutes to put together, and then I pop it in the oven. Before I know it, dinner is ready to be served.

"Feel free to do what I did when I came upon this recipe...play with the herb ingredients until they suit your family's taste. It's a basic recipe that can easily be altered for a little variety," Nancy notes.

"If your husband's like mine, you will likely be surprised at how much he enjoys the rice-and-peas side dish. Along with an easy-to-prepare vegetable—my family likes brussels sprouts—it's a wonderful way to complement the meal.

"Finally, you'll be delighted at how little time it takes you to whip up the macaroons. My family unanimously agrees these are one of the best desserts I offer. I hope your family likes them, too."

Not much has changed in the Tafoya home over the years...Nancy continues to set a fast pace, and this meal has remained a regular on her family's dinner table!

Italian Chicken

1/2 cup grated Parmesan cheese
2 tablespoons dried oregano
1 tablespoon minced fresh parsley
1/2 teaspoon garlic salt
1/4 teaspoon pepper
4 boneless skinless chicken breast halves
3 tablespoons butter *or* margarine, melted
Hot cooked brussels sprouts, optional

In a shallow bowl, combine Parmesan cheese, oregano, parsley, garlic salt and pepper. Dip chicken breasts in melted butter, then coat with Parmesan mixture. Place in a greased 9-in. square baking dish. Drizzle with any remaining butter. Bake, uncovered, at 425° for 15-20 minutes or until the chicken juices run clear. Serve with brussels sprouts if desired. **Yield:** 4 servings.

Easy Rice and Peas

2 cups water
1 tablespoon butter *or* margarine
1 teaspoon salt
2 cups uncooked instant rice
1 cup frozen peas

In a medium saucepan, bring water, butter and salt to a boil. Add rice and peas. Cover and remove from the heat. Let stand for 5-7 minutes or until all of the water is absorbed. **Yield:** 4 servings.

Coconut Macaroons

1/3 cup all-purpose flour
2-1/2 cups flaked coconut
1/8 teaspoon salt
2/3 cup sweetened condensed milk
1 teaspoon vanilla extract

In a bowl, combine flour, coconut and salt. Add milk and vanilla; mix well (batter will be stiff). Drop by tablespoonfuls 1 in. apart onto a greased baking sheet. Bake at 350° for 15-20 minutes or until golden brown. Remove to a wire rack to cool. **Yield:** 1-1/2 dozen.

A Delicious Way To Share the Day

NO MATTER how busy her family of five's day becomes, Ann Ingalls of Gladstone, Missouri strongly believes that *everyone* should sit down together at least once around a meal.

"It's an opportunity to share feelings and to tell about the happenings of the day," she explains.

With three active teenagers and her own job as a kindergarten teacher, though, attaining that goal isn't easy. So Ann regularly relies on this mouth-watering meal.

"My brother-in-law created this Breaded Pork Chops recipe several years ago, and he graciously shared it with me," Ann says. "Sometimes, for a change of pace, I'll make them 'Italian' by adding red sauce and more Parmesan cheese.

"While the chops are cooking, I begin the salad. It's one I concocted over 20 years ago when we had an abundant harvest in our big garden. Because my husband loves steamed vegetables, this one is a particular favorite of his.

"The fruit with cream is the last and fastest dish. It's such a treat that I frequently even make it for company.

"What I like most about this meal is that it allows me to provide my family with nutritious, flavorful foods even when time is short."

So gather your loved ones around the dinner table for this marvelous meal. It's the perfect way to end all of your hectic days.

Breaded Pork Chops

- **1 cup Italian-seasoned dry bread crumbs**
- **2 tablespoons grated Parmesan cheese**
- **1/3 cup bottled ranch salad dressing**
- **6 pork chops (1/2 inch thick)**

Combine bread crumbs and Parmesan cheese in a shallow dish. Place dressing in another shallow dish. Dip pork chops in dressing, then coat in crumb mixture. Place in an ungreased 13-in. x 9-in. x 2-in. baking pan. Bake, uncovered, at 375° for 25 minutes or until pork is no longer pink. **Yield:** 4-6 servings.

Green Bean Tomato Salad

- **1 pound fresh green beans, trimmed and halved**
- **2 medium tomatoes, sliced**
- **1 small onion, sliced**
- **1/3 cup olive *or* vegetable oil**
- **3 tablespoons red wine vinegar**
- **1 teaspoon Dijon mustard**
- **1/4 teaspoon salt**
- **1/8 teaspoon pepper**

Steam green beans for 6 minutes or just until crisp-tender. Immerse in cold water; drain. Place beans in the center of a large plate. Arrange tomato and onion slices around beans. Whisk together remaining ingredients and pour over vegetables. Chill until ready to serve. **Yield:** 4-6 servings.

RAVE REVIEWS. When making fresh fruit salads, mix in some frozen seedless grapes just before serving. Everyone will comment on this refreshing addition.

Fresh Fruit with Vanilla Cream

- **4 cups fresh fruit (raspberries, blueberries, strawberries *and/or* peaches)**
- **1 package (3 ounces) cream cheese, softened**
- **1/4 cup confectioners' sugar**
- **2 to 3 tablespoons light cream**
- **1/2 teaspoon vanilla extract**
- **1/4 teaspoon orange *or* almond extract**

Place fruit in a serving bowl or individual dessert dishes. Using a whisk, mix the cream cheese and confectioners' sugar. Gradually add cream and extracts; stir until smooth. Pour over fruit. **Yield:** 4-6 servings.

Welcoming Warm-Weather Menu

WITH TWO young boys, summer days—or any days throughout the year for that matter—are anything but lazy for Marilyn Dick. When that season's in full swing at her home in Centralia, Missouri, this menu's a once-a-week regular.

"The boys really keep my husband and me hopping as soon as the weather turns warm," states Marilyn. "Plus, I work as a dental assistant.

"I feel lucky to have three hungry men to feed—they don't turn down a thing I serve! I enjoy complex cooking when time allows. But, these days, time's at a premium. Because of that, I keep my eyes open for quick meals like this.

"I can put this flavorful meal in front of my family in less than 30 minutes," Marilyn adds. That dashing trait doesn't diminish how delightful the three dishes are when they're put together.

"The chicken kabobs are perfect warm-weather fare because they're done on the grill in just minutes...leaving the kitchen cool and comfortable.

"Crisp water chestnuts and cherry tomatoes add an interesting new twist to traditional spinach salad. And Strawberries with Lemon Cream is a light and sweet finale to the meal.

"Dyke and I often ask friends over for dinner on the spur of the moment," notes Marilyn. "Most everyone who's had this meal has loved it. Many have asked me for the recipes.

"People say they like the combination of tangy and sweet tastes. They also tell me they appreciate the fresh flavor and different textures."

If your days are as short on time as Marilyn's—or you simply want to spend as little time in the kitchen as possible—this meal's a satisfying way to express yourself!

Honey-Mustard Chicken Kabobs

4 boneless skinless chicken breast halves
4 small zucchini
4 small yellow squash
2 medium sweet red peppers
4 ounces small fresh mushrooms
Hot cooked rice, optional
GLAZE:
3/4 cup honey
1/2 cup prepared mustard
1/4 cup water
2 tablespoons soy sauce
2 tablespoons cornstarch
1 tablespoon cider vinegar

Cut chicken, squash and peppers into 1-in. pieces; thread along with mushrooms alternately onto skewers. In a saucepan, combine glaze ingredients; bring to a boil. Boil for 1 minute or until thickened. Grill the kabobs over hot coals for 10 minutes, turning often. Brush with glaze; grill 5 minutes more or until the chicken is no longer pink and vegetables are tender. Serve over rice if desired. **Yield:** 4 servings.

Tangy Spinach Salad

4 to 6 cups torn fresh spinach
1 cup sliced fresh mushrooms
1 can (8 ounces) sliced water chestnuts, drained
1 cup cherry tomatoes
1/4 cup bacon bits
2 green onions, sliced
DRESSING:
6 tablespoons vegetable oil
2 tablespoons vinegar
2 tablespoons sugar
1-1/2 teaspoons dry mustard
1/2 teaspoon celery seed
1/4 teaspoon salt
Pepper to taste

In a large bowl, toss the first six ingredients. In a jar with tight-fitting lid, combine all dressing ingredients and shake well. Pour over salad and toss. Serve immediately. **Yield:** 4 servings.

Strawberries with Lemon Cream

1 pint fresh strawberries, sliced
1 to 2 tablespoons sugar
1 cup whipped topping
2 cartons (8 ounces *each*) lemon yogurt
1 tablespoon grated lemon peel
Additional lemon peel and 4 whole strawberries for garnish, optional

Place sliced strawberries in a medium bowl; sprinkle with sugar. In another bowl, fold whipped topping into yogurt; add lemon peel. To serve, layer strawberries and the yogurt mixture into four parfait glasses. Top each with lemon peel and a strawberry if desired. **Yield:** 4 servings.

Mexican Food to Delight Your Brood

IT'S EASY for mother-of-three Laurie Smith Murphy of Foster, Rhode Island to describe her two top considerations in rating a recipe: Is it good...and is it *fast*?

"Both of our sons play hockey, our daughter's in gymnastics and soccer and one son's in a musical ensemble," she details. "In addition, all three take swimming lessons—and my husband also plays hockey and golf!

"Our family's hectic schedule of activities led me to put together this speedy standby supper, one that's on my menu several times a month.

"The main course, Beefy Spanish Rice, is something I adapted from a cooking show that I saw many years ago," she notes. "With rice and ground beef, it's a hearty meal that satisfies everyone at our table. Plus it can be altered to fit most any taste by adjusting how spicy and saucy you make it.

"I like varying things, too, by using ground turkey in place of the beef on occasion—or adding leftover spaghetti sauce instead of tomato paste.

"The salad is one I created...I do a lot of experimenting trying to get vegetables into everyone in my family! No one turns up their noses when they see this on the table.

"Finally, the dollop of yogurt adds just the right sweetness to top off my dessert. It's such a simple recipe that can be prepared throughout the year by using each season's finest fruit.

"It's amazing how preparation time for this meal works out so smoothly. While the main course is simmering, I'm able to toss together the salad and prepare the dessert fruit. Everything ends up being done at once."

Laurie assures that this meal will surely make life a whole lot easier in *your* home.

Beefy Spanish Rice

1 pound ground beef
1 medium onion, chopped
1 green pepper, chopped
1 garlic clove, minced
1 can (14-1/2 ounces) stewed tomatoes
1-1/2 cups water
1 cup uncooked long grain rice
1 teaspoon salt
1/2 to 1 teaspoon chili powder
1/2 teaspoon dried thyme
1/4 teaspoon dried basil
1/4 teaspoon pepper
2 tablespoons tomato paste
French bread

In a large skillet, cook ground beef, onion, green pepper and garlic until the meat is browned; drain. Stir in the next eight ingredients; bring to a boil. Reduce heat; cover and simmer for 20 minutes or until the rice is tender. Stir in tomato paste and heat through. Serve with French bread. **Yield:** 4-6 servings.

Crispy Vegetable Salad

1 bunch leaf lettuce, torn
1 cucumber, sliced
2 cups broccoli florets
1 cup cauliflowerets
1 large tomato, cut into wedges
1 large carrot, shredded
1 bottle (8 ounces) ranch salad dressing
2 tablespoons grated Parmesan cheese
1/2 teaspoon lemon pepper

In a large salad bowl, combine lettuce, cucumber, broccoli, cauliflower, tomato and carrot. In a small bowl, combine dressing, Parmesan cheese and lemon pepper; mix well. Serve with salad. **Yield:** 4-6 servings.

Quick Fruit Cup

2 unpeeled red apples, cut into chunks
1 orange, peeled and sectioned
1 banana, peeled and sliced
2 kiwifruit, peeled and sliced
1 carton (8 ounces) lemon *or* vanilla yogurt
Fresh mint, optional

Combine all fruit in a medium bowl; toss gently. Spoon into individual serving bowls; top with a dollop of yogurt. Garnish with mint if desired. **Yield:** 4-6 servings.

Down-Home Dinner's Easy as Pie

YES...she *is* retired. But, these days, Laura Odell of Eden, North Carolina needs meals that can be prepared in less than 30 minutes as much as she ever has!

"Between hobbies and my family, I don't have much time on my hands," she cheerfully relates. "I love to cross-stitch, for example.

"And my husband, Roy, and I have three grown sons and six grandchildren, all of them within a few miles. So we generally have plenty of company for supper. Add in housework, and you can see why I rely on this quick-and-easy menu at least once a month.

"The Easy Potpie really merits its name," remarks Laura. "Just about as fast as you can open a couple of cans and brown a crust, it's done.

"Loaded with chicken or turkey and vegetables, this creamy, country-style dish is a favorite in our home. We especially enjoy this casserole in winter when it comes out of the oven so hearty and steaming hot.

"While the potpie's baking, I toss together the salad ingredients. To make preparation even faster, I usually have the vegetables pre-sliced and ready to go anytime.

"Lemon Cheese Pie is a cool, refreshing treat that can be made in a jiffy. Or prepare it ahead of time and freeze for a fast dessert."

Sound good to you? Then why not find out firsthand tonight by serving Laura's quick-and-easy specialty? *Your* family will likely make fast work of it as well!

Easy Potpie

3 cups cubed cooked chicken *or* turkey
1 can (16 ounces) mixed vegetables, drained *or* 2 cups frozen mixed vegetables, thawed
1 can (10-3/4 ounces) condensed cream of celery soup, undiluted
1/4 cup chopped onion
2 tablespoons all-purpose flour
2 cups chicken broth
1/4 teaspoon dried rosemary, crushed
1/4 teaspoon pepper

BISCUIT TOPPING:
1 cup self-rising flour*
1/2 teaspoon pepper *or* lemon pepper
1 cup buttermilk
1/2 cup butter *or* margarine, melted

In a saucepan, combine chicken, vegetables, soup, onion and flour; mix well. Stir in broth, rosemary and pepper; bring to a boil over medium heat, stirring occasionally. Boil for 1 minute. Pour into an ungreased shallow 2-1/2-qt. baking dish. For topping, combine the flour and pepper in a bowl. Stir in buttermilk and butter just until moistened. Spoon over chicken mixture. Bake at 425° for 25 minutes or until golden brown. **Yield:** 6 servings. ***Editor's Note:** As a substitute for self-rising flour, place 1-1/2 teaspoons baking powder and 1/2 teaspoon salt in a measuring cup. Add enough all-purpose flour to equal 1 cup.

Tossed Salad

5 cups torn mixed greens
1 medium tomato, diced
1 cup sliced radishes
1 cup sliced red onion
1/4 cup bacon bits
2/3 cup vegetable oil
1/3 cup vinegar
1-1/4 teaspoons salt
1/2 teaspoon pepper

In a salad bowl, toss first five ingredients. In a jar with tight-fitting lid, shake the remaining ingredients until blended. Pour over salad and toss. Serve immediately. **Yield:** 6 servings.

Lemon Cheese Pie

1 package (8 ounces) cream cheese, softened
2 cups cold milk, *divided*
1 package (3.4 ounces) instant lemon pudding mix
1/2 teaspoon grated lemon peel
1 graham cracker crust (9 inches)

In a mixing bowl, beat cream cheese until smooth. Gradually add 1/2 cup milk. Sprinkle pudding mix over all. Gradually add remaining milk and lemon peel; beat until thickened, about 5 minutes. Pour into the crust. Freeze until ready to serve. **Yield:** 6-8 servings.

A Classic Family Favorite

IF you're pressed for time to prepare a filling complete meal for your family, you'll likely give Linda Young of Longmont, Colorado an A+ for her appetizing solution.

"My husband, Allan, and I have five children," shares Linda. "I home-school the youngest three, full hours Monday through Friday. Needless to say, I'm not lacking for 'assignments' to keep me busy!

"In addition, Allan's work schedule often can be unpredictable. So it's nice to have at-hand recipes like these that go from start to serving in no time.

"What makes the Pigs in a Blanket such a breeze are the refrigerated crescent rolls you wrap the hot dogs in," she notes. "The kids especially look forward to them as a special lunch-time treat. And I've yet to meet an adult who can eat just one!

"With just a handful of ingredients, the coleslaw couldn't be easier. It really lives up to its name. I have been known to double—and sometimes triple—the recipe for company and potluck suppers. It's always met with rave reviews.

"For a special beverage, I like to perk up ordinary apple juice with brown sugar and spices. It warms us up on cool fall days.

"Pumpkin Ice Cream is as simple as opening a can, stirring and freezing. Plus, if you're like me and looking for a good way of using up your home-grown pumpkins, feel free to substitute fresh-picked for canned."

Linda's cooking philosophy? "I enjoy cooking and feel I can do more of it if what I'm making is convenient and speedy." That certainly describes this meal. So does *delicious*!

Pigs in a Blanket

1 tube (8 ounces) refrigerated crescent rolls
8 hot dogs
1 egg, beaten
1 tablespoon water
Caraway seed
Carrots and celery sticks, optional

Separate crescent dough into triangles. Place hot dogs at wide end of triangles and roll up. Place on an ungreased baking sheet. Combine egg and water; brush over rolls. Sprinkle with caraway and press lightly into rolls. Bake at 375° for 12-15 minutes or until golden. Serve with carrots and celery if desired. **Yield:** 4 servings.

Quick Coleslaw

3 cups chopped cabbage
2 green onions, chopped
1 medium carrot, shredded
1/2 cup mayonnaise
1 tablespoon sugar
1 teaspoon celery seed
1/2 teaspoon dry mustard
1/4 teaspoon salt

In a medium bowl, combine cabbage, onions and carrot. Combine remaining ingredients; stir into vegetables. Chill until ready to serve. **Yield:** 4 servings.

Pumpkin Ice Cream

1 cup canned *or* cooked pumpkin
1/4 teaspoon pumpkin pie spice
1 quart vanilla ice cream, softened
Gingersnaps, optional

In a medium bowl, mix the pumpkin and pie spice until well blended. Stir in ice cream. Freeze until ready to serve. Garnish with gingersnaps if desired. **Yield:** 4-6 servings.

Harvest Apple Drink

1 can (46 ounces) apple juice
1/3 cup packed brown sugar
2 cinnamon sticks
6 whole cloves

In a medium saucepan, bring all ingredients to a boil. Reduce heat; simmer for 15 minutes. Strain. Serve warm. **Yield:** 4-6 servings.

YOU CAN dish out a hearty, country-style dinner for two without having to prepare a lot of food, as these recipes prove. Served with mashed potatoes, **Salisbury Steak** tastes just like Mom's old-fashioned recipe. **Lemon-Basil Carrots** is a satisfying side dish that will draw lots of compliments, and **Creamed Spinach Casserole** is a great way to work healthy vegetables into any menu. And for a perfect-sized dessert, try moist and delicious **Fruit Cocktail Cake**.

DOWN-HOME DINNER. Pictured are: Salisbury Steak, Lemon-Basil Carrots, Creamed Spinach Casserole and Fruit Cocktail Cake (all recipes on page 91).

COOKING FOR TWO

Preparing small-serving suppers is a snap with these savory main meals, side dishes and desserts.

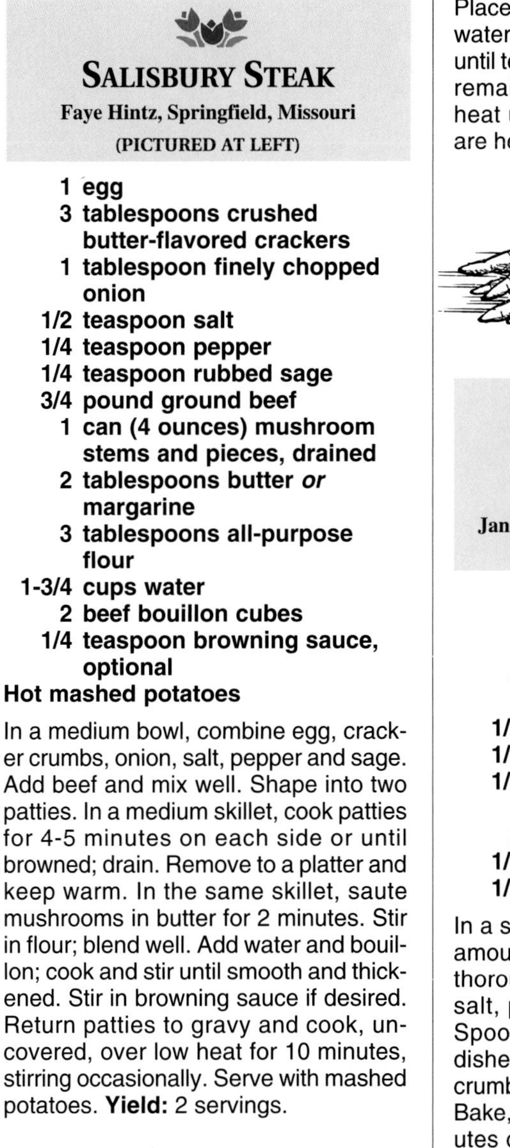

SALISBURY STEAK

Faye Hintz, Springfield, Missouri

(PICTURED AT LEFT)

1 egg
3 tablespoons crushed butter-flavored crackers
1 tablespoon finely chopped onion
1/2 teaspoon salt
1/4 teaspoon pepper
1/4 teaspoon rubbed sage
3/4 pound ground beef
1 can (4 ounces) mushroom stems and pieces, drained
2 tablespoons butter *or* margarine
3 tablespoons all-purpose flour
1-3/4 cups water
2 beef bouillon cubes
1/4 teaspoon browning sauce, optional
Hot mashed potatoes

In a medium bowl, combine egg, cracker crumbs, onion, salt, pepper and sage. Add beef and mix well. Shape into two patties. In a medium skillet, cook patties for 4-5 minutes on each side or until browned; drain. Remove to a platter and keep warm. In the same skillet, saute mushrooms in butter for 2 minutes. Stir in flour; blend well. Add water and bouillon; cook and stir until smooth and thickened. Stir in browning sauce if desired. Return patties to gravy and cook, uncovered, over low heat for 10 minutes, stirring occasionally. Serve with mashed potatoes. **Yield:** 2 servings.

LEMON-BASIL CARROTS

Donna Smith, Palisade, Colorado

(PICTURED AT LEFT)

4 medium carrots, cut into 1-1/2-inch pieces
1 tablespoon butter *or* margarine
1 to 2 teaspoons lemon juice
1/4 teaspoon dried basil
1/8 teaspoon garlic salt
Dash pepper

Place carrots in a small saucepan; add water to cover. Cook for 10 minutes or until tender; drain and return to pan. Add remaining ingredients. Cook over low heat until butter is melted and carrots are heated through. **Yield:** 2 servings.

CREAMED SPINACH CASSEROLE

Jane Everett, Pinehurst, North Carolina

(PICTURED AT LEFT)

1 package (10 ounces) frozen chopped spinach
5 tablespoons butter *or* margarine, *divided*
1/2 teaspoon salt
1/4 teaspoon pepper
1/2 cup shredded cheddar cheese
2 eggs, beaten
1/2 cup milk
1/2 cup soft bread crumbs

In a saucepan, cook spinach in a small amount of water for 2-3 minutes; drain thoroughly. Add 4 tablespoons butter, salt, pepper, cheese, eggs and milk. Spoon into two greased 8-oz. baking dishes. Melt the remaining butter; add crumbs. Sprinkle over spinach mixture. Bake, uncovered, at 350° for 20-25 minutes or until almost set. **Yield:** 2 servings. **Editor's Note:** A shallow 1-qt. baking dish can be used instead of two 8-oz. dishes. Bake for 25-30 minutes.

FRUIT COCKTAIL CAKE

Mrs. C. Cunningham, Astoria, New York

(PICTURED AT LEFT)

1 cup all-purpose flour
2/3 cup sugar
1/2 cup chopped walnuts *or* pecans
1/2 cup golden raisins
1 teaspoon baking soda
1/2 teaspoon ground cinnamon
1/4 teaspoon salt
1 egg
1 can (8-3/4 ounces) fruit cocktail, undrained
Confectioners' sugar, optional
BUTTER SAUCE:
1/3 cup sugar
1/4 cup butter *or* margarine
1/4 cup evaporated milk *or* half-and-half cream
1/4 teaspoon vanilla extract

In a medium bowl, combine flour, sugar, nuts, raisins, baking soda, cinnamon and salt. In a small bowl, beat egg; add fruit cocktail. Stir into dry ingredients just until moistened. Pour into a greased and floured 8-in. round baking pan. Bake at 325° for 55-60 minutes or until cake tests done. Cool in pan for 5 minutes before removing to a wire rack. Cool completely. Dust with confectioners' sugar if desired. For sauce, combine sugar, butter and milk in a small saucepan; bring to a boil. Cook and stir for 3 minutes. Remove from the heat; stir in vanilla. Serve warm over the cake. Refrigerate leftover sauce. **Yield:** 4 servings.

SOUTHWESTERN GRILLED LAMB

Margaret Pache, Mesa, Arizona

1 cup salsa
1/2 cup chopped onion
1/4 cup molasses
1/4 cup fresh lime juice (about 2 limes)
1/4 cup chicken broth
2 garlic cloves, minced
1 to 3 tablespoons chopped seeded jalapeno peppers
2 teaspoons sugar
4 lamb chops (1 inch thick)
Sour cream

In a saucepan, combine the first eight ingredients. Simmer, uncovered, for 15-20 minutes. Meanwhile, grill lamb chops, turning once, over medium coals for 10-14 minutes for rare, 14-16 minutes for medium or 16-20 minutes for well-done. Brush with sauce during the last few minutes of grilling. Serve with sour cream. **Yield:** 2 servings.

JUST BECAUSE you're cooking for two doesn't mean you have to curb your creativity. **Pork Chop Dinner for Two** is an all-in-one entree that can easily be adjusted to serve a larger crowd. Lots of sausage and produce...and minimal cooking time...make **Sausage and Vegetable Skillet** an attractive addition to your recipe files. **Mother's Potato Soup** is a terrific "grand-opener" to any supper. Or serve it alone as a light lunch. After one taste of **Baked Applesauce**, you'll never want to eat the store-bought variety again.

MEATY MEALS. Clockwise from top: Sausage and Vegetable Skillet, Mother's Potato Soup, Pork Chop Dinner for Two and Baked Applesauce (all recipes on page 93).

Mother's Potato Soup

Louella Kightlinger, Erie, Pennsylvania

(PICTURED AT LEFT)

RIVELS:
1 egg white
Pinch salt
6 tablespoons all-purpose flour
SOUP:
1-1/2 cups cubed peeled potatoes (3/4-inch pieces)
1 large carrot, sliced
1/2 cup chopped onion
1/2 teaspoon salt
1/8 teaspoon pepper
1-1/2 cups water
1 egg yolk
1/2 cup milk
Minced fresh parsley

In a small bowl, beat egg white lightly with a fork. Stir in salt and flour (mixture will be slightly dry); set aside. In a 1-1/2-qt. saucepan, combine potatoes, carrot, onion, salt, pepper and water. Cover, but keep the lid ajar, and bring to a boil; cook for 3 minutes. With a knife, cut rivels into soup. Cook, partially covered, for 10 minutes. Beat egg yolk and milk; add to the soup. Bring to a boil. Remove from the heat and sprinkle with parsley. Serve immediately. **Yield:** 2 servings.

Sausage and Vegetable Skillet

Ruby Williams, Bogalusa, Louisiana

(PICTURED AT LEFT)

1/2 pound fresh Italian sausage, cut into 1/2-inch slices
1 tablespoon cooking oil
1 cup cubed yellow summer squash (3/4-inch pieces)
1/2 cup chopped green onions
2 garlic cloves, minced
1-1/2 cups chopped fresh tomatoes
2 teaspoons Worcestershire sauce
1/8 teaspoon cayenne pepper

In a medium skillet, cook sausage in oil over medium heat until no longer pink; drain. Add squash, onions and garlic; cook for 2 minutes. Stir in tomatoes, Worcestershire sauce and cayenne pepper; heat through. **Yield:** 2 servings.

Pork Chop Dinner For Two

Shirley Lazor, Colorado Springs, Colorado

(PICTURED AT LEFT)

2 pork loin chops (3/4 inch thick)
1 tablespoon cooking oil
2 medium potatoes, peeled and sliced
1 medium onion, sliced
1 medium carrot, sliced
1 tablespoon butter *or* margarine
1/2 teaspoon salt
1/4 teaspoon pepper

In a skillet, brown the pork chops in oil. Place in a greased 8-in. square baking pan. Layer potatoes, onion and carrot over chops. Dot with butter. Sprinkle with salt and pepper. Cover and bake at 350° for 55-60 minutes or until pork chops are done. **Yield:** 2 servings.

Baked Applesauce

Mary Mootz, Cincinnati, Ohio

(PICTURED AT LEFT)

2 large tart apples, peeled and sliced
3 tablespoons sugar
1/4 to 1/2 teaspoon ground cinnamon
1/4 teaspoon vanilla extract

Place apples in a greased 1-qt. baking dish. In a small bowl, combine sugar, cinnamon and vanilla; mix well. Sprinkle over apples. Cover and bake at 350° for 40-45 minutes or until apples are tender. Uncover and mash with a fork. Serve warm. **Yield:** 2 servings.

Speedy Steak Sandwiches

Ruth Page, Hillsborough, North Carolina

4 slices French bread (3/4 inch thick)
Butter *or* margarine, softened
Prepared mustard
1/2 pound uncooked lean ground beef
1/4 cup milk
1 tablespoon minced onion
1 tablespoon steak sauce
1/2 teaspoon garlic salt
1/4 teaspoon pepper

In a broiler, toast one side of the bread. Spread untoasted sides with butter and mustard. In a small bowl, combine remaining ingredients; spread evenly over buttered side of bread. Broil 6 in. from the heat for 5-7 minutes or until beef reaches desired doneness. **Yield:** 2 servings.

Macaroni and Cheese

Betty Allen, East Point, Georgia

1-1/2 cups cooked elbow macaroni
1 cup (4 ounces) shredded sharp cheddar cheese
1/2 cup milk
1 egg, lightly beaten
1/2 teaspoon salt
1 tablespoon butter *or* margarine

Combine macaroni, cheese, milk, egg and salt; mix well. Pour into a greased 1-qt. shallow baking dish; dot with butter. Bake, uncovered, at 350° for 30-35 minutes or until a knife inserted in the center comes out clean. **Yield:** 2 servings.

Peanut Butter Parfaits

Mildred Sherrer, Bay City, Texas

1/2 cup packed light brown sugar
3 tablespoons milk
2 tablespoons light corn syrup
2 teaspoons butter *or* margarine
2 tablespoons creamy peanut butter
Vanilla ice cream
1/4 cup peanuts

In a saucepan, combine brown sugar, milk, corn syrup and butter. Cook and stir over medium heat until sugar is dissolved and mixture is smooth, about 4 minutes. Remove from the heat; stir in peanut butter until smooth. Cool to room temperature. Spoon half into two parfait glasses; top with ice cream. Repeat layers. Sprinkle with peanuts. **Yield:** 2 servings.

Individual Meat Loaves

Kim McMurl, Fargo, North Dakota

1 egg
3 tablespoons milk
1/2 teaspoon Worcestershire sauce
1/2 teaspoon onion salt
1/4 teaspoon pepper
1/4 cup cracker crumbs
1/2 pound uncooked ground pork
1/3 cup packed brown sugar
1/4 cup ketchup
3 tablespoons vinegar
1/2 teaspoon prepared mustard

In a medium bowl, beat egg; add milk, Worcestershire sauce, onion salt, pepper and crumbs. Add the pork and mix well. Shape into two 5-in. x 2-1/2-in. loaves; place in a small baking pan. Combine remaining ingredients; pour over loaves. Bake, uncovered, at 325° for 1 hour or until no longer pink. **Yield:** 2 servings.

THE TWO of you don't need to be celebrating a special occasion to enjoy these delicious dishes. Dress up your weekday dinner table with juicy **Cornish Hens with Rice Dressing** or easy-to-prepare **Sausage-Stuffed Squash.** No matter what main dish you serve, **Mother's Sweet Pea Salad** is an ideal accompaniment. And you'll both enjoy a tasty treat like **Cinnamon Apple Dumplings**.

PERFECTLY PORTIONED. Clockwise from bottom: Cornish Hens with Rice Dressing, Mother's Sweet Pea Salad, Cinnamon Apple Dumplings and Sausage-Stuffed Squash (all recipes on page 95).

Cornish Hens with Rice Dressing

Geraldine Grisdale, Mt. Pleasant, Michigan

(PICTURED AT LEFT)

1-1/3 cups chicken broth
1/2 cup uncooked long grain rice
1/2 cup sliced fresh mushrooms
1/4 cup chopped celery
2 tablespoons chopped onion
1/2 teaspoon dried marjoram, *divided*
1/2 teaspoon salt, *divided*
2 Cornish hens (1 to 1-1/2 pounds *each*)
1 tablespoon vegetable oil
Pepper to taste

In an ungreased 9-in. square baking dish, combine broth, rice, mushrooms, celery, onion, 1/4 teaspoon marjoram and 1/4 teaspoon salt. Place hens on rice mixture and brush with oil. Sprinkle with pepper and remaining marjoram and salt. Cover and bake at 350° for 1 hour. Uncover and bake 25-35 minutes longer or until juices run clear. **Yield:** 2 servings.

Cinnamon Apple Dumplings

Marie Hattrup, The Dalles, Oregon

(PICTURED AT LEFT)

1 cup all-purpose flour
1/4 teaspoon salt
1/3 cup shortening
3 tablespoons ice water
2 medium baking apples
3 tablespoons sugar
1/2 teaspoon ground cinnamon
Half-and-half cream
SAUCE:
1/3 cup sugar
2 tablespoons red-hot candies *or* 1/4 teaspoon ground cinnamon
1/2 teaspoon cornstarch
2/3 cup water
1 tablespoon butter *or* margarine
Additional half-and-half cream, optional

In a medium bowl, combine flour and salt. Cut in shortening until mixture resembles coarse crumbs. With a fork, stir in water until dough forms a ball. Roll out on a floured surface to a 14-in. x 7-in. rectangle; cut pastry in half. Peel and core apples; place one on each square of pastry. Combine sugar and cinnamon; spoon into apples. Moisten edges of pastry and gather around apples; pinch and seal. Place dumplings in an ungreased 9-in. x 5-in. loaf pan or a shallow 1-1/2-qt. baking dish. Brush with cream. In a small saucepan, combine the first five sauce ingredients; bring to a boil over medium-low heat, stirring frequently. Boil for 3 minutes. Pour between dumplings. Bake at 400° for 35-45 minutes or until the pastry is golden brown and the apples are tender. Serve warm with cream if desired. **Yield:** 2 servings.

Mother's Sweet Pea Salad

Nellie Dulin, Concord, North Carolina

(PICTURED AT LEFT)

1/3 cup mayonnaise
1/4 teaspoon dry mustard
1/4 teaspoon sugar
1/4 teaspoon salt
Dash pepper
1 cup diced cooked salad potatoes
1 cup frozen peas, thawed
1/2 cup chopped sweet pickles
1 hard-cooked egg, chopped
1 cup shredded lettuce

In a bowl, combine mayonnaise, mustard, sugar, salt and pepper. Add potatoes, peas, pickles and egg; mix gently. Chill. Serve over lettuce. **Yield:** 2 servings.

Sausage-Stuffed Squash

Linda Gaido, New Brighton, Pennsylvania

(PICTURED AT LEFT)

1 acorn squash (2 to 2-1/2 pounds)
Salt and pepper to taste
12 ounces bulk pork sausage
1 egg
2 tablespoons brown sugar
2 garlic cloves, minced
1/3 cup dry bread crumbs

Cut squash in half lengthwise; remove seeds. Sprinkle with salt and pepper. In a small bowl, combine the sausage, egg, brown sugar, garlic and bread crumbs; mix well. Spoon into squash halves; place in a small shallow baking dish. Bake, uncovered, at 350° for 1-1/2 hours or until the squash is tender. **Yield:** 2 servings.

Saucy Stuffed Zucchini

Barbara Edgington, Frankfort, Ohio

3 to 4 medium zucchini (1-3/4 to 2 pounds)
12 ounces Italian sausage, browned and drained
1/2 cup chopped sweet red pepper
1/2 cup chopped green pepper
2 tablespoons chopped onion
1-1/2 teaspoons Italian seasoning
1 can (8 ounces) tomato sauce
2 tablespoons butter *or* margarine
2 tablespoons all-purpose flour
1/4 teaspoon salt
1-1/4 cups milk
1/2 cup grated Parmesan cheese, *divided*
1 teaspoon Dijon mustard

Drop whole zucchini into boiling water; boil for 5 minutes. Drain. Rinse under cold water; cool. Cut in half lengthwise; scoop out pulp, leaving a 1/4-in. shell. Place pulp in a saucepan; add sausage, peppers, onion, Italian seasoning and tomato sauce. Bring to a boil. Reduce heat; cover and simmer for 5 minutes. Place zucchini shells in a greased 13-in. x 9-in. x 2-in. baking dish. Spoon filling into shells. In a saucepan, melt butter; add flour and salt. Stir until a smooth paste forms. Gradually add milk; bring to a boil, stirring constantly. Boil 2 minutes. Remove from the heat. Add 1/4 cup of Parmesan cheese and the mustard; mix well. Pour over zucchini. Sprinkle with remaining Parmesan. Bake, uncovered, at 350° for 25-30 minutes or until heated through. **Yield:** 3-4 servings.

Tuna Egg Salad

Daisy Brocato, Raceland, Louisiana

✓ This tasty dish uses less sugar, salt and fat. Recipe includes *Diabetic Exchanges*.

1 hard-cooked egg, chopped
1 can (3 ounces) tuna in spring water, drained and flaked
1/4 cup chopped celery
1/4 cup chopped sweet pickles
3 tablespoons mayonnaise
2 teaspoons prepared mustard

Combine all ingredients in a small bowl and mix well. Spoon into tomatoes, use as a sandwich filling or serve with crackers. **Yield:** 3 servings (1-1/4 cups). **Diabetic Exchanges:** One serving (prepared with light tuna and mayonnaise) equals 1-1/2 meat, 1 vegetable; also, 129 calories, 396 mg sodium, 86 mg cholesterol, 7 gm carbohydrate, 11 gm protein, 6 gm fat.

A MEAL FROM MOM. Clockwise from top right: Hearty Corn Chowder, No-Fuss Chicken, Apple Lettuce Salad and Whole Wheat Bran Bread (all recipes on page 97).

Memorable Meals

With these eight complete meals, it's easy to make some mouth-watering memories of your own.

Winter Menu Warms The Heart

"WHEN the winter winds blow here in the Midwest, this hearty meal warms you right to the toes," says Mark Twiest of Allendale, Michigan.

"Just remembering this special meal prepared by my mother-in-law, Mae Eaton, makes me feel warm all over. Perhaps that's because she cooks with her loved ones in mind.

"My mother-in-law devised her No-Fuss Chicken when her children were growing up and schedules were hectic. It was a favorite Sunday dish because it could be cooking while the family was at church.

"These days, she invites us to her house on our birthdays to celebrate with this fried chicken dinner. With its creamy sauce, I think you'll agree it's a finger-licking-good entree.

"Everyone in my wife's family is a corn lover, so her mom created this wonderful Hearty Corn Chowder to satisfy their appetites. Loaded with bacon, sausage and potatoes, it really rounds out the menu. I've also served it alone for a meal in itself.

"Nothing can beat the fresh-from-the-oven goodness of homemade bread, and Mom's original Whole Wheat Bran Bread is no exception. It's a winning combination of everyday ingredients. Around here, we gobble up one loaf right away. I freeze the other loaf to enjoy later.

"Mom tells me she could get her children to eat lots of lettuce when it was combined with apples, nuts and mayonnaise. This refreshing Apple Lettuce Salad still appeals to the kid in all of us. It nicely complements the rich, hearty chicken. I think you'll agree the surprisingly simple dressing adds just the right amount of sweetness.

"Mom's an extraordinary cook who uses her talents to serve others. She makes an unending supply of cookies for her grandchildren, she's in charge of church suppers, and she volunteers for an organization that teaches young mothers how to cook."

Why not welcome your family in from the cold with this down-home dinner?

No-Fuss Chicken

2/3 cup all-purpose flour
1 teaspoon dried sage
1 teaspoon dried basil
1 teaspoon seasoned salt
1 broiler/fryer chicken (2-1/2 to 3 pounds), cut up
1/4 cup butter *or* margarine
2 cups chicken broth

In a shallow bowl, combine flour, sage, basil and seasoned salt; coat chicken. Reserve remaining flour mixture. In a large skillet, melt butter; brown chicken on all sides. Transfer to a slow cooker. Add 1/4 cup reserved flour mixture to the skillet (discarding the rest); stir until smooth. When mixture begins to bubble, stir in chicken broth and bring to a boil; boil for 1 minute. Pour over chicken. Cover and cook on high for 2 to 2-1/2 hours or until chicken juices run clear. **Yield:** 4 servings.

Hearty Corn Chowder

1/2 pound sliced bacon
1 cup chopped celery
1/2 cup chopped onion
2 cups diced peeled potatoes
1 cup water
2 cups frozen corn
1 can (14-3/4 ounces) cream-style corn
1 can (12 ounces) evaporated milk
6 ounces smoked sausage links, cut into 1/4-inch slices
1 teaspoon dill weed

In a large saucepan, cook the bacon until crisp. Remove to paper towels; crumble and set aside. Drain all but 2 tablespoons of the drippings. Saute celery and onion in drippings until onion is lightly browned. Add potatoes and water. Cover and cook over medium heat for 10 minutes. Stir in corn, milk, sausage, dill and bacon. Cook until the potatoes are tender, about 30 minutes. **Yield:** 4-6 servings (1-1/2 quarts).

Whole Wheat Bran Bread

1-1/2 cups water, *divided*
3/4 cup milk
1 cup all-bran cereal
6 tablespoons butter *or* margarine
1/3 cup dark molasses
3 tablespoons sugar
4 teaspoons salt
2 packages (1/4 ounce *each*) active dry yeast
2 cups whole wheat flour
3-1/4 to 3-3/4 cups all-purpose flour

In a saucepan, combine 1 cup water and milk; bring to a boil. Remove from the heat; stir in the cereal, butter, molasses, sugar and salt. Cool to lukewarm. Heat remaining water to 110°-115°; pour into a large mixing bowl. Sprinkle with yeast; stir until dissolved. Add cereal mixture and whole wheat flour; beat well. Add enough all-purpose flour to make a stiff dough. Turn out onto a floured surface; knead until smooth and elastic, about 6-8 minutes. Place in a greased bowl, turning once to grease top. Cover and let rise in a warm place until doubled, about 1 hour. Punch the dough down. Shape into two loaves and place in greased 8-in. x 4-in. x 2-in. loaf pans. Cover and let rise until doubled, about 1 hour. Bake at 400° for 25-30 minutes. **Yield:** 2 loaves. **If Cooking for Two:** Wrap one loaf in heavy-duty aluminum foil and freeze to enjoy later.

Apple Lettuce Salad

3 cups torn lettuce
2 unpeeled red apples, diced
1/2 cup diced celery
1/4 cup raisins
1/4 cup chopped walnuts
DRESSING:
1/2 cup mayonnaise *or* salad dressing
2 tablespoons pineapple juice
1 tablespoon sugar

In a large salad bowl, toss lettuce, apples, celery, raisins and walnuts. In a small bowl or jar with a tight-fitting lid, combine dressing ingredients; mix or shake until well blended. Pour over salad and toss. Serve immediately. **Yield:** 4-6 servings.

APPEALING ASSORTMENT. Clockwise from bottom: Baked Ham and Apples, Skillet Herb Bread, Holiday Gumdrop Cookies and Minty Peas and Onions (all recipes on page 99).

Mothers Made Magic In the Kitchen

HERE four cooks share their most treasured recipes from their mothers. Make them alone or serve them together as they're shown at left.

"When Mother wanted to serve ham, she went to the smokehouse, took a whole ham down from the rafters and sliced off as much as we needed," recalls Marjorie Schmidt of St. Marys, Ohio. "Nowadays, folks can run to their local butcher.

"Baked Ham and Apples is great if you use real smoked ham with no water added. When Mother prepared it this way, the flavor was especially sweet and buttery, and the apples were delicious."

Skillet Herb Bread comes from Shirley Smith. She explains from her Yorba Linda, California home, "We had a lot of family get-togethers when I was growing up. My grandmother, aunts and mom were all good cooks, and each had her own specialty when it came to bread.

"But Mom's was my favorite—she started making it 40 years ago. The flavors call to mind the taste of cornbread stuffing. I like to serve it with a number of my family's most-requested main dishes."

Says Santa D'Addario from her Brooklyn, New York home, "When my mother was in a hurry and needed a quick side dish, she could rely on Minty Peas and Onions. It's a delightfully delicious way to dress up ordinary frozen peas.

"Besides being easy to prepare, this dish was loved by everyone in our family. It was handed down to my mother by my grandmother."

Letah Chilston of Riverton, Wyoming proves that cookies always make a fantastic dessert. "Whenever I make this recipe, I feel like I'm keeping my mother's festive spirit alive," she explains.

"Holiday Gumdrop Cookies were her special treat each year at Christmas. In addition, these cookies are great for keeping children busy—they can cut up the gumdrops and eat all the black ones (they turn the dough gray)."

Good cooking is just moments away with these wonderful recipes!

Baked Ham and Apples

1 slice center-cut smoked ham (1 inch thick and 2 to 2-1/2 pounds)
2 teaspoons dry mustard
1/2 cup packed brown sugar
3 medium baking apples
2 tablespoons butter *or* margarine
Pepper to taste

Place ham in an ungreased 13-in. x 9-in. x 2-in. baking dish. Rub with mustard and sprinkle with brown sugar. Core apples and cut into 3/4-in. slices; arrange in a single layer over ham. Dot with butter and sprinkle with pepper. Cover and bake at 400° for 15 minutes. Reduce heat to 325°; bake for 45 minutes. Uncover and bake 15 minutes longer or until apples are tender. **Yield:** 6-8 servings.

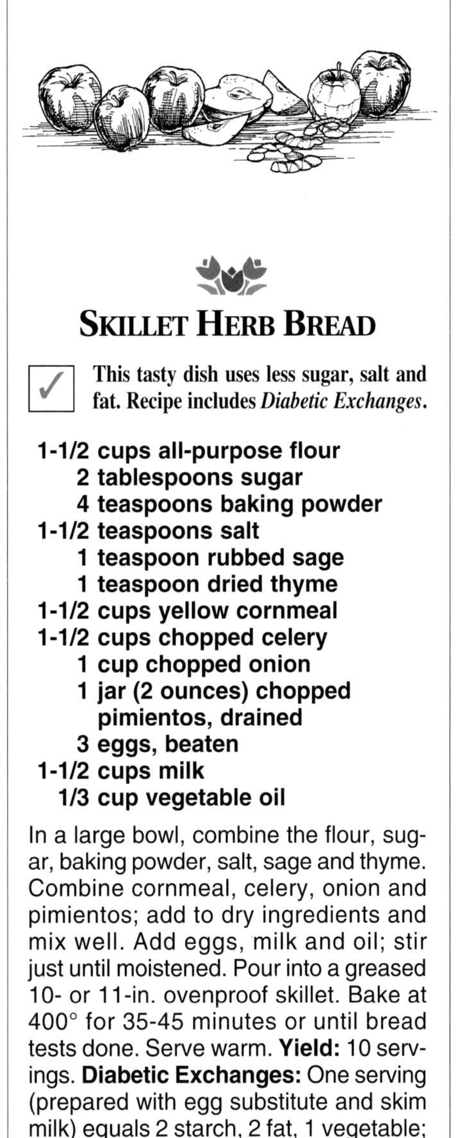

Skillet Herb Bread

✓ This tasty dish uses less sugar, salt and fat. Recipe includes *Diabetic Exchanges.*

1-1/2 cups all-purpose flour
2 tablespoons sugar
4 teaspoons baking powder
1-1/2 teaspoons salt
1 teaspoon rubbed sage
1 teaspoon dried thyme
1-1/2 cups yellow cornmeal
1-1/2 cups chopped celery
1 cup chopped onion
1 jar (2 ounces) chopped pimientos, drained
3 eggs, beaten
1-1/2 cups milk
1/3 cup vegetable oil

In a large bowl, combine the flour, sugar, baking powder, salt, sage and thyme. Combine cornmeal, celery, onion and pimientos; add to dry ingredients and mix well. Add eggs, milk and oil; stir just until moistened. Pour into a greased 10- or 11-in. ovenproof skillet. Bake at 400° for 35-45 minutes or until bread tests done. Serve warm. **Yield:** 10 servings. **Diabetic Exchanges:** One serving (prepared with egg substitute and skim milk) equals 2 starch, 2 fat, 1 vegetable; also, 278 calories, 595 mg sodium, trace cholesterol, 39 gm carbohydrate, 7 gm protein, 10 gm fat.

Minty Peas and Onions

✓ This tasty dish uses less sugar, salt and fat. Recipe includes *Diabetic Exchanges.*

2 large onions, cut into 1/2-inch wedges
1/2 cup chopped sweet red pepper
2 tablespoons cooking oil
2 packages (16 ounces *each*) frozen peas
2 tablespoons minced fresh mint *or* 2 teaspoons dried mint

In a large skillet, saute onions and red pepper in oil until onions just begin to soften. Add peas; cook, uncovered, stirring occasionally, for 10 minutes or until heated through. Stir in mint and cook for 1 minute. **Yield:** 8 servings. **Diabetic Exchanges:** One serving equals 1 starch, 1 fat; also, 114 calories, 118 mg sodium, 0 cholesterol, 15 gm carbohydrate, 6 gm protein, 4 gm fat.

Holiday Gumdrop Cookies

1-1/2 cups spice gumdrops
3/4 cup coarsely chopped walnuts
1/2 cup golden raisins
1-3/4 cups all-purpose flour, *divided*
1 cup packed brown sugar
1/2 cup shortening
1 egg
1/4 cup buttermilk
1/2 teaspoon baking soda
1/2 teaspoon salt

Cut gumdrops into small pieces, reserving black ones for another use. Place gumdrops in a bowl. Add the walnuts, raisins and 1/4 cup flour; toss to coat. Set aside. In a mixing bowl, cream the brown sugar and shortening. Add egg; beat in buttermilk. Combine baking soda, salt and remaining flour; stir into creamed mixture. Add gumdrop mixture and mix well. Chill for 1 hour. Drop by rounded teaspoonfuls 2 in. apart onto ungreased baking sheets. Bake at 400° for 8-10 minutes. Cool for 2 minutes before removing to a wire rack. **Yield:** about 3 dozen.

BACKYARD BONANZA. Clockwise from the bottom: Old-Fashioned Swiss Steak, Chef's Salad, Feather-Light Biscuits and Baked Carrots (all recipes on page 101).

Menu Items Stood the Test of Time

AFTER owning a restaurant in Fresno, California for 19 years, Eleanore Hill and her husband decided to retire and spend some time near Lake Tahoe.

"Of course, the kids came to visit us often," notes Eleanore. "Whenever I asked what they'd like to eat, their response never varied—they requested my hearty Swiss steak, chef's salad, carrots and biscuits.

"I soon realized these dishes had been the kids' favorite foods on the menu at our restaurant years ago. So it was easy for me to make this meal for them to enjoy again and again.

"This Old-Fashioned Swiss Steak features tender beef in a hearty tomato sauce. The kids enjoyed this so much they would often look forward to eating any leftovers the next day!

"Now when I make this just for my husband and myself, I freeze serving-size portions in airtight containers or freezer bags for a fast future meal.

"The traditional Chef's Salad makes a nice side dish as well as main meal. At the restaurant, we offered three dressings with this salad that were made fresh every morning. At home, I had to serve all three dressings, too. The kids could never make up their minds which dressing they wanted, so they'd put a tablespoon of each on their salads. I share a Thousand Island dressing with you here.

"Baked Carrots are compatible with most any meal. The chicken broth gives them great flavor. Whenever I serve this dish, they quickly disappear. For a variation, this vegetable combination is delicious mashed in with potatoes.

"The kids couldn't resist my Feather-Light Muffins. I usually used a glass or baking powder can lid as a cutter so the biscuits would be larger than average size...and I always baked some extras for them to take home. They liked to split them and fill them with cheese or peanut butter and strawberry jam.

"My memories of working in our restaurant, as well as the relaxing dinners we enjoyed as a family at Lake Tahoe, help make this my most memorable meal."

Old-Fashioned Swiss Steak

1/2 cup plus 2 tablespoons all-purpose flour, *divided*
2 teaspoons salt, *divided*
3/4 teaspoon pepper, *divided*
1/2 teaspoon garlic salt
2 pounds boneless round steak, cut into serving-size pieces
3 tablespoons cooking oil
1 garlic clove, minced
2 cups chopped green pepper
1 cup chopped celery
1 cup chopped onion
2 cans (14-1/2 ounces *each*) diced tomatoes, undrained
1 cup beef broth
1 tablespoon soy sauce
1/4 cup cold water

In a large plastic bag, combine 1/2 cup of flour, 1 teaspoon salt, 1/2 teaspoon pepper and garlic salt. Add beef and toss to coat. Remove meat from bag and pound with a mallet to tenderize. Heat oil in a Dutch oven; brown the meat. Add garlic, green pepper, celery and onion; cook and stir for 10 minutes. Add tomatoes, broth, soy sauce and remaining salt and pepper. Cover and bake at 325° for 2 hours. Remove from the oven and return to stovetop. In a small bowl, combine water and remaining flour; stir into juices. Bring to a boil over medium heat, stirring constantly until thickened. **Yield:** 6-8 servings. **If Cooking for Two:** Freeze serving-size portions in airtight containers or freezer bags.

Chef's Salad

1/2 head iceberg lettuce, torn
1 can (15 ounces) garbanzo beans, drained, optional
1 small red onion, chopped
1/2 cup sliced radishes
1 small cucumber, chopped
1 small tomato, chopped
1 cup julienned fully cooked ham
1 cup julienned Swiss *or* cheddar cheese

DRESSING:

1 cup salad dressing *or* mayonnaise
1/2 cup *each* ketchup, sweet pickle relish and chopped onion
Dash garlic salt

In a large salad bowl, toss lettuce, beans if desired, onion, radishes, cucumber and tomato. Arrange ham and cheese on top. Cover and refrigerate until serving. In a small bowl, combine all dressing ingredients; stir until well blended. Chill for 1 hour. Serve with the salad. **Yield:** 6 servings.

Baked Carrots

1 pound carrots, cut into sticks
1 bunch green onions with tops, chopped
1 cup chicken broth

Place the carrots and onions in an ungreased 1-qt. casserole; pour chicken broth over all. Cover and bake at 325° for 1 hour. **Yield:** 6 servings. **Editor's Note:** This dish may be placed in the oven along with the Old-Fashioned Swiss Steak during the last hour of baking.

Feather-Light Biscuits

6 cups buttermilk baking mix
1/4 cup sugar
1 package (1/4 ounce) active dry yeast
1/3 cup shortening
1 to 1-1/4 cups warm water (110° to 115°)
1/4 cup butter *or* margarine, melted

In a large bowl, combine the baking mix, sugar and yeast. Cut in shortening until mixture resembles coarse crumbs. Stir in enough warm water to make a soft and slightly sticky dough. Turn onto a floured surface; knead gently 3-4 times. Roll dough to 3/4-in. thickness; cut with a 2-1/2-in. round biscuit cutter. Place on ungreased baking sheets. Brush tops with melted butter. Bake at 400° for 10-12 minutes or until lightly browned. **Yield:** about 2 dozen.

SPRINGTIME TEMPTATIONS. Clockwise from top left: Leg of Lamb, Mixed Greens Salad, Mother's Manicotti and Easter Pie (all recipes on page 103).

Easter Dinner... Italian-Style!

"SO MANY of my mother's recipes were passed down to become traditions in our family," says Barbara Tierney of Farmington, Connecticut. "But the dishes I think of first are those that Mother made for Easter dinner.

"Unlike most folks', Mother's holiday menu had a true Italian flair. The first course was always her cheesy manicotti. It's so good we had to remember to save our appetites for the rest of the meal!

"People are surprised to hear that instead of using pasta, Mother made crepes. We kids had fun helping her fill them with lots of smooth ricotta cheese.

"Of course, Easter Sunday just wouldn't be the same without Leg of Lamb. Served with gravy and mint jelly, it was one of Mother's many masterpieces.

"Not only is the Mixed Greens Salad crisp and refreshing, it features an authentic Italian dressing that puts store-bought dressings to shame.

"The variety of greens and produce makes it eye-appealing as well. It was a dish we enjoyed not only on holidays but throughout the year.

"The crowning glory to Mother's meal was her golden Easter Pie. This dessert is a specialty in many Italian homes, so mothers make sure their daughters master the recipe to ensure that the tradition continues.

"Friends and relatives often urged Mother to go into business selling her pie because it was so irresistible, but she wouldn't hear of it. That would have turned her pie-making into a common trade. Mother thought only family and friends should enjoy her Easter Pie.

"But I can't resist sharing her Easter Pie recipe—and all other recipes from my most memorable meal—with you," admits Barbara.

Mother's Manicotti

CREPES:
1 cup all-purpose flour
1 cup water
2 eggs
1 tablespoon vegetable oil
Dash salt
FILLING:
1 carton (15 ounces) ricotta cheese
3/4 cup shredded mozzarella cheese
3 tablespoons grated Parmesan *or* Romano cheese
1 tablespoon chopped fresh parsley
1 egg, beaten
1 jar (28 ounces) spaghetti sauce
Additional shredded Parmesan *or* Romano cheese

Place flour in a bowl; whisk in water, eggs, oil and salt until smooth. Pour a generous 1/8 cup into a greased hot 8-in. skillet; turn to coat. Cook over medium heat until set; do not brown. Repeat with remaining batter (makes 10 to 12 crepes). Stack crepes between waxed paper; set aside. For filling, combine the cheeses, parsley and egg; mix well. Spread half the spaghetti sauce in the bottom of a 12-in. x 8-in. x 2-in. baking dish. Spoon 3 tablespoons of the cheese mixture down the center of each crepe; roll up. Place seam side down over spaghetti sauce; pour remaining sauce over crepes. Sprinkle with Parmesan or Romano cheese. Bake, uncovered, at 350° for 30 minutes or until bubbly. **Yield:** 6-8 servings.

Leg of Lamb

1/2 leg of lamb (3 to 4 pounds)
5 garlic cloves, minced
1 teaspoon salt
1 teaspoon pepper
1/4 teaspoon ground thyme
1/4 teaspoon garlic powder
1/4 cup all-purpose flour

Cut five slits in the meat; insert garlic. Combine salt, pepper, thyme and garlic powder; rub over meat. Place on a rack in a roasting pan. Broil 5-6 in. from the heat until browned; turn and brown the other side. Turn oven to 350°. Add 1/2 cup water to pan. Cover and bake for 25 minutes *per pound* or until internal temperature reaches 160° for medium or 170° for well-done. Remove to carving board and keep warm. Pour pan drippings into a large measuring cup, scraping browned bits. Skim fat, reserving 1/4 cup in a saucepan; add flour. Add water to drippings to equal 2 cups; add all at once to flour mixture. Bring to a boil; cook and stir until thickened and bubbly. Cook and stir 1-2 minutes more. Slice lamb and serve with gravy. **Yield:** 6-8 servings.

Mixed Greens Salad

1/2 small head iceberg lettuce, torn
1/2 small bunch escarole *or* endive, torn
1/2 small bunch romaine, torn
1 small tomato, cut into chunks
1/2 small cucumber, sliced
1/4 cup olive *or* vegetable oil
1/4 cup red wine vinegar
1/4 teaspoon salt
1/4 teaspoon pepper

In a large salad bowl, toss greens, tomato and cucumber. Combine the oil, vinegar, salt and pepper in a jar with a tight-fitting lid; shake well. Pour over salad and toss. Serve immediately. **Yield:** 6-8 servings.

Easter Pie

CRUST:
1-2/3 cups all-purpose flour
2 tablespoons sugar
1/2 teaspoon salt
1/4 teaspoon baking powder
1/4 cup butter *or* margarine
1/4 cup shortening
2 eggs, lightly beaten
FILLING:
1 carton (15 ounces) ricotta cheese
1 cup sugar
1 tablespoon all-purpose flour
1/4 teaspoon grated lemon peel
1/4 teaspoon grated orange peel
Dash salt
4 eggs
2 teaspoons vanilla extract
1/3 cup semisweet chocolate chips
1/3 cup diced citron, optional
1/8 teaspoon ground cinnamon
Dash ground nutmeg

In a bowl, combine the flour, sugar, salt and baking powder; cut in butter and shortening until mixture resembles small crumbs. Add eggs; stir until moistened and mixture forms a ball. Cover and refrigerate for 1 hour. On a lightly floured surface, roll out dough to a 10-in. circle. Place in a 9-in. pie plate; flute crust. Refrigerate. For filling, beat the ricotta, sugar and flour in a mixing bowl. Add peels and salt; beat until smooth. In another bowl, beat eggs until thick and lemon-colored, about 5 minutes; slowly fold into ricotta mixture. Gently mix in remaining ingredients. Pour into the crust. Bake at 350° for 55 minutes or until a knife inserted near the center comes out clean. Cool. Store in the refrigerator. **Yield:** 6-8 servings.

SUNDAY SUPPER STAPLES. Clockwise from bottom: Butter Roast Chicken, Cool Cucumber Salad, Asparagus Supreme and Pineapple Cheesecake Squares (all recipes on page 105).

A Collection of Newfound Favorites

A LIFELONG interest in cooking led Elisabeth Garrison to begin her cookbook collection. She now has nearly 200! In addition, she's written a food column for her local paper and has compiled a cookbook of her own.

"With all of these sources, I can easily come up with recipes to make memorable meals," says the Elmer, New Jersey cook.

"But my most treasured meal didn't come from a book. Instead, each of the four recipes in this special meal was given to me by a family member or a friend—so these dishes are near and dear to my heart.

"I began collecting recipes when I was newly married and very interested in cooking. My sister-in-law's mother sent me this family-favorite Butter Roast Chicken recipe, and I knew it was destined to be a favorite in our household. The lemon-butter sauce makes this a great dish.

"People are surprised to hear that this refreshing molded lime salad also features cucumbers. Whenever I'm asked to bring a dish to a potluck dinner, I prepare this salad because it looks so attractive on the table and tastes delicious. I often make it for at-home dinners with family and friends, too. It's always much appreciated.

"Because we live in 'The Garden State', our produce is top-notch in season. Spring is the time of year to enjoy asparagus, and I serve it several times a week. Preparing Asparagus Supreme is one of my favorite ways to use it.

"Pineapple Cheesecake Squares are often requested in our home, perhaps because they're not too sweet. A cousin gave me the recipe a long time ago, much to the delight of my children, who always enjoyed it."

Concludes Elisabeth, "Whenever I reach for any of these recipes, I'm filled with warm memories of the people who shared them with me."

Why not share them with your friends and family and create some memories of your own?

Butter Roast Chicken

1 broiler-fryer chicken (2-1/2 to 3 pounds), cut up
1/2 cup butter *or* margarine
1/3 cup lemon juice
1 tablespoon paprika
2 teaspoons salt
1 teaspoon pepper
1 teaspoon brown sugar
1/2 teaspoon dried rosemary, crushed
1/8 teaspoon ground nutmeg
1/8 teaspoon cayenne pepper

Place chicken in an ungreased 13-in. x 9-in. x 2-in. baking pan. Combine remaining ingredients in a small saucepan; bring to a boil. Remove from the heat and pour over chicken. Bake, uncovered, at 325° for 1-1/2 hours or until juices run clear, basting occasionally. **Yield:** 6 servings.

Cool Cucumber Salad

1 medium cucumber
1 package (3 ounces) lime-flavored gelatin
1 teaspoon salt
1/2 cup boiling water
1 cup mayonnaise
1 cup cottage cheese
1 small onion, grated
Sliced cucumbers and fresh parsley, optional

Peel and halve cucumber; remove the seeds. Shred and pat dry; set aside. In a bowl, combine gelatin and salt with boiling water; stir until dissolved. Add mayonnaise and cottage cheese; mix well. Stir in the onion and shredded cucumber. Pour into an oiled 5-cup mold. Refrigerate until firm. Unmold onto a serving platter. Garnish with cucumbers and parsley if desired. **Yield:** 6 servings.

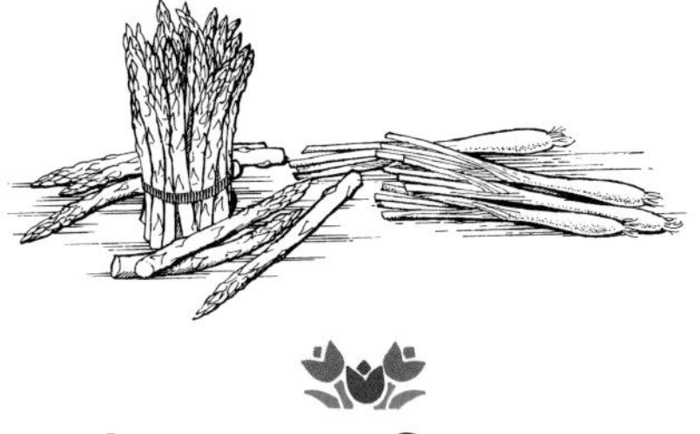

Asparagus Supreme

1-1/2 pounds fresh asparagus, cut into 1-1/2-inch pieces
2 tablespoons butter *or* margarine
2 tablespoons all-purpose flour
1/2 teaspoon salt
1/4 teaspoon pepper
1 cup milk
4 hard-cooked eggs, diced
1 jar (2 ounces) diced pimientos, drained
1 cup (4 ounces) shredded cheddar cheese
Dry bread crumbs

Cook asparagus in boiling water until nearly tender; drain and set aside. In a small saucepan, melt butter. Add flour, salt and pepper; cook and stir until smooth and bubbly. Gradually add milk; cook and stir until thickened. Remove from the heat. Place half of the asparagus in a greased 1-1/2-qt. baking dish. Top with half of the white sauce, eggs, pimientos and cheese. Repeat layers. Sprinkle with bread crumbs. Bake, uncovered, at 325° for 30-35 minutes. **Yield:** 6 servings.

Pineapple Cheesecake Squares

1/2 cup all-purpose flour
3 tablespoons sugar
1/4 teaspoon salt
1/4 cup butter *or* margarine

FILLING:

1 can (8 ounces) crushed pineapple
1 package (8 ounces) cream cheese, softened
3 tablespoons sugar
1 tablespoon all-purpose flour
1 egg
1 cup milk
1 teaspoon vanilla extract
Ground cinnamon

In a bowl, combine the flour, sugar and salt; cut in the butter until crumbly. Press into the bottom of an ungreased 8-in. square baking pan. Bake at 325° for 12 minutes. Cool. Meanwhile, drain pineapple, reserving juice; set pineapple and juice aside. In a mixing bowl, beat cream cheese, sugar and flour. Add egg and mix until smooth. Add pineapple juice. Gradually add milk and vanilla. Sprinkle pineapple over crust. Slowly pour filling over pineapple. Sprinkle with cinnamon. Bake at 325° for 1 hour or until a knife inserted near the center comes out clean. Cool to room temperature. Chill; cut into squares. Keep refrigerated. **Yield:** 9 servings.

FABULOUS FALL FARE. Clockwise from bottom right: Greens with Hot Bacon Dressing, Buttermilk Oatmeal Muffins, Hearty Beef Stew and Cranberry Apple Crisp (all recipes on page 107).

Terrific Tastes From Around The Country

SAVOR the flavors of yesteryear with these treasured recipes from four cooks from coast to coast.

"I discovered this Hearty Beef Stew recipe several years ago when we belonged to a newcomers group," relates Virginia Brown of Hudson, Florida. "It's a real lifesaver when company comes to visit...and when you live in Florida, you have company often!

"Put it in the oven, forget it and be gone for the day with your guests. It's loaded with meat and vegetables, so when you return home, just fix a side salad and warm some bread. Dinner is ready to be served! I've found the men especially love this hearty meal."

Robert Luebke of Appleton, Wisconsin suggests you serve his fresh-from-the-oven Buttermilk Oatmeal Muffins with the stew. "These moist and delicious morsels bake in no time for a wonderful addition to your favorite main course," he shares.

"When my wife and I were courting, these muffins were a significant part of the first dinner we had together. She's an excellent cook, and that first meal was truly a gourmet's delight. Now whenever she plans a menu and asks for my suggestions, I make sure these muffins are on it."

For a nice salad that complements any meal, why not try Robert Enigk's Greens with Hot Bacon Dressing? "I grew up in a German community, and we had this salad often," explains Robert from his Canastota, New York home. "It's an old traditional dish—I recall my grandmother talking about her mother making this recipe.

"As a variation, the 'old-timers' in my family enjoy cutting up some boiled potatoes on dinner plates, then serving the warm salad mixture on top of the potatoes."

Cranberry Apple Crisp comes from Martha Sue Stroud of Clarksville, Texas. "A dear friend from California shared this recipe with me years ago, and it's always been a big hit whenever I've served it," she says.

"I especially like to prepare this in fall when both cranberries and apples are in season. The fruits are quite compatible in flavor and color, and they help make any table look festive and inviting."

No matter what time of year you serve these dishes, you'll be showered with compliments from everyone!

Hearty Beef Stew

2 pounds beef stew meat
6 to 7 medium potatoes, peeled and cut into 1-1/2-inch pieces
2 medium onions, cut into wedges
8 medium carrots, cut into 1-inch pieces
4 to 5 celery ribs, cut into 1-inch pieces
1 can (4 ounces) sliced mushrooms, drained
1/3 cup quick-cooking tapioca
1-1/2 teaspoons salt
1 beef bouillon cube
1 teaspoon sugar
2 bay leaves
1-1/2 teaspoons dried thyme
3 cups tomato juice

In a 4-qt. Dutch oven or baking dish, layer the first 12 ingredients; pour tomato juice over all. Cover and bake at 300° for 3 hours, stirring occasionally, or until the meat and vegetables are tender. Remove bay leaves before serving. **Yield:** 6-8 servings.

Buttermilk Oatmeal Muffins

1 cup quick-cooking oats
1 cup buttermilk
1 egg, beaten
1/2 cup packed brown sugar
1/4 cup vegetable oil
1 cup all-purpose flour
1 teaspoon baking powder
1/2 teaspoon baking soda
1/2 teaspoon salt

In a bowl, soak oats in buttermilk for 15 minutes. Stir in egg, sugar and oil. Combine flour, baking powder, baking soda and salt; stir into oat mixture just until moistened. Fill greased or paper-lined muffin cups three-fourths full. Bake at 400° for 16-18 minutes or until muffins test done. Cool in pan 5 minutes before removing to a wire rack. **Yield:** about 8 muffins.

Greens with Hot Bacon Dressing

4 cups torn fresh spinach
4 cups torn iceberg lettuce
3 celery ribs, sliced
1/2 cup chopped red onion
4 bacon strips, diced
1 egg
2/3 cup water
1/3 cup cider vinegar
2 teaspoons sugar
2 teaspoons cornstarch
1/2 teaspoon salt
1/4 teaspoon pepper

In a salad bowl, toss spinach, lettuce, celery and onion; set aside. In a large skillet, cook bacon until crisp; remove with a slotted spoon to paper towels to drain. Discard all but 2 tablespoons drippings. In a small bowl, beat egg; add water and mix well. Add to the drippings. Combine vinegar, sugar, cornstarch, salt and pepper; add to the skillet. Bring to a boil, stirring constantly. Remove from the heat; pour over salad. Add bacon. Toss and serve immediately. **Yield:** 6-8 servings.

Cranberry Apple Crisp

3 cups chopped peeled baking apples
2 cups fresh *or* frozen cranberries
1 cup sugar
3 tablespoons all-purpose flour

TOPPING:
1-1/2 cups quick-cooking oats
1/2 cup all-purpose flour
1/2 cup packed brown sugar
1/2 cup butter *or* margarine, melted
1/4 cup chopped pecans

Combine apples, cranberries, sugar and flour. Place in a greased 11-in. x 7-in. x 2-in. baking dish. In a bowl, mix topping ingredients until crumbly; sprinkle over apple mixture. Bake at 350° for 50-55 minutes or until the fruit is tender. **Yield:** 6-8 servings.

GRADUATION DAY DINNER. Pictured are: Broiled Fish, Roasted New Potatoes, Blue Cheese Salad and Baked Lemon Pudding (all recipes on page 109).

Reel in Raves with Flavorful Fish

"THE VERY FIRST MEAL that my mother made for me when I came home after I graduated from college was one I couldn't wait to enjoy," remembers Ann Berg of Chesapeake, Virginia.

"When Mother put her familiar broiled fish and all the trimmings on the table, it wasn't only a festive meal, it made me feel I was *home*. I'd felt some homesickness while I was away at school, and I'd been yearning to taste some of Mom's down-home cooking.

"Mother's secret in preparing her Broiled Fish was to butter the fish first before dusting it with flour. She told me that if you don't, the flour will fall off. It also seals in the moisture of the fish, which makes it succulent and absolutely delicious. Even folks who aren't fond of fish enjoy it prepared this way.

"Roasted New Potatoes are simple to make but anything but plain. Flavors of garlic and herbs combine to add extra zip to tender new potatoes. I can still smell these 'spuds' baking in Mom's oven! This side dish goes hand in hand with the delicate taste of the fish.

"There's nothing like a fresh salad to round out a meal, but the colorful combination in the Blue Cheese Salad has eye appeal as well. I love the crispy crunch of croutons and tangy touch of dill in this recipe.

"It was always a treat when Mom made Baked Lemon Pudding for dessert. The tart taste of lemon brings the perfect finish to this meal.

"Mother often made her fish dinner when I was growing up. Since we lived on the West Coast, there always seemed to be an abundance of wonderful-tasting fish, and I had always taken it for granted—until I went away to college. When she served this delicious fish dinner to me after graduation, I instantly associated it with fond feelings of home."

In the years since, Ann has started her own home-style custom by serving this wonderful dinner to her own family. When she first met her husband, he really didn't care much for fish. But after tasting this flavorful recipe, he quickly learned to love it. Now he even requests this particular meal, and Ann is only too happy to oblige.

Now your family can enjoy this mouth-watering dinner, and you'll be sure to get rave reviews from them every time you serve it.

CRACK THE CASE. If you crack the shells of hard-cooked eggs slightly and let them stand in cold water for 5 minutes, they'll be much easier to peel.

Broiled Fish

4 orange roughy, red snapper, catfish *or* trout fillets (1-1/2 to 2 pounds)
6 tablespoons butter *or* margarine, melted, *divided*
1 tablespoon all-purpose flour
Paprika
Juice of 1 lemon
1 tablespoon minced fresh parsley
2 teaspoons Worcestershire sauce

Place fish on a broiler rack that has been coated with nonstick cooking spray. Brush tops of fish with 3 tablespoons of the butter; dust with flour and sprinkle with paprika. Broil 5-6 in. from the heat for 5 minutes or until fish just begins to brown. Combine lemon juice, parsley, Worcestershire sauce and remaining butter; pour over the fish. Broil 5 minutes longer or until fish flakes easily with a fork. **Yield:** 4 servings.

Roasted New Potatoes

1-1/2 pounds new potatoes, quartered
2 tablespoons olive *or* vegetable oil
2 garlic cloves, minced
1/2 teaspoon dried rosemary
1/2 teaspoon dried thyme
1/2 teaspoon salt
1/8 teaspoon pepper

Combine all ingredients in a plastic bag; toss to coat. Pour into an ungreased 13-in. x 9-in. x 2-in. baking pan. Bake, uncovered, at 450° for 35 minutes or until potatoes are tender. Remove from the oven and cover with foil to keep warm while broiling the fish. **Yield:** 4 servings.

Blue Cheese Salad

1/4 cup white wine vinegar
1/4 cup olive *or* vegetable oil
1 garlic clove, minced
1/4 teaspoon pepper
1/4 teaspoon seasoned salt
1/2 teaspoon dill weed
1 small bunch romaine, torn
3 hard-cooked eggs, chopped
1 cup croutons
1/2 cup crumbled blue cheese

In a small bowl or jar with tight-fitting lid, combine the first six ingredients; mix or shake until well blended. Place romaine in a large salad bowl; top with the eggs, croutons and blue cheese. Add dressing and toss. Serve immediately. **Yield:** 4 servings.

Baked Lemon Pudding

1 cup sugar
3 tablespoons all-purpose flour
3/4 cup milk
Juice of 2 lemons, strained
1 tablespoon butter *or* margarine, melted
2 teaspoons grated lemon peel
2 eggs, *separated*

In a medium bowl, combine sugar and flour. Stir in milk, lemon juice, butter and lemon peel. Beat egg yolks; add to the lemon mixture. Beat egg whites until stiff peaks form; fold into the lemon mixture. Pour into a greased 1-qt. baking dish; set in a larger pan with 1/2 in. of water. Bake, uncovered, at 350° for 55-60 minutes. Serve warm. Refrigerate any leftovers. **Yield:** 4 servings.

REGIONAL RECIPES. Clockwise from bottom: Liver Dumplings, Pickled Beets, Banana Applesauce Cake and Spinach Greens (all recipes on page 111).

Ethnic Meal Features Down-Home Dumplings

AS Sara Lindler's traditional German dinner proves, foods that have been in the family for years certainly make for memorable times.

"Mother served this meal all the time, and I continued the custom in my own home," reports this Irmo, South Carolina cook.

"Many people in my community love these Liver Dumplings, which are also called 'nips'. It is an ethnic dish that was first brought here by settlers who came to this part of South Carolina many generations ago.

"Through the years, I've revised the recipe slightly to suit my family's tastes. Now all my relatives like the way I fix them. Serve the dumplings in beef broth, or thicken the broth like gravy and serve this dish as a stew. Either way, they are hearty, delicious and different.

"Greens make the best salad to serve with this meal because the flavors are so compatible with the main course. We often use collards here in the South, but spinach or beet greens are good substitutes.

"The beets Mother served came from our garden and were canned for the winter months. Even as a child, I loved beets because they were so colorful. Their tangy flavor is a great complement to the rest of the foods in this meal.

"Banana Applesauce Cake was always Mother's special treat for her six children. It's a delectable 'mountain' of cake and fruit, and very moist. In addition, since it looks so impressive on the table, it's perfect for entertaining.

"I find it rewarding to pass on my heritage to future generations by sharing family recipes like these with relatives, friends...and you!"

Liver Dumplings

1/2 pound uncooked beef liver
1 large onion, cut into eighths
1 teaspoon salt
1-1/2 teaspoons ground sage, *divided*
1/2 teaspoon ground coriander
1/2 teaspoon dried basil
1/2 teaspoon pepper, *divided*
3 cups all-purpose flour
1/4 teaspoon baking powder
3 egg whites
1 egg yolk
5 cans (14-1/2 ounces *each*) beef broth
1/2 cup cornstarch

In a food grinder or processor, combine liver, onion, salt, 1 teaspoon of sage, coriander, basil and 1/4 teaspoon pepper; process until smooth. Add the flour, baking powder, egg whites and yolk; process until well mixed. Batter should be thick and spoonable. (Add a little water if too thick or a little flour if too thin.) Set batter aside. In a 5-qt. Dutch oven, combine broth, cornstarch and remaining sage and pepper; bring to a rolling boil, stirring constantly. Reduce heat to a gentle boil. Drop batter by heaping teaspoonfuls into broth, dipping spoon in broth to release dough. Gently boil, uncovered, for 20 minutes or until dumplings are no longer sticky. Stir occasionally. **Yield:** 8-10 servings.

Quick & Easy

Spinach Greens

4 bacon strips
12 cups torn fresh spinach *or* beet greens (1 pound)
1 tablespoon sugar
3/4 teaspoon salt

In a large skillet, cook the bacon until crisp; remove to a paper towel to drain. Add greens to drippings; cook, stirring constantly, just until wilted. Stir in the sugar and salt. Crumble bacon and stir into greens. Serve immediately. **Yield:** 6-8 servings.

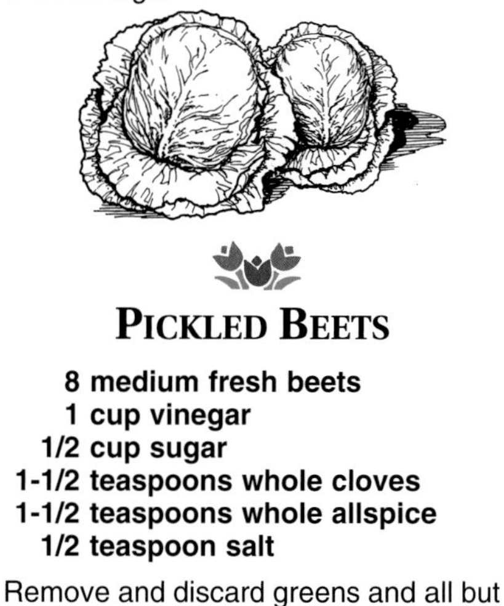

Pickled Beets

8 medium fresh beets
1 cup vinegar
1/2 cup sugar
1-1/2 teaspoons whole cloves
1-1/2 teaspoons whole allspice
1/2 teaspoon salt

Remove and discard greens and all but 1/2 in. of the stems from beets. Cook beets in boiling water until tender; drain and cool. Peel and slice; place in a bowl and set aside. In a small saucepan, combine vinegar, sugar, cloves, allspice and salt. Bring to a boil; boil for 5 minutes. Pour over beets. Refrigerate at least 1 hour. Drain before serving. **Yield:** 6-8 servings. **If Cooking for Two:** Undrained beets may be stored in a covered container in the refrigerator for several months.

Banana Applesauce Cake

1 cup butter *or* margarine, softened
2 cups sugar
4 eggs, *separated*
3 cups all-purpose flour
2 teaspoons baking powder
1 cup milk
1/2 teaspoon vanilla extract
1/2 teaspoon lemon extract

FILLING:

2 cups sweetened applesauce
3 medium firm bananas, sliced
3 tablespoons lemon juice

FROSTING:

1 cup sugar
2 egg whites
3 tablespoons water
1/2 teaspoon cream of tartar
1/4 teaspoon salt
1 teaspoon vanilla extract
1/4 cup flaked coconut, toasted

In a mixing bowl, cream butter and sugar; beat in egg yolks. Combine flour and baking powder; add to creamed mixture alternately with milk. Beat in extracts. In a small bowl, beat egg whites until soft peaks form; gently fold into batter. Pour into three greased 9-in. round baking pans. Bake at 350° for 25-30 minutes or until cake tests done. Cool for 10 minutes; remove from pans to wire racks to cool completely. Divide applesauce and spread over two of the cake layers. Dip bananas in lemon juice; arrange over applesauce. Stack on serving plate with plain layer on top. For frosting, combine sugar, egg whites, water, cream of tartar and salt in the top of a double boiler over boiling water. Beat for 7 minutes or until stiff peaks form. Beat in vanilla. Remove from the heat; continue beating until frosting cools. Frost sides and top of cake. Sprinkle with coconut. Store in the refrigerator. **Yield:** 16-20 servings.

INDEX